Praise for *Endpapers*

"It's thoughtful and nuanced and full of gender exploration we rarely get to see."   —*LGBTQ Reads*

"Achingly evocative and thoroughly satisfying, Jennifer Savran Kelly's *Endpapers* follows a genderqueer bookbinder through post-9/11 New York as she searches the city for answers about a long-hidden love letter and the outlines of her own identity. Part historical mystery, part meditation on the shifting nature of creativity and self, *Endpapers* is a story that bursts with warmth, community, and the sometimes-heartbreaking decisions we make when we begin to stitch together the spine of our lives."   —Katy Hays, author of *The Cloisters*

"Part portrait of the artist, part queer coming of age, and part investigative puzzle, this intimate, emotional novel parlays romance, passion, politics, and history into a compelling tale, beautifully and insightfully told. Jennifer Savran Kelly is an exciting, empathetic new voice."   —J. Robert Lennon, author of *Subdivision* and *Let Me Think*

"Jennifer Savran Kelly's *Endpapers* is an accomplished, moving novel where the search for answers to a literary mystery doubles as the search for queer authenticity in a world of bindings: book bindings, artistic bindings, social bindings. With humor, tenderness, and honesty, Savran Kelly lays bare the struggle to find our brilliant, beautiful selves—and the courage to go forth boldly with them."
                              —Zak Salih, author of *Let's Get Back to the Party*

"A mystery wrapped in a love story wrapped in an artist's coming of age, *Endpapers* is an ode to queer joy and the messiness of selfhood. With tenderness and insight, Jennifer Savran Kelly explores what we lose when we keep our innermost selves hidden—and what it means to forge an authentic life through art."   —Antonia Angress, author of *Sirens & Muses*

"The mystery of Gertrude and Marta converges beautifully with the artwork that Dawn begins to conceive. Savran Kelly is a bookbinder and book production editor, and the novel's details of book and print restoration ground and add depth to Dawn's story."   —*BookPage*

"Sometimes the hardest thing to be is our authentic selves. How do we do that when society has hidden and erased any path that could show us the way? Dawn Levit finds that heroic path by believing in hunches and looking for clues. Not quite a mystery novel, this is a story of following one's own inner desire for belonging through art and surprising friendships. Savran Kelly creates a story full of humans whom we long to be friends with after the last page is read. Love is acceptance, and this book is that and more."

—Amy E. Wallen, author of *When We Were Ghouls*

"Richly imagined . . . Kelly populates the novel with a roundly developed cast . . . and while the mystery of why Gertrude's letter was bound into the book will keep the reader turning pages, it's Dawn's evolution as an artist and a person that gives the novel its beating heart. Readers will find lots to love."

—*Publishers Weekly*

"A dizzying, intimate mystery, an exploration of how we become engrossed in the stories of others in order to tell ones of ourselves."   —*Electric Literature*

‖ENDPAPERS‖

‖ENDPAPERS‖

a novel by

Jennifer Savran Kelly

ALGONQUIN BOOKS OF CHAPEL HILL   2023

Published by
ALGONQUIN BOOKS OF CHAPEL HILL
Post Office Box 2225
Chapel Hill, North Carolina 27515-2225

an imprint of Workman Publishing
a division of Hachette Book Group, Inc.
1290 Avenue of the Americas
New York, New York 10104

Printed in the United States of America. Design by Steve Godwin.

Library of Congress Cataloging-in-Publication Data
Names: Savran, Jennifer, author.
Title: Endpapers / a novel by Jennifer Savran Kelly.
Description: First edition. | Chapel Hill, North Carolina : Algonquin Books of Chapel
Hill, 2023. | Summary: "In 2003 New York, a genderqueer book conservator who
feels trapped by her gender presentation, ill-fitting relationship, and artistic block
discovers a decades-old hidden queer love letter and becomes obsessed with tracking
down its author"—Provided by publisher.
Identifiers: LCCN 2022040937 | ISBN 9781643751849 (hardcover) |
ISBN 9781643753706 (ebook)
Subjects: LCGFT: Genderqueer fiction. | Novels.
Classification: LCC PS3619.A89 E53 2023 | DDC 813/.6—dc23/eng/20220912
LC record available at https://lccn.loc.gov/2022040937

ISBN 978-1-64375-540-3 (PB)

10 9 8 7 6 5 4 3 2 1
First Paperback Edition

For Mom,
for believing in me, always

For Chris and Elijah,
for everything

‖ENDPAPERS‖

PART I *Buchbinder*

‖ ART

BECAUSE I'M NOT ready to go home. Home to Lukas. Because lately I get more pleasure from spreading open the covers of a book than my own legs. Because the pungent smell of ink and the soft touch of paper. I linger here—in the book conservation lab, after hours, after everyone has gone off to rejoin loved ones, even our boss, who usually stays because she has a project on the side.

Pausing, I inhale the quiet. Soon my hand cool against the heavy wheel of the press, loosening and turning. ...e that's finally my fingers. Soon I'll know if this book ...ything to say. worthy of exhibiting. Or even one newsprint and then for Book Arts earlier

Carefully I free the protect... ...rday and stacked in the the pages, which I printed ...ne was here to see. I take this week and folded an...

press today during...

a moment to enjoy the uncomplicated thrill of a newly pressed book block. Perfectly flat, perfectly compact, a first hint of the separate coming together into one whole.

If only it were that easy.

I carry it to my workbench, where I've set out thread, dyed tan to match the paper, and black leather sewing tapes, lined with Japanese tissue. I promised myself I wouldn't look at the content before sewing the folios together. I don't want to talk myself out of finishing. But I peek at the first page, the letter-pressed words smooth and black against thick, nubby paper. It's pretty.

Pretty isn't art.

For a long time, art had been my savior. Lately it's my spectacular failure. I'm supposed to be showing my work by now, like my former classmates, only there is no work. I've been vacant—of ideas, of images and words. So lately I've taken to spying, sitting in coffee shops and bars to eavesdrop on conversations. It's amazing what you overhear people talking about in New York City—an old window washer who's also an evangelist trying to convert a teenage girl; a mortified cop who had to spend his first few hours on duty investigating dolls that had been left in weird places, creating a fire hazard.

Turning the pages, I scan my drawings. The window washer squeegee-izes from his platform high above the street, pretty teen girl dripping water onto his adoring masses. A girl. Such sadness responds to his question: Yeah, I'm a good porcelain dolls face. The police officer rounds up blocking sewers, street. Exquisitely dressed toy girls with feminist slogans and fire hydrants, donning signs officer, more cops attempt to go about their business with arms full of dolls announcing: *My body, my choice; The future is female; Resist.*

Somehow it's not working. The renderings are competent and the scenarios interesting, but none of it has anything to do with me. I've been trying to find out what can happen, what I can make, if I forget everything the world wants to see when it looks at me. But under these bright fluorescent lights, my images only remind me once again that I've become more invested in hiding who I am than expressing it. Heart sunk, I brush my bangs across my forehead, the way the woman who cuts my hair instructed. "More feminine," she'd said.

Good girl.

Am I though? I wonder to the empty room. *Good? A girl?*

As if to save me from my own thoughts, my phone buzzes and it's Jae. *Crappy day at work. Don't let me smoke alone?*

I laugh. At least I still have my sense of humor. *Nice try,* I write, and flip my phone closed. Jae knows I hate being high. His obsession with weed almost killed any possibility of us even becoming friends when we met a couple of years ago. I turn back to my book and rack my brain for a way to save it.

My phone buzzes again. *How about we dress in drag and go dancing at Pyramid? Lukas and I wear makeup, you smoke. Deal?* I shake my head and start to type, *You're joking, right?* But looking down at my book, I pause. Jae knows I've been thinking about this for a while.

I type, *Lukas would never*, hit send, and close my phone.

A few minutes later: *Fine. You and me then.*

Ignoring him, I continue to scan my book. More drawings. More people in the city who appear to be living double lives. A businessman holding his dry cleaning high over his shoulder on a crowded sidewalk like Jesus carrying the cross. A homeless woman selling amateur magic tricks who, finally, disappears behind a cloud of smoke. Who are these people? What do they want? More important, what do I want from them?

What do I want?

I turn the page and my angel stares up at me, as if waiting for an answer. "Sorry to disappoint," I say. "I don't know how to save you."

Though I hate to admit it, maybe Jae's invitation has come now for a reason. Maybe the way to fix this, to make art again, is to face what I've been avoiding. Eyeing the book, I flip my phone back open. Before I change my mind, I type, *Fine, you're on.*

My heart speeds up.

LEAVING THE METROPOLITAN Museum of Art, I submit to the crowd on the sidewalk, keeping its erratic pace as I take a left onto Fifth Avenue and walk four blocks to catch the 5 train downtown toward Brooklyn. When the doors of the train slide closed, I catch sight of my reflection in the window. I let my hair fall over my left eye and observe how the bulk of my coat erases my curvy hips and D-cup breasts. With my new Prohibition haircut, in my jeans and engineer boots, I can almost believe I've taken on the male form.

It's still a bit jarring. For the last few years, I've been erring on the side of female. On the train, however, somewhere on the border of real life, where everyone's a stranger and I can hide inside my coat, it's easier to let myself slip. At the next stop, a seat opens. I sit, leaning back, widening my legs like men do. A woman across the way looks at me and, feeling emboldened, I wink. When she smiles, I look away, horrified by my transgression, my hands already on my bangs, sweeping them to the side.

BACK AT MY apartment, as I zip Jae into my dress, I'm impressed by how easily he wears it, how much he never seems to care what people think. He primps in front of the mirror while Lukas looks on, amused—or perhaps interested—and I rummage through Lukas's half of the closet, looking for something that will work for me. Trying on the second of his two button-up shirts, I study myself in the mirror and don't know what's worse: that I feel like a weird, misshapen man or a woman playing dress-up. Meanwhile, Lukas is helping Jae pick out makeup colors. Even though Lukas won't go out dressed like a woman, he's always eager for an excuse to get into makeup at home, as long as it's around people he trusts. He looks happy helping Jae. And I should be glad to see them having fun, but my heart feels suddenly heavy. I've been avoiding Lukas all day, worried he'll notice me brooding about yet another thing I can't shake off. Earlier this week I tagged along to a party he was working at the Manhattan New Music Project, a reception for a local musician who'd won some indie award. While Lukas and I have become too practiced in our impression of a heterosexual couple—there I was in my black dress with the white collar and high-heeled Mary Janes, he in his button-up and tie—the musician still sashayed flamboyantly straight to Lukas. For most of the night, his hand was living it up on Lukas's shoulder, and me, I may as well have not been there. Lately I've been missing when our love was easy. When the only way his touch felt was right.

"This isn't working," I say.

Lukas turns to me. "What do you mean? You look . . . nice." He hesitates over the last word. I know how hard it is for him to give such a direct compliment, especially in front of someone else, and I soften a little.

Turning back to the mirror, however, I wish I could see what he sees. Sometimes it gets lost. Fed up with myself, I walk over to Jae and pull some lipstick and eyeliner from the makeup bag.

"What do you think you're doing?" he says.

"The plan was for you to wear makeup. We never said I couldn't."

He looks from me to Lukas. "Seriously? The straight dude is the only one willing to go out in drag?"

Lukas laughs. "I have band practice."

"Right, convenient," I say. I lean toward the mirror and start to line my eyes. They both watch as if they're going to stop me, but then return their attention to Jae's face. When my own is complete, I reexamine myself and decide the shirt isn't actually too bad, though it needs a tie. I throw one on, but instead of pants, I grab a pencil skirt from the closet and head to the bathroom. When I reemerge, Jae shakes his head. "What?" I say. "I'm in drag. I'm a man in a skirt and makeup."

But I actually don't hate what I see in the mirror. I pull my bangs back with a barrette. Maybe it's not a cop-out after all but something closer to who I am. At least today. Lukas and Jae still look disappointed. I try to brush it off as nothing more than my imagination and hold my arm out for Jae, whose transformation is now complete. Before he comes to me, he turns to Lukas to say goodbye, batting his fake eyelashes and putting his hand out for a kiss.

Lukas takes it with a bow.

"Oh my god, stop being so cute and let's go," I say.

FINALLY, A COUPLE of hours later, Jae and I are here, packed tight on the dance floor, me remembering why I hate being high and Jae looking ridiculously pretty in dark eyeliner, sparkly shadow, and cherry-red lipstick. His drag may be a bit rough, but he's beautiful on the dance floor, in the colored smoky light, his body mingling with strangers, contorting to "Crazy in Love." As I sweat in Lukas's button-up, I envy how ordinary Jae looked on the subway ride here, as if this is a regular way for him to be out in the world. But of course for him it's only drag, a costume. Meanwhile, I keep regretting my skirt, more concerned that people will see what I'm not than what I am.

After a few songs, Jae's winded and we go to the bar for a second drink. His eyeliner is already running, and one of his fake lashes has come loose. I peel them both off, one at a time, as he shouts over the music about his crappy day at work, his coworker who insists on backseat-driving all his copyediting. I yell back at him to try to let it go for the night, enjoy the music, when some half-dressed dude reaches over us to signal the bartender. As he excuses himself, he laughs—at us—and says, "Fun outfits." Then, to me, "You know, the city's full of straight bars. It's too bad you've wandered into the wrong place."

Jae ignores him and tries to lead me back to the dance floor, but I pull away, my mood fallen like a brick. "Nah, let's go," I say, loud enough for the guy to hear. "I'm done with goddamn queers."

"Whoa, take it easy," says Jae. "I'm pretty sure he was kidding."

"Fuck that. I'll accept them when they accept me."

Jae looks apologetically at me, and then at the guy, who's not even paying attention anymore.

Outside, I feel pot-sick, out of control of myself in a way that makes breathing impossible. Suddenly I need out of my skin, out of Lukas's shirt that's straining to contain my body. This is exactly why I stopped hanging out with queers when I moved in with Lukas, why it was so comfortable to slip back into the closet. Trying to break myself to fit in, even among the marginalized, was exhausting. Now I can't stop thinking about the dude at the bar, his self-important, patronizing face. Stupidly, I start to cry.

"Hey," says Jae. "Hey, Dawn, it's all right."

"Whatever, fuck that guy. Come on, let's walk." I put two cigarettes in my mouth, light them, and offer him one.

"Where are we going?"

"Nowhere. I just need to keep moving."

Jae is unfazed by my anxiety. He's quiet and calm as ever, and as I walk next to him, my body grows solid again.

After several minutes we're walking past Marble Cemetery, and even though I haven't planned any of this, I stop and say, "Here we are."

I peek through the bars of the gate, but I can't see much in the dark. Jae joins me.

After a moment, he pulls his head back and blows out smoke. "That was fun. What next?"

"I barely saw anything," I say.

"What do you want to do? Break in?"

I laugh like *of course not*, but the night has me feeling adventurous. I actually wouldn't mind breaking a few rules. Quickly, I scan the street to see if anyone's paying attention to us. There are hardly any people out at this hour. "Yeah, why not."

"Very funny." He grinds his cigarette butt into the sidewalk.

"I'm not joking."

He shakes his head, but as he looks back at me, a hint of a smile animates his face. "In our dresses?" he says.

"Technically mine's a skirt." Before I lose my nerve, I hike it up to the tops of my legs and start climbing the gate.

"Holy shit," says Jae. But soon he's following.

JAE IS CONTENT to poke around the graves with me. We wander, reading tombstones until they all sound the same. Then we come to one with a fist carved into it, reaching straight up.

"What does that mean?" I say.

"Not sure," says Jae. "Hands mean different things depending on which way they're pointing. But I don't know about a fist."

"It looks like someone's trying to get out."

"Smart corpse." Jae starts walking again. "Speaking of getting out," he says as I fall into step with him, "there's another protest coming up. Some friends and I are making signs this weekend. You should come."

I consider it for a moment. I've been feeling like I should do something tangible to protest what's happening in Iraq instead of wasting my time trying to find a voice through art. But it's the first time in a while I've dared to make anything at all.

"Maybe," I say. "I've finally been playing around with some ideas for a new piece, and . . ." I'm afraid if I tell him about my recent failed attempt, it'll sound so dumb, I'll give up entirely. "Anyway, so far it's been a mess, but I'm hoping to take time over the weekend to try to save it."

He puts his arm around my shoulder. "No problem, bro. We make our own statements."

We walk quietly with our arms around each other, and I want to capture the extra love and gratitude I feel for him tonight, so I pull out my camera and take a picture of us.

When we look at it, something about Jae's glittery eye-shadow sparkling among so much cold, dead marble strikes us both as funny. Also, the way he's standing, with no regard for the fact that he's in a dress, makes me laugh out loud. "Oh my god, how can you look like such a dude in that outfit?"

"I don't know what that means," he says, pulling a cigarette from his boot. "Should I be offended?" He lights it and lets it hang from his mouth like a hard-boiled detective.

Laughing harder, I snap a picture. Then I take his cigarette so he can take one of me. It's late, but we're both energized, so we hop back over the gate and head to Tompkins Square Park, to a playground, to some old church, everywhere we go taking pictures of ourselves and each other, pretending to be tourists. We're having so much fun we've forgotten about dancing. And Jae says now I have blackmail photos of him, so he has no choice but to trust me forever.

WE RIDE BACK to Brooklyn on the subway and he walks me home. And then outside the door of my apartment building, I freeze up, wondering if Lukas might be awake. My mood still too fragile to be alone with him.

"Come on," I say. "It's too early to turn in. Let's go get a drink."

"Dawn, it's way past midnight," he says.

"So? When has that stopped you before?"

He shakes his head. "Okay, let's have it. Did something happen with Lukas?"

I look away. "Nah, everything's fine."

Jae waits for me to say more.

"It's nothing. Really. Just a crappy day. Just another crappy artist's book."

His face softens. He kisses me on the cheek. "I get it," he says. "But for now, you should go drink some water. And tell Lukas I say good night."

‖BOOK

IN THE MORNING I watch Lukas from bed with half-open eyes. For once he's woken before me, and it looks like he made breakfast. He's standing at the stove, dishing something into a bowl. It smells fruity.

Carrying it over, he says, "Good morning. Did you have fun with Jae?"

I sit up against the wall and take the bowl, moving over to make room for him. My bag is next to me on the floor. I pull out my camera, toss it onto his lap, and take a spoonful of hot oatmeal. "Oh wow, is this mango?"

Lukas scrunches his face. "It's weird, I know. I threw in a pinch of cinnamon, but I'm not sure if it's good." He sets the camera down. "Anyway, before I look at these, I wanted to give you something." He reaches under his pillow and pulls something out.

"What is it?" I say.

"Just a mixed CD. I made it for you. Last night." He gives it to me and looks away. It has a handmade cover, and on the front he's written *For Dawn. You're the bee's knees.* Below, he's drawn a beautiful burgundy bumblebee that looks like a woodcut print.

My face flushes. Even though it's kind of goofy, he rarely says anything so clearly. I guess he knows I've needed to hear it.

I kiss him.

"It's not a big deal," he says.

"You know it is. And I love it. Also, I thought you had practice with Pete last night."

"I did, but it only went for an hour, and you were out late." He kisses me back. Then picks up the camera and scrolls through the pictures Jae and I took, shaking his head and smiling.

"Aha," I say, poking his side. "Seems fun, right?" It's become a little game, me trying to prove that Lukas is enjoying something anyone else also enjoys.

"Whatever, looks like you two had a good time. You gonna post it on Friendster?" He's teasing, but his tone is still warm.

"Make fun all you want, but I got you." I take the camera from him and pull him close, moving the bowl and CD out of the way, and bury my face in his long dark hair, resting my cheek against his neck. The smell of sleep is strong between us. Sleep and nicotine and sweet, old T-shirt. As I breathe him in, all the doubt from yesterday is already melting away.

He kisses me and then frees his arms and heads to the bathroom. I shovel the rest of the oatmeal into my mouth and leave the bowl in the sink as I make for the shower.

AT WORK IT'S right to business. There's been a small accident in the stacks, a tiny leak in the ceiling that's left at least one book water damaged. It's an important one, Katherine said, so she wants me and my careful hands right there with some tools for quick repair and a cart to work on, in case I detect any more books that need a hand. I was more than happy to comply, to get away from her meddling stare, her complaints that I look too boyish today.

"What does that mean?" I'd asked.

"Depressed," she'd said.

Bending over the cart and the book, I draw in stale, regulated air, run my fingers over the intricate design on the cover—a work of art in itself—and the indent made by each gold-stamped line. It's an illustrated survey of art deco and art nouveau architecture, *Building Beauty*, bound in the early 1950s.

I ease open the cover to reveal water-stained endpapers splitting and yellowing along the gutter. Gently turning each page, I arrive at a photograph of Gaudí's Casa Batlló—the hollow eye cavities of his skull balconies staring up at me from beneath a wavy roof that shines iridescent in the light captured by the photographer. Below the skulls, the building is a body, both shapely and skeletal, open through the middle to reveal the life inside. Pillars carved into bones frame windows rounded into organic shapes, colorful organs of stained glass. Everywhere my gaze falls, new details emerge. When finally I lift my eyes, I feel as if I've been transported back to the library stacks from somewhere far away. It takes me a few moments to return to myself.

With my hand still holding the lifting knife, I brush my bangs across my forehead.

More feminine.

Less depressed.

Then, placing my tool between my teeth, I continue my inspection of the book. The water damage appears to be limited to the outer spine. The text block is intact aside from one loose signature. A new lining on the spine will be enough to hold it in place.

I open my strop and draw my lifting knife across it in figure eights as Katherine has taught me, until the round tip of the blade tapers into near invisibility. Then I open the back cover of the book and make a light incision with my scalpel along the inner edge of the board. The cover separates cleanly. In order to reattach it later, I'll need to create a new hinge and slide it underneath the original endpaper. Slowly, I pass my lifting knife under the freshly cut edge to ease it away from the board as I hold the cover steady.

That's when I notice a discrepancy in the feel of the board. Almost half of the endpaper has already come unglued, and looking closely, I detect a faint rectangular outline just inside the loose area.

With a sudden eagerness I crouch and bring my eyes down level with the book. Attempting to keep my lifting knife steady, I run it back and forth under the paper until I catch a glimpse of something underneath. I hold my breath. A few more strokes of the knife and I'm able to jiggle it free, leaving only one tiny tear behind.

What I finally hold in my hand confuses me. It's a severed

paperback cover for a book called *Turn Her About*, with a campy illustration of a woman looking into a handheld mirror and seeing a man's face. The tagline reads "What was her dark secret? A powerful novel about a tragic love." What is this doing here? I laugh. But then a trickle of fear descends as I remember my night out with Jae. What if someone from work saw us and is pranking me? I walk to both ends of the aisle, scanning the stacks, but there are no signs of life. The only sound aside from my footsteps is the hum of the HVAC system.

Back at the cart I examine the book cover again and flip it over. Handwritten on the back in tight script with light blue ink is a letter, written in German. Aside from a bit of glue in one corner where it had attached to the endpaper and some mild discoloration, the whole thing is undamaged. Putting the lifting knife back between my teeth, I turn the cover over in my hands several more times. Assuming it's not a cruel joke, what are the chances that this particular image would have been hidden in a book that Katherine assigned to me?

The letter is addressed *Liebe Marta*, and signed *Ich liebe Dich, Gertrude*. I wish I could read it, but I don't speak German. These opening and closing words are the only ones I recognize.

With the feeling I'm holding a ghost in my hands, I bring it up to my face and inhale the sickly sweet odor of animal glue. Despite the absurdity of the illustration and how I found it, for a brief moment I think I'm going to cry.

I know I should bring it straight to the lab, show it to Katherine and encase it in Mylar, but, as if it's a rare treasure like I used to find in the woods as a kid—a four-leaf clover or the feather of a blue jay—I don't want to let it go. Carefully, I sandwich it between two pieces of scrap paper and slip it inside my notebook.

After surveying the surrounding books and determining that none of them need repair, I take the cart and *Building Beauty* back to the basement, to the conservation lab, where everyone is working quietly. I slip in and go straight to my workbench, trying not to attract attention as I move the book cover from my notebook into the back pocket of my messenger bag.

As soon as I begin to work, Katherine walks in. I don't see her right away, but I know by the change in the room's energy—everyone suddenly more alert. Instinctively I take my lifting knife from between my teeth because she hates it when I hold my tools in my mouth.

"Dawn," she says in her unmistakably posh British accent, coming over to see my progress. "How'd it go?"

I touch the pocket of my bag, eye the knife resting on my bench next to the book. The handle shiny with my saliva. "Fine," I say. "Just one to repair. An end-cap. I can reback it this week."

Katherine beams. "You look better. Being with the books did you good—you got some nice pink in your cheeks."

Out of the corner of my eye, I see my colleague Amina across the room shooting me a knowing look. Katherine has no filters. Although we usually commiserate later, we forgive her most things because she treats us well, having the museum pay for us to take special workshops, encouraging us to use the lab equipment to make our own books in our downtime, and going fiercely to bat for us if anyone at the museum threatens any of our daily comforts—like the time she fought against the school tours they wanted to bring through so students could watch us working. "We're a room full of women," she'd said. "What if we need to fix our bras? It's not a peep show."

So we're used to laughing away Katherine's insensitivity. But this afternoon I'm not getting the joke. The book cover I've found is working hard on my imagination, mutating back and forth from a romantic gesture to a practical joke to the last remnant of someone's deep internal conflict, their desire to both reveal themself and hide at the same time.

As I stand there saying nothing under Katherine's gaze, before her model-perfect frame and the shiny red braid hanging over her shoulder, I grow awkward and messy and hold my arms tight to my sides in order to avoid unleashing a wave of body odor.

Setting the book on my workbench, I return the cart to its corner of the room and keep to myself for the next hour until it's time to go home. I leave with the cover of *Turn Her About* still in my bag.

‖ BODY

MORE THAN AN hour has passed by the time I reach Park Slope and navigate the two and a half long blocks to my apartment. Dragging my feet up all four flights of stairs, I smell myself with every step.

I walk in the front door to find Lukas cooking dinner in the pink blouse my mother gave me when I left for college, the one with the ruffles at the ends of the sleeves. He has it tied at the waist like I've shown him.

The smell of curry fills the kitchen.

"Mmmm," I say.

Lukas has made up his eyes with teal eyeliner and dark pink shadow, and he's looking at me with a coy, uncertain smile. He's never sure whether he wants me to find him this way, and it excites me all the more to see him so vulnerable, waiting for my approval. Also, finally, it means I can give in to the boy inside—the one both Katherine and I have been trying to discourage out of me all day.

"Chana masala," says Lukas.

Dropping my bags to the kitchen floor then pulling off my coat, I step behind him and put my hands on his hips, press my mouth against his shoulder blade, enjoy the slight roughness of the polyester blouse against my lips. He stops stirring the food and leans against me, making me wish, as usual, that I were half a foot taller so I could take his full weight. I stand as tall as I can, holding him from behind, breathing him in, until I can't wait anymore, and turn him toward me. I unbutton his blouse, run my hands through his long hair, over his smooth face and his jaw. I look into his deep brown eyes dressed in their bright colors, take the spoon from his hand, and pull him away from the stove. I've never enjoyed the taste of anyone so much. Within minutes I have him undressed and he's on his knees fumbling with my belt.

With our clothes out of the way, I take his hand and lead him to the futon, feeling his eyes on my broad shoulders, the nape of my neck where my hair is cut close—his favorite view. Yet even as he kisses his way down my body, I'm aware of his disappointment over my full breasts, my bald upper lip, which I refuse to stop tweezing. I push against the thoughts and lie back, giving in to the pressure of his head on my inner thigh, and dream ashamedly of having his whole body between my legs, imagining him inside me as we tangle ourselves into impossible shapes.

Afterward, lying next to each other, bodies raw and mouths sour, Lukas puts his head on my shoulder and holds my hand.

It makes me think again about the book cover I found—about secrets and longing—and it spurs me to ask the question I've been too afraid to voice for some time. I unwind my hand from his and run one finger down his nose, letting it rest at the tip.

I close my eyes. I say, "I want to have sex with you. Intercourse."

Lukas is quiet.

"Intercourse?" he says. "Why now?" Though he doesn't seem put off by the question.

I picture Lukas and the musician at the party last week, picture the careful, intricate handwriting on the back of the book cover. I haven't been able to stop thinking about what secrets it holds, ones the author may never have gotten the chance to reveal. "I don't know," I say. "Forget it."

"Why didn't you say anything?" He takes my hand again.

"I was afraid you'd think I'm a pig."

"You are a pig," he says. "Dawn, the pig. That's what I like about you." He kisses my chin.

I put my head against his. "Oink."

He closes his eyes.

I wait. Play with my bangs. Pretend his answer isn't that important, even though my insides are chewing themselves up.

The first time we fooled around, we didn't even make it to my bed. Tangled in the pile of clothes we'd wrestled out of on the floor, there was no letting go, no coming up for air until we'd kissed every inch of each other. Then as soon as everything went still and the only thing I could hear was our breathing, I realized he was crying. My desire quickly turned into shame. I was afraid I'd hurt him or done something wrong.

But he covered his eyes with his hand and explained that intercourse felt too much like a violation, so he couldn't do it and he hoped I would be okay with that.

It had been music to my ears—Lukas offering me something I'd never believed anyone else would want, a way to be close without worrying about who should play what role or what our bodies could or couldn't do. No boy, no girl. I was so relieved that I cried too, and we fell asleep next to the bed, holding each other. I didn't stop to wonder if there was something more behind his hesitation.

Now, waiting for his answer, my body has grown to ten times its size. Enormous and smothering. It was a stupid thing to ask for. I don't know how to be a woman any more than I know how to be a man.

And of course there's Lukas's familiar silence. The one that speaks volumes. That draws out, long and painful, while I wait for him to say something he can't. Which is usually whatever he knows I want to hear. As far as he's concerned, if people say what's expected of them, the words lose their meaning. But often he can't find words of his own, so instead he says nothing.

Faced with that silence, I do what I always do. End it before he has to open his mouth. "Ich liebe Dich," I say.

"What?" says Lukas.

"Ich liebe Dich. That means 'I love you' in German, right?"

"I think so. Why?"

"I found something today." I untangle myself from him and slide out of bed. I want to be far away from him. "In a book I was fixing. I think it's a love letter."

The chana masala is puffing and splattering tiny red dots

all over the stove. I grab the wooden spoon and stir, let the steam warm my face. Then I turn the heat off. I'm ravenous, but I can't wait anymore to show him what I've found. Pulling my T-shirt and jeans back on, I find my bag on the floor and dig through it. Lukas is still naked, but he's covered himself with the sheet. We're moving on.

"Look at this," I say. "Be careful." I place the book cover on the futon between us.

He laughs. "Wow."

"I know, right? I love how cheesy it is."

He picks it up. Turning it over, he finds the letter and scans it in silence.

I watch him. "Don't you think it's a wild mystery?"

He shrugs, sets it back down on the futon. "Sure."

I pick it up. "Really? That's it? You're not even impressed by the coincidence? The fact that this particular book cover was bound into the one book Katherine asked me to fix?"

"Of course I am," he says, leaning back against the wall. "But life is full of coincidences. The ones we notice are just the ones we pay attention to—because we happen to find meaning in them."

"Okay, Mr. Roboto," I tease. But irritation has pushed its way into my voice. I scoot to the edge of the futon and stand.

"Come on," he says, pulling me back down by the hand. "The handwriting is nice." He puts his head against my shoulder.

"Nice try," I say. But his attempt to mollify has worked. I lean close to him, the letter in front of us.

"What's it say, anyway?"

"I don't know. Just these few words. Of course *liebe* is

'love.' And if it's the same as Yiddish, I think *Bild* is 'picture,' and *Vater* sounds like 'father.' I was hoping you might be able to recognize some of the others."

Lukas laughs again. "I don't speak German."

"Your father never taught you any?"

"No. He teaches Spanish and French."

I know he isn't laughing at me, but I'm still feeling ashamed from before, over wanting what I'm not supposed to want. Technically, Lukas and I don't even have a word for our relationship. We're only monogamous because neither of us has met anyone we're more attracted to. At least that's what Lukas says. For a while he had me convinced that monogamy only means something when it isn't enforced, but as the years have gone on and it's become increasingly hard for him to say the word *love*, I've begun to fear he's just afraid of committing.

Also, his casual remark about his father is a reminder that after the two years we've been together, I still don't know anything about his parents aside from the fact that his dad teaches some foreign languages and that neither of them has much tolerance for anyone who isn't white and Catholic. Even though I'm not religious, I'm still too Jewish for them.

"Anyway, no problem," I say, the harshness returning to my voice. "I'll ask Jae."

Lukas sits up. "Don't be mad," he says. "I agree it's cool, all right?"

I pick it up and run my hand over the first line of writing. *Liebe Marta.*

"It's more than that," I say. "It's probably a love letter. Based on when the book was bound, it must have been written in the 1950s, so can you imagine what kind of courage it had

to take for a woman to write a love letter to another woman—
especially on the back of an illustration like this—even if she
hid it?"

"I don't know. Didn't people use flowery language in letters
to their friends all the time? Besides, if you want to know what
it says, just try Babel Fish."

"Why would someone go through the trouble of hiding a
letter to a friend?"

"Maybe it was the friend who hid it. Also, you just said so
yourself. The illustration."

"Fine. But either way, you have to admit there's something
about it. I mean, yeah, it's campy, but it's also kind of beautiful. Like, it feels too . . . special or something to have a computer translate."

Lukas peels back the sheets and retrieves his underwear and
pants from the corner of the kitchen. While I look around for
a safe place to store my artifact, he's on to the chana masala.

‖LIEBE

I MET LUKAS at the end of my final year at SUNY Purchase, at the overcrowded senior art exhibition. He was the pretty dark-eyed boy who kept returning to my painting in the corner, a nude self-portrait, mostly of my back, with my face partially turned toward the viewer. Excited by my discovery of Hannah Gluckstein, the early-twentieth-century Jewish artist who donned men's clothing and signed her paintings as Gluck ("no prefixes, suffixes, or quotes allowed"), I'd exaggerated the broadness of my shoulders and definition of my muscles while rendering my face as classically feminine—pink cheeks and red lips. But I lost my nerve to show it. Just before I had to hand it in for a final grade, I painted clown makeup over the face.

A friend brought me over to the painting to introduce me to Lukas, and when Lukas learned I was the artist, he blushed.

I knew right away I wanted to bring him home. By morning, I'd learned only a handful of things about him—he lived in Brooklyn and worked at a music nonprofit, he was vegan, and he had a very old cat named Angela Davis. It was all I needed to know.

WHEN I GRADUATED, I didn't move in with Lukas so much as I went to visit him in Brooklyn and never left. It was winter, only a few months after 9/11, and I returned to a city I barely recognized. A New York haunted by debris, every breeze still carrying the smell of burnt metal and tar. The city's many moods were nowhere more evident than in its graffiti, which I relied on to guide me through this new reality—the Twin Towers resurrected everywhere, memorialized with candles and flowers. American flags looming larger than life. Firefighters in heroes' capes. George W. Bush a terrorist and a wanted man. It had become a city obsessed with remembering, even as the line between memory and belief was being erased. The streets vibrated with equal parts love and fear, demanding both *9/11TRUTH* and *MUSLIMS GO HOME*.

It was strange to feel so free coming back here during that time. Lukas seemed like a rare bird that had found its way to me, if only for a moment. It wasn't long after our first night together that I started to trust him with everything. I told him things I never thought I'd say out loud, like, "Isn't it funny that we met at my final art show, because the last time I saw my parents was at last year's juniors' show?"

"How is that funny?" he'd said.

"Because my ex-girlfriend stopped by to give me flowers, and my dad walked out. Then my mom, who hadn't chosen a side for years, finally chose. She said, 'I'm sorry, but what do you want, Dawn? Do you want me to be alone for the rest of my life? Is that what you want?' And I said, 'Of course not,' and she walked out after him. Ha ha."

Lukas said that wasn't funny at all, that was fucked up.

I explained how I was an only child of parents who wanted a big family until God or science interfered with their plans, and how they liked to tell me that they never adopted because I was enough for them. When I was a kid, we'd host big dinner parties, during which I got to stay up late enjoying the attention of grown-ups. My mother was a school nurse, and sometimes she invited the art teacher, Mrs. Bainbridge, and those were always my favorite nights because we'd pull out my sketchbooks, and Mrs. Bainbridge would go through every page, asking me questions and offering tips for improvement. "She has a real talent," she would say, and my parents would beam.

It wasn't until I signed up for a half-day high school program at the School of Visual Arts in Manhattan that my parents started to worry. It wasn't the art itself. They'd always believed I would marry a Jewish doctor or lawyer and wouldn't need to make a stable salary of my own. It was the influence that studying art seemed to have on me, because as far as they could see, that was when I changed, when I gave up pink and boys. That was when they started sending me to therapists. For a while they called it depression because they didn't want to call it what it was, and they pretended like they just wanted to find out what could be done to restore me to my true self, to a time when I was happy. "But I am happy," I'd say as Dad downed his second Scotch of the evening and Mom retreated to a room in the basement that she had turned into her "office," where she could "go over paperwork" in silence.

"What's funny," I'd told Lukas, "is how happy they would be if they knew I was still here with you, even though you're not Jewish, or a doctor. What's funny is how much they say they want me back in their life even though my father hates what I am and my mother resents me for putting her in the middle."

I asked him if he knew what it felt like to have parents that wanted to do the right thing, that wanted to love and accept you for who you are, but just couldn't.

Lukas didn't. His parents had shut him out with far more conviction, kicking him out of the house when he was in high school for nothing but cutting class a few times to smoke. They didn't even need to know that sometimes he wanted to wear makeup and women's clothes, or that he liked to look at men. Eventually their fear of who he might become without their intervention overrode their anger and they asked him to come back, but he refused. Now they barely talk.

Nothing about Lukas is straightforward. Lukas, who believes fiercely in people's right to arm themselves but captures our roaches with leftover take-out containers and walks them seven blocks to the park to set them free. Lukas, who will never promise anything but is always there when it counts. Who always tries to live the way he wishes the rest of the world would, which inevitably leaves him disappointed.

Lukas is impossible not to love. He challenges my ideas of what it means to be a good person and makes me believe that all of my sadness and anger are justified.

• • •

AFTER ONLY A month together in Brooklyn, he asked me to travel to Europe with him. His job gave him two weeks of vacation, and he said he wanted me to see the works of art I'd studied, to get up close to them and breathe in their history. It would help with the creative block I'd been struggling with since finishing my program, he said. And it wouldn't cost us much because ticket prices were still down after 9/11 and we could stay in hostels.

It wasn't until we were at the airport that I realized how scared I'd become to fly. I was convinced the plane would go down and I'd die in the middle of nowhere, alone. Of course Lukas would be there, but still. My parents had no idea where I even was. And how many friends had I stayed in touch with since arriving in the city? We could be halfway across the Atlantic and go down in the middle of the ocean, and no one would know or care. It was that idea, the image of crashing to my lonely death, that I couldn't handle. As I arrived at the gate with a bite of cheese Danish in my mouth, suddenly everything went dry. I couldn't chew for lack of saliva. It hurt to blink.

"I can't do it," I said. I was sure my body had ceased to function, had no way to get me on the plane.

"What are you talking about?" Lukas said.

"I can't. I can't do it."

He took my bags and told me to sit. "What's going on?"

I started to shake. The tears came in a rush. "I want to, I really do," I said. "But I can't."

"Can't what?"

"I can't get on the plane. I can't."

He was unperturbed. He looked out the big window at the

plane that was pulling up to the ramp. He looked back at me. "Yes, you can."

"I can't." I was sobbing now, everyone staring.

Lukas was silent. He didn't try to quiet me. And even though he didn't try to comfort me either, strangely I felt taken care of, being with someone who seemed so at ease with my public breakdown. After a few minutes he put his face close to mine and said gently but firmly, "I'm getting on the plane. I want you to come with me. So if you don't, I'm going to knock you out and drag you."

It stunned me out of my panic. I laughed, almost choking on a sob. "Fuck you," I said.

"I'll do it." He was holding his forehead against mine.

In that moment, I understood something about Lukas. Although he would probably never be there for me in ways anyone else could recognize, he would be there in his own ways, ways that perhaps meant something more. He made me feel safe enough to get on the plane, safe enough to cry my way to Paris, and safe enough to trust that the adventure ahead was worth it.

We spent those two weeks hopping from city to city and museum to museum, checking in and out of hostels, eating the best food our limited budget would allow. When we'd had enough of one place, we left for another, each day inventing and reinventing ourselves together. We were strangers everywhere, free to be who we wanted, without anyone's expectations based on who we'd been the day before.

We carried that sense of freedom back home with us, and at the time I believed we could sustain it.

LUKAS WAS RIGHT about another thing too. The trip got my art unstuck, at least in theory. In college, I'd studied oil painting, hoping that if I examined the nude figure, I could understand it, even find ways to subvert it, making everyone else see what I saw. I wanted to depict the strange suppleness of flesh, bodies that were infinitely malleable and hard to pin down. But I couldn't do it. My art became reduced to a technical exercise in rendering what our teachers called the "ideal human form." Another way to fix bodies into categories.

Lukas had majored in music and gender studies, and he was always talking about the likes of Anaïs Nin, Kathy Acker, and Judith Butler. I hadn't been a big reader as a kid, or even in college. But I was desperate for a world filled with shades of gray, and on his bookshelves I found it.

At first, it didn't occur to me that I could make my own books, so instead I made paintings of them, books stacked one on top of another, spread open on a table, left behind on a chair, pages dog-eared. But it was never right. I couldn't get at the thing about them that I was trying to capture. And I was too embarrassed to show Lukas.

Then one night when I thought I had it figured out, I painted a portrait of him holding a book, a biography of Assata Shakur, but no matter what I did, I couldn't make it work. I got so frustrated that an actual scream escaped from my mouth and I stabbed the canvas with an X-ACTO knife.

Lukas laughed. "What the hell are you doing?"

I was breathing heavily. The knife still in my hand, I plunged it into the easel and, in a great show of futility, it fell to the floor. "It's not funny."

Lukas put the book down and reached for his tobacco and

rolling papers. "Yeah, it is." He was naked and unashamed as he sat there rolling his cigarette, snapping the rubber band back around the pouch of tobacco. He put one foot up on the chair he was sitting in, leaning onto his raised knee, his long, muscular limbs arranging themselves into an odd *K*.

I looked at the canvas, at the slice I'd made through his hand, the book. I looked at him sitting there naked and smoking, and even though I wanted to yell at him, I couldn't. "It was a dumb fucking painting," I said.

Lukas reached for me and pulled me onto his lap, burying his face in my neck. He rubbed my head and explored his way down my back.

I looked again at the torn canvas. His hand—the one holding the book—had curled under, deforming the lower part of his arm.

I touched his real arm, felt it solid around me.

He said, "Don't be an idiot like me and try to get everything perfect. You'll never finish anything."

"Okay," I said. "I won't be an idiot like you."

"Promise me," he said.

By then I understood that words only meant something to him if they were unexpected, and I'd learned to translate. He was saying he believed in me, that I shouldn't give up. *Thank you*, I wanted to say. *I believe in you too.*

"I promise," I said.

‖MESSAGE

AWAKE AT 7:24 the next morning, I get out of bed and take a quick, hot shower while Lukas sleeps, then riffle through my closet to find the right thing to go with my mood, which is *Anything is possible*. Despite Lukas's skepticism, I'm sure I've found a love letter. It's put me in a curious, restless mood. I pull my bangs back into something like a pompadour, fasten them with a clip, and paint my lips a rich plum color. By 8:45, I'm dressed and out the door, Lukas still snoring gently. I've taken the book cover and left a note.

Off to solve the mystery. xx D.

JAE LIVES ONLY five-and-a-half blocks away, and I love the walk when it's quiet. It's Saturday, and most of the people out and about are still waking up, moving slowly, nowhere yet to rush to. Store owners are raising gates, unlocking doors. There's a spring chill in the air, and today I'm feeling good—unusually comfortable in my skin, enjoying the full curve of my hips and the way they add extra movement to my steps.

Arriving at Jae's place, I open the door with my non-coffee hand and step into the cramped foyer. I press the edge of my cup against the buzzer to his apartment. When I texted him last night, he was less than thrilled about the early hour, and I'm hoping he's awake.

"Be right down, bro," comes his voice over the static. It's a small thing, but one I don't take for granted, that Jae is the only person I know who calls me both sister and brother, even though we've never talked about it.

I step back out into the crisp air and look at the church across the street. It looks as old as Brooklyn and reminds me of Gaudí's Sagrada Família. I wonder what kind of people worship there, and I'm waiting for someone to come or go when I hear the door open behind me.

"How's it going?" Jae wraps me in a one-arm hug. "And what's so fucking important you had to get me up early?"

I punch his arm. "Come on, I'll take you to Fuerte. All the coffee you can drink."

His face brightens into that contented look of his that isn't quite a smile.

I start walking east to Fifth Avenue and hear his footsteps catch up behind me. He lights a cigarette and offers me a drag, which I accept. We walk and smoke in silence.

CAFE FUERTE IS a giant space filled with mismatched furniture and the smell of coffee and split pea soup. Jae and I sit by a front window, where the tables are raised on platforms like mannequins in store displays. Tom Waits's voice comes husky over the speaker in the corner: *The girl behind the counter has a tattooed tear.* "One for every year he's away," she said.

In the morning light, watching Jae eat a cinnamon roll, I notice that his face has taken on a soft glow.

"How long has it been now?" I say. "Since you showered."

"Almost eight weeks." It's the first time he smiles for real all morning.

"Looking good, dude," I say.

Jae has stopped washing as an experiment. He read somewhere that if you go long enough without using soap, your body adapts—stops producing the bacteria that cause body odor and blemishes. "I'm telling you. Soap is one of the biggest scams of all time," he'd said. "Just watch." This is one of the things I love about him. All the small, personal ways he finds to buck the system.

"You're pretty quiet for someone who needed to see me so urgently," he says. "What's this thing you couldn't wait until noon to have me translate?"

"Just giving you a minute to wake up." I open my messenger bag and pull out the book cover, sandwiched between protective sheets of paper. The cover is still safe inside. But the truth is, now that I'm sitting in front of Jae and the mystery is about to be revealed, something inside me is resisting. I've built it up too much and don't want it to be over.

I set the book cover in front him, and it looks delicate and strange resting in the bright light between us, as if it's been plucked out of time.

He picks it up. "This is amazing. Where did it come from?"

I knew he'd be excited. I explain how I found it and he

examines the front, smirking at the campy image of the woman/man looking in the mirror. Then he flips it over and studies the ornate cursive, every now and then pausing to scrawl in his notebook.

"What is it?" I say. "Happy? Sad?"

"Let me finish. Most of the German I know is from my mom talking to me, so I'm not that fast."

Jae's parents met on some research trip abroad, his mom there from Germany, his dad from Korea. I've often wondered if his multicultural background is what makes him so good at getting along with lots of different people. But probably it's just him.

Finally he finishes and slides the notebook in front of me. "You were right. It's a love letter." He scrubs his face with his hands.

His expression makes me nervous. I slide the book cover carefully back into my bag and, drawing a deep breath, look down at Jae's writing.

Dear Marta,

Darling, forgive my bluntness. There are things I've been wanting to tell you, and this picture says it better than I can. For a long time I've feared that the way I see myself, the things I desire, are wrong, and that somehow it means I'm sick. So although I cherish your friendship, I've been afraid of how I truly feel around you because, of course, you're a girl, and if this feeling is love, then what does that make me? Lately, however, I've dared to hope. I've met others like me, and for the first time it seems possible that when I see you at school and your face lights up with that smile, there's some code in it, a special signal that you feel it too.

If this is a figment of my imagination, I pray you can forgive me. More important, I pray you understand how crucial it is to keep my secret. But if it's true that you feel as I do, please accept this invitation to visit Father's bindery. I have something wonderful to show you. This Sunday at three? Please say yes.

I love you,
Gertrude

I read it through twice before lifting my eyes. "Wow," I say.

"Yeah."

"Did something about this disturb you?"

Jae scratches his head. "Don't you think it has a desperate, almost ominous feeling to it?"

"Maybe. It is pretty melodramatic."

We sit quietly for a moment, looking from each other to the table and back again. Above Jae's head, in a vintage beer ad, a man with gray hair and round red cheeks raises his glass. Laughter erupts from somewhere across the cafe.

Jae says, "Want to go have a cigarette?"

I nod.

He tears the translation out of his notebook and hands it to me. I fold it and nestle it between two books in my bag. We leave our half-eaten baked things on the table, gather our stuff, and leave Cafe Fuerte. Jae starts toward Flatbush Avenue, but after half a block I stop walking. I drop my bag on the sidewalk and sit on it.

You're a girl, and if this feeling is love, then what does that make me? It's one thing to have found this—the weird coincidence of it all—but a whole other thing to know that I'm holding someone's most personal feelings in my hand. A younger person than I'd pictured too. A girl, and perhaps even one like me—who wasn't even sure what *girl* means.

Jae stops walking and turns around. "Dude," he says. "You okay?"

"Yeah." I can't look at him. I thought this was going to be fun, but now for no reason I'm overwhelmed with sadness and once again I feel dumb in front of him, out of proportion. That was the phrase my father always used to describe my behavior. *Out of proportion.*

"It's all right," Jae says. "Just take a minute."

"I'm sorry," I say. "I'm fine."

He sits next to me on the sidewalk, offers me a drag of his cigarette. I shake my head. We sit there, letting people pass us by. I observe all the ways they have to change course in order to avoid stepping on us.

‖IMPRESSION

I WALK JAE home, apologize for the hundredth time, and promise I'll call later. He puts his hand on my back and disappears through the tiny foyer.

On my phone I find a text from Lukas. *Recording studio with Pete. Back this afternoon. xx.*

Good luck! I write. And then don't know what to do with myself. I've moved on from overwhelmed with sadness to just overwhelmed, with a parade of questions racing through my mind: Who hid the letter? Was it Marta, or did Gertrude lose her nerve to send it? Did Gertrude ever get to tell Marta how she felt? What did she want to show Marta at her father's bindery? I look down the street, as if the answers will be coming around the corner. A cab with red graffiti scrawled on the trunk drives by, and I decide to take it as a sign.

Going scouting, I type into my phone. *CU later. xx.*

When I'm looking for inspiration to make art and don't feel like spying on people, sometimes I walk around the city and try to focus my gaze. Because I moved to Brooklyn shortly after 9/11, I'd escaped the horror of watching pieces of my home rain from the sky. But I stepped right into the aftermath. Everywhere I went, signs of destruction or loss followed, pictures hanging from telephone poles, notes from children, siblings, parents, begging, *Have you seen my father, my mother? Have you seen my brother, my sister? Have you seen my husband, my daughter, my cousin, my friend?* American flags waved as far as the eye could see, but it was impossible to tell which ones were meant to suggest love and which ones hatred. The only thing that felt straightforward was the street art—whatever feelings it inspired, at least the messages were clear. Like those of the original graffiti artists—the Black and Latino kids who wanted to create a nonviolent way to connect and make their voices heard. I still can't help but appreciate the irony in how the city tried to silence them for decades only to end up lauding street artists for their displays of patriotism after 9/11. And even though it's mostly the sanctioned murals by gallery artists that get celebrated, it feels right that these works still have to share space with the graffiti covering overpasses, poles, and dumpsters. So I've been focusing on that, and it makes me feel safer. And although it hasn't been sparking any brilliant ideas, it's allowed me to process the grief that's been all around me that I've felt I have no right to partake in.

Thinking again about Gertrude's letter and that uncanny illustration, it feels like I practically fished her story out of my dreams, and I need to clear my head. I pick a direction and walk. The sidewalk is crowded, so I turn off on a side street, keeping my eyes alert. I pass fruit stands, Chinese take-out restaurants, a long row of brownstone apartments. I don't know what I'm looking for but when I find it, I want to get a picture.

When I'm walking in the city and not paying attention, all I see is the sheer volume of things. The endless gum on the sidewalk. Too many road signs crammed onto the corners. Shops packed so tightly together they blend into one. With a city this full, you have to look closely to see anything else, even the big graffiti murals painted across walls and overpasses. But especially the small intrusions, the paper figures left hanging from fire escapes and sewer gratings. The mosaics used to fill in cracks on sidewalks and walls. The images and messages left where they would be so easy to miss—under bridges, along the bottoms of walls, on dumpsters. For me, street art makes the city feel smaller, a little friendlier even.

I come to a street corner where the brick wall on my right has been painted in neon colors. Two shapely woman's legs tower over me, landing on stiletto-heeled feet, a strawberry ice cream cone melting over one shoe. I cross the street to get enough distance to fit the image in the viewfinder of my camera and snap a few pictures. The tag says CREAMNYC.

Then I walk and walk until I land on the other side of Park Slope, at the uptown F train. There, on the wall next to me, a giant pink angry man's face rises from a gargantuan chest and shoulders. Behind him an American flag flies. Spray-painted in large green letters over his head: UNITED WE STAND. I cringe. Just last week the paper said that something like three hundred hate crimes have been committed against Muslims in the last year. Almost as scary to me as that number was my initial reaction to it. Instead of being upset for the victims, I was mad at the media, suspecting they'd underreported the numbers to downplay the threat. It made me see how on edge I've been living, so aware that any difference can make you a target—to think that three hundred hate crimes sounded like too few.

I shiver and snap a photo. Yeah, united we stand.

As I make my way down the steps to the platform, I spot a small hole in the brick, which someone's painted a sideways face around, turning the jagged edges of the remaining brick into teeth. I squat and snap another photo. No tag.

I walk through the turnstile, push my way onto the train, and sit, cradling my camera. I close my eyes and picture the illustration on the book cover. The light blue handwriting on the back, so tight and neat to make every word fit. *The way I see myself, the things I desire, are wrong. . . . Lately, however, I've dared to hope. . . . It seems possible . . . there's some code . . . a special signal that you feel it too.* I imagine a teenage girl questioning (fearing) everything about herself: her gender, her sexuality. Was she trans? Or something else, like me? I imagine her writing feverishly at night, in the dark, so she wouldn't get caught, and I understand what it takes to hide feelings like that every day. I used code to communicate with the girls I dated in high school, a secret language we believed was keeping us safe from view.

I stand and lean against the pole in the middle of the subway car, press the base of my skull against the cool metal.

You're a girl, and if this feeling is love, then what does that make me?

Closing my eyes again, I try to clear my mind, but instead I remember a day I haven't thought about in a long time. I was in high school, kissing my girlfriend Alice in my bedroom, and the door opened. After sending her home, my father slapped me hard across my face. I'll never forget that particular sting, the sensation of something so intense yet so alien. The ringing in my ear, the prickles along my jaw. The look on my father's face as he said, "So help me, God."

He'd looked me up and down. *So help me, God.*

The next thing I knew he was pulling me down the hall by my arm, the Turkish runner buckling under our feet. It was a Friday, which meant it was nearly time to head to schul for Shabbat services. I wondered if he was going to pull me the whole way there until he opened the door to the front porch and ordered me to sit. Then he disappeared into the garage and returned moments later with handcuffs. I didn't even know we had them. Before I could process what he was doing, my chair was against the peeling green banister at the front of the porch and my left wrist was cuffed to one of the rails. Then he was walking away, back to the garage.

He stopped to look at me, only for a second. But that moment is what sticks with me. How soft and kind he looked. Everything about my father looks soft and kind, and the more disappointed he is with me, the softer and kinder he looks. That's his trick. His way of making me feel that he's not just in the right, he's doing me a kindness.

"This is what happens to people who think they're too special to live by the rules," he said.

A moment later I heard his car starting, and he was gone.

Stunned, at first I did nothing. None of it made sense. My

father was sometimes cruel, but he had never been violent. But after I sat there for some length of time I can't recall, reality came into focus. My cheek stung. He'd hit me. He'd left me trapped. No one was home, and I had no idea when they'd be back.

I held in a scream, scared our neighbors would hear. But no one would probably even respond. Our neighborhood was a true picture of Long Island suburbia, where your neighbors were none of your concern unless their weeds had invaded your carefully manicured lawn. I pulled hard with my cuffed hand, straining against the metal with every ounce of energy I could muster, but it was no use. So I shook my arm violently until it hurt too much to keep going.

The sun was already starting to set, but a late school bus turned onto our street and stopped a few houses before ours. I watched my neighbors' son get off and run up the path to his house, backpack jostling behind him. When he disappeared inside his front door, I let out breath.

Soon more neighbors pulled into their driveways, gathering things from their cars and waving to me as they collected their mail, and I was still too embarrassed to call for help. From a distance it must have looked like I was just enjoying a mild evening outdoors. I had to have been there an hour, struggling on and off with the cuffs, counting the seams between the wooden floorboards, crying from confusion and fear, before my dad's car finally returned, Mom's trailing behind.

It was almost dark when the garage door squealed shut. My mother's thin frame appeared, her hair a frizzy halo. She pulled a chair next to mine and reached for my wrist, then produced a key and slid it into the cuffs, not looking at my face until I was free. In the dim light, I could make out the tears shining around her eyes.

I said, "Where's Dad?"

Mom sat back, dropped the key on the table as if it were a dead spider. "Your father thought it would be better if he cooled down a bit more before seeing you."

"You mean you thought it would be better," I said.

Mom didn't say anything.

I hated that silence. It always preceded an apology for something my dad did. Rather than defending me, rather than standing up for me—or even for herself—all she could do was make his excuses. I stood up and pushed past her to go inside, but she followed, and as soon as the door was shut behind us, she choked back a sob.

"What?" I said.

"Please, Dawn." She picked at something on her skirt. "Please. You have to understand."

"No, I don't."

"He loves you. He's not a bad person."

"He handcuffed me to the fucking porch," I said.

Mom pressed her lips together and looked up at the ceiling. The corner was riddled with cobwebs.

I said, "Is that all?"

Mom reached for my hand. I pulled it away.

Crying openly now, she said, "No, it's not all. I was hoping you could tell me what you're doing. You know, what is all of this? Can you tell me that?" She gestured to me as she said *all of this*.

"All of what?"

"The clothes, the hair. You know."

"I don't know."

"You don't know?"

"No. That's the whole goddamn point," I said. "I don't know."

Mom pulled a tissue from her pocket. "Well, what your dad and I know is that you need to watch yourself. It's one thing to have certain feelings, but when you broadcast them to the world without a care, you invite a reaction. Sometimes a dangerous one. How are we supposed to help you if you don't know what you want?"

"I don't need your fucking help."

"Watch your language."

"Fuck that."

"Dawn," she said.

But I was already on my way to my room, where I kneeled in front of my bed, pushed my face into the mattress, and sobbed.

THE SUBWAY RATTLES and I have to steady myself to keep from falling. As it slows to a stop, the conductor announces York Street. I gather my bags and fight my way off the train. Secret codes, keeping us safe. Nothing but the naive thoughts of a child. I wonder if Gertrude was safe, writing her note to Marta. Leaving a record of her feelings. I wonder if Marta was.

As I step out onto the sidewalk, the light burns my eyes. I cross to the shady side of the street and duck into a deli for another coffee. By the time I come out, the sun has passed behind a mass of gray clouds.

I end up almost under the Brooklyn Bridge, on my left a wall peppered with illegible spray-painted words. Something about a good night's scare. I snap a few pictures and continue on under the bridge, toward the East River. It's the time of day when families are gathering. Mothers and fathers holding tiny hands that are trying to break free. Siblings chasing each other.

I turn back and make my way under one of the bridge's stone archways, my stomach complaining for food, my hands shaking from too much caffeine. A chilly breeze comes off the water, so I set my bags down and button my jacket, pausing for a moment to hug my arms across my chest. My gaze lands at the base of the arch. In the dim light, a small image comes into focus: A simple face, painted in purple. Long eyelashes, a few light vertical strokes above the top lip hinting at a mustache. The hair short, but longer in the front like mine. Beneath the face, in uneven letters, *Transitioning is freedom. Protect freedom N*●*W.* The face has been painted over in a few spots with illegible red marks so that it looks like blood has been smeared across the person's forehead, left cheek, and left eye.

I think about Lukas's words, how we notice things when we find meaning in them. I crouch in front of it, run my fingers along the mustache and every letter in *Transitioning is freedom*. The surface of the stone looks smooth, but it's rough and grainy to the touch.

I look for a tag. None.

As if the image might disappear if I look away, as if I've conjured it with my imagination, I keep my eyes on it while I back up to my bag and pull out my camera. Then, inching slowly back toward the face, I take a few photos, capturing a handful of details. The blood-smeared eye. The vague mustache. *Protect freedom N◉W.*

N◉W.

◉.

I start shivering so badly, I can barely get a decent shot. I'm cold and sweating and too caffeinated to think straight.

My phone vibrates. Another text from Lukas. *Still recording. We have the studio til dinner. Should I bring home Sangam?*

I look at the time. Almost 1:30. I've been wandering for close to three hours. I text *:)*.

In the distance I spot a brightly painted sign. *Diego's Restaurant and Bar.* I pick up my pace.

When I step inside the dimly lit dining room of Diego's, the air is thick with the taste of chili. My mouth watering, I drop into the first seat at a well-worn bar, mostly empty, except for a small group who look like regulars. Their punctuated laughter dissolves easily into the Spanish music that's pumping in through the speakers.

The bartender wears a black T-shirt with *DIEGO'S* written across the chest. The muscles in her skinny arms flex as she serves two mason jars full of bright blue liquid to a pair of women at a table across the room. Eventually she returns to the bar.

"What'll it be?" She has dark eyes and a pretty smile.

"Can I order food?" I have to raise my voice to be heard over the music.

She grabs a menu and sets it in front of me. Leaning over it, she brings her face closer to mine. "You can order anything you like."

I shift in my seat. As she walks away, I watch the slight

back and forth of her hips, the shape of her neck as she brushes a dark curl away with her fingers. She turns back to smile at me, and I welcome her flirtation.

Then I catch a glimpse of myself in the mirror over the bar and see that, in the dim light, under my woolen newsboy cap, with my lipstick long chewed off, I've turned into a guy.

But here's what I really see. The words from one of Lukas's books, *Woman's Mysteries*, by a student of Carl Jung. It said that at one time the moon's essential quality was considered to be unrepresentable by a single or static emblem because it was always changing. And because of its changeability, it was believed to possess a special kind of knowledge—one "too strange for man to bear," so strange, in fact, that it could blast their minds into madness. Hence the word *lunacy*.

So when the bartender returns, I keep the cap on, keep my face partially shaded. But this time she stops to look at me more closely before taking my order.

"So what'll it be?" she says again. I detect new color in her cheeks.

I clear my throat and order a burrito and a margarita.

She attempts another smile, but I can tell she's trying to erase any trace of flirtation.

It's not that I'm looking to be unfaithful to Lukas, whatever that even means for us. Watching the bartender, I'm not really planning anything. Just enjoying the surprise of a pretty woman who likes what she sees when she looks at me. Or at least she seemed to, until she realized what I am.

I take out my camera, scroll through my new photos, and then pull out my sketchbook to begin drawing some of the interesting details. She sets a margarita in front of me, but I don't look at her this time.

When she comes back with the food, however, my head's buzzing pleasantly. I notice a turquoise-and-orange beaded flower hanging from a beaded chain and obscuring the letters on her chest.

"I like your necklace," I say.

She looks down. "Thank you. A friend made it."

"Can I see it?"

"Sure." She takes the charm between her fingers and holds it out, careful not to get too close.

"Beautiful." I look up at her.

"If you'll excuse me," she says, and heads to the other end of the bar.

I sip my margarita, the buzz in my head growing stronger. "What's your name?"

"Perla." she says, without turning around.

What's wrong? I want to say. *You have nothing to fear.* But I'm still sober enough to recognize that I just want to make her the uncomfortable one.

I look down at my uninspired doodles, lick the salt from my glass, and scoot back in my stool, my appetite gone. I take out a mirror and reapply my lipstick. Without waiting for Perla to return with the check, I drop enough cash to cover the bill and collect my things.

I wrap myself up against the gray that has consumed the city and make for the door while one of the women with the blue drinks whispers something to Perla. As I step outside, they all share a good laugh.

‖HOME

A FEW HOURS later, I step out of the subway station in Park Slope and into a hard evening rain. I've spent the twenty minutes on the train sketching more things I'd seen on the street after lunch, trying to imagine how I could incorporate the cover of *Turn Her About*. But all I'm doing is copying other people's work. My own so-called art still going nowhere. And what was the point of finding the book cover if it's not meant to help me break free from this creative block?

I arrive home in a shitty mood, go to the bathroom, and curse my way out of sticky, damp clothes. I've gotten into the habit of changing away from Lukas so I don't have to see him avoid looking at my female parts. But I have to walk past him in the living room to get to my dry clothes. In our studio apartment, the only separation between rooms is the arch between the kitchen and the bedroom/office/living room. He doesn't even raise his head from his synth until I'm facing my dresser, my back to him. Then he comes over and traces my shoulder blade with his finger.

"What's wrong?" he says.

"Nothing." No matter how much I don't want to give in, every sensation in my body concentrates under his touch. I ignore it and push his hand away. He surrenders—too easily. I pull on a pair of underwear, a minimizing bra, a pair of boxer shorts, and a tank top.

Lukas is already back to his synth, with his headphones on. He never lets me hear him play until he thinks it's good enough.

I feel like he's ignoring me, and I can't stand the thought of being invisible right now. "What are you doing that I really can't hear?"

"Practicing."

"What about dinner?" I say. An accusation.

"What about it?"

"So I guess I'm supposed to go get Sangam."

Lukas finally pushes his chair away from the desk and looks at me. "What's wrong with you? I was just waiting until you got home."

"Me? I'm not the one practicing when it's time to get dinner on the table." I go to the kitchen and start slamming things around. After what feels like an hour but in reality is probably a few minutes, I stop and hold my hands out in front of me, spreading the fingers as if they'll open a pathway to release my anger. Instead they just look weird, like part of someone else's hands. I cross my arms and lean against the refrigerator, disgusted with myself for trying to bully Lukas into paying attention to me. I'm acting like my mother.

I mumble, "I'm sorry."

His hands fidget with knobs on the synth. "Whatever, it's fine."

I bring my bag to the bed, pull out my sketchbook, and open it to my terrible drawings. By way of explaining my behavior, I say, "Hours of chasing art, and this is all I can fucking do."

Lukas gets up from the desk and comes to sit next to me. His face softens. He says, "Dawn, who cares? You're onto something with the scouting. Just go with it."

"I'm onto a bunch of crappy drawings." I close the book and toss it onto the floor. "Jae invited me to help make signs for a protest, and I refused so I could finally do some art-work, and I've done nothing. While he's off making an actual difference."

Lukas makes a face. "Well, it's awesome that Jae wants to do something about the war, but trust me—protesting is not making much of a difference."

"You don't know that," I say. "Just because none of yours ever seemed to work. What if they did and we just don't know it yet? It's not like change happens overnight."

"Yeah, maybe that's the problem. It makes more sense to me to put my energy where I can see results."

I sigh. I don't want to fight about this. "Yeah. I mean, I know all of it is important. Composting, making stuff instead of buying it. It's just that sometimes I worry those things are invisible."

"In a capitalist society, choosing where to spend your

money is plenty visible. And so is art. Think about all the art that's made a difference to you."

"But that's work that's actually shown somewhere."

"Yours will get there. You just have to keep at it."

Something deep inside me sinks. "Is that supposed to make me feel better?"

Lukas looks confused. "I'm telling the truth."

"Right, that I'm not good enough yet but keep trying."

"No," he says. On the neck of his dark red T-shirt, the fabric has dissolved into tiny valleys.

"I might as well give up, then." I look at him sitting next to me but leaning into the wall, his arms crossed over his chest. His fingers stained with tobacco. His face tired. I'm exhausted from trying to please him—and everyone else. I want to cry, but not in front of him.

"I don't know what to do. I'm sorry," I say. I don't know whether I'm talking about politics or art or him, the fact that I know he's just trying to make me feel better and I won't let him. "I'm sorry," I say again. I pull his arms open, rest my head against his chest, and ball my hand into a fist, which I push against his warm, hard stomach. After a beat, he closes his arms around me and presses his lips against the top of my head.

When he holds me, it never feels like I thought being in a man's arms would feel. It isn't wrap-you-up-in-strong safe. It's the kind that says *You belong here.* He lifts my face and kisses me softly, and it feels so good to let everything go.

‖FOIL

ON MONDAY MORNING I wake with my art no further along and Gertrude's words back in my head. *You're a girl. . . . What does that make me?*

If Gertrude's father worked at a bindery, it must've been Gertrude who put that note in the book. Which means she must never have sent it to Marta after all. And now, years later, it's me who finds a queer—and maybe trans—person's voice from the past, an unspoken yearning she (he?) couldn't reveal to anyone except, by some long shot, a stranger in the distant future. And yes, maybe I'm only noticing the coincidence because it feels meaningful to me, maybe I'm drawing conclusions that are entirely beyond reason, but I can't get over the idea that, somehow, my fate is tied to Gertrude's.

It's time to investigate.

THE BOOK IS still on my workbench. I'd left it out so the spine could dry over the weekend. Maybe it will at least point me to the bindery where Gertrude's father worked.

The radio says it's a warm April day, and I'm feeling girly, so I throw on a vintage black dress with small embroidered pastel flowers, along with Mary Jane sandals. Opaque green tights cover the hair on my legs.

When I'm ready to leave, Lukas is showering. I enter the steamy, windowless bathroom and open the curtain. He leans his head out and kisses me as tiny warm drops tickle my face.

"Nice dress," he says.

I smile. It's unusual for him to compliment me when I'm female. I've always liked that he isn't the kind of guy to comment on a woman's appearance, but lately I've been needing to hear it. I want him to be attracted to the woman I am too.

As I reach for the door to leave, I hear his voice over the running water. "It would look better on me though."

I swallow, steam catching in my throat.

AS USUAL, I arrive at the museum fifteen minutes late. Amina and Stacey are already working at their benches. Katherine's on the phone, talking loudly to Celeste, the chief librarian, a jewel-green silk shawl peeking through the red waves of her hair.

The book is where I've left it. A sense of relief washes over me.

Katherine laughs at whatever Celeste said on the other end of the line. "Talk soon," she says. Then she hangs up and looks at me. "Well, good morning." She pauses to take in my dress while adjusting her shawl, then walks out of the bindery.

I say good morning to Amina from my end of our shared workbench, over the glue bowls and brush holders. She's scraping old glue off the spine of a book, gentle with her binder's knife.

"How was your weekend?" I say, my hands already on *Building Beauty*, peeling it away from the supports I'd set up to keep it in a safe position while the spine dried. I want to check the covers inside and out for a binder's stamp.

"My friend Khadija visited, and I took her to the planetarium. It was fun. Her first time to New York City."

I've removed all of the boards and weights from the book and am turning it over in my hands. "Whose?"

"Earth to Dawn," says Amina.

"Sorry," I say. "Just distracted."

"What are you doing?"

I'm staring at the bottom-right corner of the back cover, where I've found three tiny stamped words. Much of the gold foil has flaked off, making them hard to read. The first two look like *American Book*.

"Trying to make out this last word," I say. "Can you help me?"

Amina comes over and stands next to me. She takes the book and looks closely, moving it around in the light. "Hmm, too hard to tell," she says. We stand there staring at it. Then she says, "Wait." She sets a piece of repair tissue over the word and grabs a pencil from my drawer. As she rubs lightly over the letters with the pencil, the full word appears on the tissue. *Stratford*. "Voilà," she says, and returns to her end of the workbench.

"Thanks."

I want to tell her what I'm doing. We've gone on so many little adventures together that I know she would be excited to help. Like the time we were curious about the price of the fine chocolate some library donors buy for us every holiday season and we spent our lunch hour on a mission to the chocolatier. I'll never forget the look on the woman behind the counter's face after she said $295 and we laughed so hard, we thought she was going to kick us out of the store. And then there was the time I won the gift certificate to a fancy restaurant in a museum-employee raffle and, since Lukas is vegan, I took Amina as my date. The two of us had never felt so out of place, but the more we inadvertently broke the rules of etiquette— piling our coats and bags by the table rather than handing them over to be checked in the coat room, fumbling through the tasting of the wine, guessing over which utensils to use for which course—the more fun we had.

But this feels different. Technically I've stolen museum property, and I don't want to get her in trouble. I say, "Did she like it? Khadija?"

"She told me it's no Dakar." Amina turns to the wall behind her, takes a large roll of green binder's silk off the shelf, and cuts a small rectangle. She holds it up and smiles. "Matches your legs."

AMERICAN BOOK-STRATFORD.

I turn the words over in my mind. Maybe Stratford is Gertrude or Marta's last name, but it doesn't sound German.

At 11:30 Katherine goes to a meeting, and I seize the opportunity to do some Web searching. When I type *American Book-Stratford* into the browser, a handful of matching results appear. I click on the first listing—an entry in *Encyclopedia Britannica*: "Founded ca. 1899 by Russian immigrant Louis Satenstein in Chelsea, NY, the American Book Bindery company later expanded, becoming American Book-Stratford Press. . . ." The remainder of the text fades from light gray to white, and a note tells me to subscribe to read the full article.

I return to the search results. The next entry, *Oxford Reference*, doesn't get me much further. Before it cuts off, however, it lists three more names associated with American Book-Stratford: Sidney Satenstein, Geraldine Burr, and Hermann Kleber. My first small win: a German name.

I type each of the three names into the search bar and come up with the same results I got for American Book-Stratford. I'm at a dead end.

Sitting at the computer, I run through every source I can think of that might have information on historical bookbinders. The New York Public Library. Our own museum library. The universities. But searching them turns up only a few records, and it's unclear whether they're relevant. Then I remember the Grolier Club, the private bibliophile society that Katherine belongs to. They publish all sorts of papers and exhibition catalogs about obscure topics in bookbinding. I go to their website and search for American Book-Stratford Press. Two library records surface, one for a paper called "The Changing Story of American Bookbinding in the Twentieth Century." The description lists the names of the binders I've discovered and even a few more. It looks like I'm sure to find more information in at least one of these. There's only one problem. I need a member to access them for me—which means I'll have to ask Katherine, and I don't want her to know I've stolen the book cover.

Then I remember she's recently written a catalog introduction for a Grolier Club exhibition. For weeks she cared about nothing but researching a short-lived British organization from the turn of the twentieth century called the Guild of Women-Binders, so if I told her I was writing something on an old bindery, she'd probably be jazzed to help.

In the meantime, I don't want to attract attention, so I clear the browser's search history and return to my bench to make a new spine for *Building Beauty*.

WHEN KATHERINE RETURNS, I try to sound casual as I tell her that lately I've become interested in the American Book Bindery and, funny coincidence, the book I've been repairing was bound there.

"I've been wanting to write an article on them," I say. "But it's been hard to find information. So if I were going to look them up, where would be the best place?" I want her to think that looking in the Grolier library is her idea. She tends to be more generous with favors when she's the one to offer.

"Most likely the Grolier Club," says Katherine. "I can look into it if you want."

"Really? I would love that," I say.

"Brilliant." Looking very pleased, Katherine begins to type. So as not to hover, I return to my book-patient.

A few minutes later, she calls me back. "I found two records." She pulls a piece of paper from the printer and sets it on her desk. "I have a meeting at Grolier tomorrow after work, so I'll see what I can find for you."

"Awesome. Thank you," I say.

She fishes a compact and a tube of lipstick from her purse, and after she applies the lipstick, she turns back to me. "What do you think? It's a sample I got yesterday, but it seems like a better color for you, so if you like it, it's yours."

In the painting above her desk, three red hens strut proudly behind silver glittery barbed wire.

‖PARALYSIS

ON MY WAY home from the museum, I remember Amina's birthday is in a few days, so I take a detour to the Village to look for a gift. I find a monograph on Jenny Holzer and get excited thinking about how much Amina will love her work. Then I look for something nice to wrap it in and walk back toward the subway feeling accomplished. With the book and a rolled-up sheet of bright orange paper tucked under my arm, I'm thinking about Holzer's work and what makes people respond differently to words than to images, especially when they encounter them in unexpected places. I scan graffiti as I go, looking for writing, for the messages that artists are trying to shout to the rest of us, and I catch sight of a small bright spot in the middle of a crumbling plaster wall. I stop to inspect it. Someone has filled in a crack with a perfect little eye, shiny and round and painted in rainbow colors. Around the corner there are three more, but the thing that catches my attention this time is the tag: *DYC*. I have to look twice to make sure I'm not misreading it.

I haven't seen that tag since my junior year of high school, when every morning I left my little suburban town of East Rockaway behind for the School of Visual Arts in New York, where every day until lunch I worked hard to fit in by pretending to know all the things the city kids knew. It was the 1990s, and the student who made the biggest impression on me was Alice because she was the first teenage girl I'd ever met who had short hair. Every day she hunched over her workbench in her gray hoodie and thick-rimmed glasses and scribbled in her notebook, sketching comics about girls. Alice was one of those people who didn't go out of their way to socialize yet everyone wanted to be their friend. A few days into the program I learned what made her so cool. While the rest of us were home watching sitcoms with our parents after dinner, she was out sneaking around with graffiti artists, tagging bridges and tunnels with her signature, *DYC*, a combination of *NYC* and *dyke*.

These delicate little eyes in the wall are something new. A disruption, to be sure, but much more subtle. Something to make the city more welcoming perhaps, because it almost feels like these eyes are not here to watch us but rather to see us. They seem to have been made by another Alice, one I no longer know, but want to.

Back in high school I fell hard for Alice. She became the sun around which I orbited, the promise of what I could someday be—a girl who didn't fit the mold. Then one day in life-drawing class she asked to borrow a pencil and returned it with her phone number wrapped around it. That night I tried at least half a dozen times to call her, but my heart was beating so fast I was afraid it would take off before I could get the words out.

The next day in school she kept her head down as usual, giving no sign she'd expected to hear from me. Then, between life drawing and oil painting, we both ended up in the girls' bathroom, and as I was washing my hands she came over and stood right next to me.

"Did you get my note?" She was looking down, and I couldn't tell if she was nervous. It made me want to reassure her.

"Yeah," I said. "I was planning to call, but it got late."

"Yeah?" She lifted her gaze, and her eyes were intense behind her glasses. She was an inch or two shorter than me, but she felt so much bigger as she reached up and put her hand on my arm, just above my elbow. "It's not late now."

I shook my head, afraid to move, afraid that whatever was happening would stop as quickly as it had started. Alice took my hand and led me into one of the stalls. She ran her fingers through my long hair, placing it behind my shoulder, and pressed her lips to mine. It was the softest thing I'd ever felt, the fullness of her mouth, the tickle of the fine hair above her lip. My nipple hardened against her arm.

She said, "Call me tonight," and left me in the stall.

After that we were inseparable—and I began to emulate all the things I loved about her. That was when things began to change. First I cut my hair short, and afterward, as I got undressed for bed that night, I looked in the mirror and saw someone new, someone that both exhilarated and terrified me. The short cut had accentuated the squareness of my jaw and broadness of my shoulders. If I turned to the right angle, put my head down just enough, I could see a boy staring back at me, and he seemed to be thanking me for opening the door.

At sixteen, I was struggling madly over my attraction to a girl and didn't want to face what this boy inside me might mean. But once I'd let him out, he became impossible to ignore. I ditched my floral dresses for fatigues and boots, and the kids at SVA took notice. The more I hung around with Alice and fed the boy inside, the more friends I made.

Makeup became the last anchor to my femininity, so I held on tight to it, using it to exaggerated effect, outlining my eyes with thick charcoal and blue liner.

But as the months passed, I began to lose my sense of self. There were days when I woke up and no sign of the boy could be felt, when I wanted the dresses and lipstick back. But I thought it was only because I was weak—scared of what I was becoming, scared of what people were thinking of me, of the pain on my parents' faces. I didn't want to give anyone false illusions, or false hope. Besides, I was convinced that giving in to any urge to be feminine would amount to selling out. I was afraid of losing Alice and the acceptance I'd won at SVA.

At the same time, back home in my regular high school, my friends were talking about me behind my back. Rumors and half-truths circulated quickly. Just as things were becoming unbearable there, Alice began to turn icy. As soon as we finished eating lunch, she'd head back to her own school instead of walking me to the subway, and her weekends began to fill with all kinds of plans that didn't include me. I assumed she was jealous of my new popularity and I became resentful and self-righteous.

"It's like you don't want me to be happy," I said. "Did you just like me because I was quiet? Because I wouldn't give you any competition?"

"Is that what you think of me?" Her hands were in the pockets of her hoodie. Her faded black backpack crumpled at her feet.

I knew there was nothing I could say that would make her want me again and I hated her for it. I said, "How the fuck am I supposed to know? You've been avoiding me. Acting like a jealous baby."

Alice picked up her backpack and slung it over her shoulder. Her glasses fell down the bridge of her nose. She said, "I don't need this crap. If you want to know the truth, the Dawn I fell for looked like a girl, okay? If I wanted to date a guy, I wouldn't have wanted you."

As soon as the words were out, I could tell she was sorry, but it didn't matter. It was too much—this tenuous world I'd built crashing and burning at my feet. All I could do was walk away first so that Alice wouldn't see how much she hurt me, and once I left, neither of us tried to find our way back.

Without Alice, I was lost. I wanted to tell her to give me another chance, that the girl she fell in love with was still inside but I'd been keeping her locked away because I didn't know what else to do.

It was as if the world had made a promise the day she kissed me in the bathroom—that I would finally know who I was and there would be somewhere I belonged. That promise had been broken. My sixteen-year-old self lost trust in everything. Not only had I lost Alice, I'd turned my whole life upside down. No matter whether people loved or hated me for it, I'd locked myself into a new identity. I had no choice but to keep playing the bull dyke.

WHEN I OPEN the door to our apartment, it's silent. I kick off my boots and make for the bed, where I sit and rub my feet, then pull out my sketchbook and stare at a blank page. I make a couple of half-hearted swipes with some colored pencils, trying to capture Alice's rainbow eyes, but it doesn't look right.

Frustrated, I collapse onto the pillow.

It seems like only a few moments later that I feel a soft tickle on the back of my neck. Confused, I swat it away and open my eyes. The room is mostly dark, but I can make out Lukas.

"Get up, sleepy head. Time for Hunan," he says.

"I just laid down. What time is it?"

"Eight."

"Whoa, I must have been out for over an hour."

"Hungry?"

"I don't know yet." I close my eyes.

Footsteps. The soft orange glow of a light turning on. Bags rustling. The smell of Hunan Delight.

I roll onto my side and push myself up to sitting, nearly crushing my sketchbook.

Lukas is at the table already eating, pulling veggie Shanghai peanut wontons from a plastic container.

"Where were you?" I say, joining him.

"Recording studio." He has the unusual look of a good music day.

"How'd it go?"

"Okay, I guess."

"Good," I say. "You going to let me hear any of it?"

"Maybe."

I throw one of my chopsticks at him. Without missing a beat, he picks it up and adds it to the two he's been using, making one a double.

I reach for a wonton and put the whole thing in my mouth. "How's Pete?"

"Neko needs a tooth pulled."

The food is spicier than usual. I take a swig of water. "How do you pull a cat's tooth?"

"Anesthesia. How about your day?" says Lukas.

I stumbled into some artwork by the girl who broke my heart in high school, I want to say. I pick up a fork and stab some tofu. "My day was fine. Actually, I don't think I told you that on Saturday Jae translated the letter I found. But it sort of raised more questions than it answered, so today I did some investigating."

Lukas spoons more rice onto his plate, offers me the container. "Are you going to tell me?"

"Only if you don't make fun."

He's still using three chopsticks. I grab mine back from him and stand up to get my bag, where Jae's translation is.

"You want the last wonton?" he says.

I unfold the paper from Jae's notebook and look at what he's written. The messy handwriting, the cross-outs. I don't want to read it out loud so I hand it to Lukas.

When he finishes reading, he's still raking lo mein into his mouth. He says, "So, you were right."

Taking the paper from him, I bring it to our desk and put it in the drawer.

"It sounds like mystery solved though." He reaches over to my plate, steals a piece of tofu. "So what are you investigating?"

"Really?" I say, sitting back at the table. "You're not the least bit curious about who wrote it? Or why it was hidden? Or whether Gertrude ever had a chance to tell Marta how she felt, or come out as trans, if that's what she was?"

"Not really. I mean, it would be interesting, but so is whatever you can guess about her."

"Right," I say. I let out a sound that's meant to be a sarcastic laugh but comes out as a balloon deflating. "I don't know why I'm even talking to you about it."

"Hey, you know what I mean. Just because I don't care about the exact circumstances of these exact people doesn't mean I don't care that you find it interesting."

"It's the fact that they're actual people that makes it interesting," I say. I push my plate away and escape to the futon, covering the embarrassment that my sketchbook has become with the blanket.

"Why are you getting bent out of shape?"

"Why do you care more about fucking wontons than people?"

Lukas drops his chopsticks and starts to clear the table.

"Come on, don't do that," I say. I know I'm not being fair, but I'm too caught up in whatever I'm feeling to back down.

He pauses, holding our dishes in midair. "What do you want me to say, Dawn?"

"I don't know. Maybe just care whether these people got to be together. Or whether they might even be now. You know, when Gertrude wrote that letter, being gay was illegal. Can you imagine living through that? And then making it to now?" Lukas looks at me like I'm some kind of naive child, and I say, "I mean, yes, things are intensely shitty, but at least that law has changed, and for the first time gay marriage is actually a conversation."

Lukas shakes his head. "Maybe, but it's not like gay marriage is any kind of real win. It's just that gay people might now be allowed to live, as long as they do it like straight people."

"Wow," I say. "You're really missing the point."

"What? I'm just saying that if we get gay marriage, it'd only be because it makes people feel good about themselves so they can keep the oppression going in other ways."

"Okay, fine, I get it. I'll call our reps tomorrow and tell them to put the breaks on gay marriage."

"Whoa. Don't twist my words."

"I don't need to. That's basically what you said."

Lukas sighs and drops the dishes next to the sink. He jams the covers on the take-out containers and shoves them in the fridge. Then he grabs his pouch of tobacco from his jacket pocket and disappears onto the fire escape to roll a cigarette.

I sit in the corner of the futon—something I've started doing lately when I feel like Lukas doesn't want to be around me. Try to make myself invisible. All these years since I became repulsive to Alice for just trying to be myself, I'd finally begun believing I found a way to do it right. But lately I'm no longer sure. What if, like water, I've just been desperate to take the shape of whatever container will hold me? When it comes to Lukas, we're so busy trying not to conform to anyone's expectations that we've already agreed never to commit, never, god forbid, to marry. I'm exhausted from always having to stand for something rather than let myself want things.

The tip of Lukas's cigarette glows outside the window. Every time he takes a drag, the bottom of his face and his fingertips light up pale orange. He's squatting, hugging himself. I want to go out there and put my arms around him.

Eventually he stands and stamps out his cigarette butt, lingering in the dark. After a few moments, he opens the window and climbs inside. I wait for him to come over to me, but he makes for the desk, turns on his synth, and puts his headphones on. In our apartment it's the only way to be alone.

I lie back down and turn to face the wall.

‖CHARGE

THE NEXT DAY, I get a text from Jae to meet after work outside the Empire State Building. When I step outside to call him, I'm surprised he's serious. "It's the one touristy thing that everyone who lives in New York should have to do," he says. "For a sense of scale."

"Right. So work's not going any better today?"

He sighs. "Come on, it'll be awesome. You in or not?"

Despite his ignoring my question, I figure he might tell me what's up in person. "Of course I'm in."

But by the time I find him among the bustle of West Thirty-Fourth Street, I have all the sense of scale I need. "I don't know about this," I say. "Fear of heights and all."

He punches my shoulder. "Perfect. Then this is exactly what you need."

Reluctantly I follow him in—more convinced by the minute

that we're going to plunge to our meaningless deaths. But he looks so purposeful, and I feel like I owe him after waking him early on Saturday and then bailing on him. "I wouldn't do this for anyone else," I say.

Jae answers with his smile that's not a smile. Around us, people in their best sneakers, toting their best cameras, press in on us from all sides, chattering about all of the things they've seen in New York. We make it up to the observation deck alive, and I'm prepared to keep far from the railing, but it turns out there's a certain unreal quality up here. My legs still wobble, but I'm able to follow Jae through the crowd. We push through bodies and stake our claim on a small empty spot in front of a pair of pay binoculars.

Jae says, "I wouldn't bother with those. It's way more interesting to see how everything really looks from up here, and also it's kind of cool to see at what point individual objects and buildings start to merge together."

He's quiet again as he looks out over NYC. But he seems so content that after a little while I almost forget I'm supposed to be scared. He'd been right about getting a sense of scale. On the ground, the city swallows me whole. Up here, all of New York could fit in my arms if I spread them wide enough. The only thing I can't see is the people down below.

"It's like a bunch of toys, right?" Jae says, practically to himself. "Nothing but a giant playset. And when it's that small, how small are we?"

"Good question," I say. "And how small's your job?"

He nudges me in the ribs with his elbow, but then puts his arm around me. "Yeah, yeah," he says, his gaze still fixed somewhere in the distance.

But for me, being up here is different. With the city so small, it has no more power over me. I'm enormous.

We stay there for a long time, not talking, just looking. Eventually, Jae taps me and nods toward the door, and we make the long trip back down to the real world. He seems much lighter than he did on the way up.

On the street, we find a falafel truck. Then, finally, as we start eating, I break our bubble of silence.

"I'm sorry again about Saturday," I say, trying to keep my falafel in the pita. "Falling apart on you like that after you did me a favor." I get the sense he still doesn't want to talk about work.

"No worries here."

"Did you at least have a good turnout for the protest?"

"It's not for a few weeks. In fact, we're prepping again this weekend, making more signs to hand out. It's not too late to join us."

"You know I think it's great that you're trying to make a difference, but seriously, rallies aren't my thing."

"It's just signs. And maybe it would, you know, be fun for you to get out."

"Ah, I see what you're doing." Yogurt drips from my falafel onto my hand, and I hold it out to show him the sauce, then lick it off. "But don't worry about me, friend. Life is A-okay."

"Yeah, dude, you're a terrible liar. Also you're gross."

I set the sandwich down and bite into my baklava. It's warm and tastes like it just came from the oven. "Holy shit, you have to try this," I say, offering him a piece.

"Nah, I'm off sugar."

I roll my eyes.

"Seriously. That stuff's more addicting than cocaine. And they put it in everything just to tempt us to buy crap we don't need. Then little by little, it destroys your liver."

I take another bite. "You're right. Best to focus on your deep-fried sandwich, then."

Jae shrugs. "It's not all or nothing, sister," he says. "Anyway, if you and Lukas are around at the end of the month, I need someone to check on my plants."

"Wow, I'm flattered you trust me enough to ask," I say. I've unintentionally killed every plant Jae's given me except for a habanero pepper plant, which is only hanging on because Lukas assumed custody. "I'll send Lukas."

Jae nods. "Good idea."

"Where are you going—vacation or work conference?" I ask, forgetting I'm not supposed to talk about his job.

But he looks unfazed. "It's a work thing, and they're lucky I'm even going." He runs his fingers through his hair. "I mean, if no one cares about the quality of the writing inside our books, what the hell am I even doing there?" He tears into his falafel. "Whatever, I'm not going to pass up an opportunity to let them buy me a plane ticket to New Orleans and a few good meals."

"Fair enough." I want to say something helpful, but Jae's job hasn't gotten any less miserable in the two years I've known him, and I'm not sure it will. I wish he would just find a new publisher to work for.

As we eat, however, my mind keeps getting distracted—going back to the top of the Empire State, imagining again a city, a life I could take charge of. Like Jae is trying to do at work and with protesting a war that's bigger than we can even comprehend. I wonder if Gertrude was trying to take control of her fear by revealing herself to Marta. Looking up at the building again, I can still picture what it's like to hold New York in my arms. To feel power over something, to feel enormous. I want to keep that feeling close. It gives me an idea.

"Listen," I say. "Can you tell me a good place to get men's shoes?"

"I can do better than that. There's a consignment shop a couple blocks down." He stands.

"Wait, now?"

"After you finish licking yourself clean."

I eat the rest of my food in two big bites and stand. "After you."

Jae still has half his falafel. He eats as we walk.

"Let me see that," I say, pointing to his sandwich.

"What?" He holds it out, looking underneath to see if something is dripping.

I grab his wrist and pull it to my mouth for a bite.

"Fuck you," he says.

"You wish."

WE ARRIVE AT a little shop on Thirty-Second Street called Gentleman's Exchange. It's packed dense with racks of mildew-scented clothing and hats. The glass cases that line the walls display men's jewelry, and a well-dressed, gray-haired gentleman stands behind the counter in half-glasses, sorting small objects in velvet boxes.

"Good afternoon," he says, without looking up.

Suddenly self-conscious, I say nothing.

Jae leads me to the back corner, to a tight spiral staircase that only goes down. I follow him as he descends, and we land in a large basement full of shoe racks.

"What size are you?" he says.

"I don't know. I've never bought men's shoes before."

He looks at my feet. "I'm guessing six or six and a half."

I walk over to the black sixes. It's the smallest section, except for the extra-large sizes. I pull a pair of black-and-white Oxfords off the rack and sit on a red vinyl bench to put them on.

"Sharp," says Jae.

"As a tack." I stand and look in the mirror on the wall. "And they fit."

Walking back and forth, I admire the shoes, while Jae looks at the size tens. But I want something more practical that I can wear with everything. I settle on a more subdued black-and-gray pair.

The shopkeeper comes downstairs. "So, you're interested in a pair of shoes."

"Yes," I say, the word barely escaping. But when I turn to him, I see he's talking to Jae.

Jae says, "Not me. Just looking."

Confused, the salesman turns to me, then looks down at my feet. "Ah, very nice."

"Thanks."

"Going to a costume party, are we?"

My cheeks fill with heat. "Something like that."

"Nice choice, but a bit expensive if you're only planning to wear them once. You should check the bargain bin in the corner. I might have a pair with a similar look in there."

I don't know what my face is doing, but Jae looks at me with concern. He says, "We're fine, thanks."

"Yeah," I say to the salesman, "you're probably right." I pull off the shoes and put them back on the rack. I turn to Jae. "I'm all set."

"Dawn," he says.

"No, I'm good. Let's go."

He looks me hard in the eye. "All right. I'll catch up with you in a sec."

I have to walk past the salesman to get to the staircase. I make my way up and out of the store, moving out of view of the shop window. Then, pressing my fists against the wall, I spit on the ground.

A few minutes later Jae comes outside holding a beaten-up plastic Macy's bag. "Dude, sorry about that," he says. "That guy didn't know what he was talking about."

"Whatever." I don't want him to see how red my face has probably gotten.

"Here." He hands me the bag. "I got you the shoes."

I stare at the plastic straining at the corners of the shoebox and my throat tightens, so I keep my head down.

"So?" Jae nudges me with the bag.

I take it. But I don't look at him.

He puts a cigarette in his mouth and punches my shoulder.

"Fuck you," I say.

He offers me his elbow, and we walk to the subway arm in arm.

‖BUCHBINDER

FIRST THING NEXT morning I remember it's Wednesday, the day Katherine had said she would bring the articles from Grolier Club to work. I shower quickly. When I open my closet, the Macy's bag is right there, staring at me. I take the shoes out and set them on top of my feet before the mirror, looking at myself in my bathrobe and two-tone Oxfords.

Lukas is drinking a cup of coffee at the kitchen table, across the room. "What are those?" he says.

"I got them yesterday."

He stands and pours me a cup, then kisses me on the back of the neck and goes to shower.

I take off my robe and pull Lukas's blue button-up shirt from the closet, then an undershirt from his drawer. I find the pair of gray men's slacks that I'd bought the day I got this haircut. I step into the pants, slide on the shirts and shoes, and grab a necktie from the top drawer of Lukas's dresser.

When the outfit is complete, I study myself in the full-length mirror again, pressing my hands over my breasts in a futile attempt to flatten them, turning right and left to see how the pants are doing with my hips. It's not perfect, but it's close. Unlike my night out with Jae, this time it looks right. Or maybe it feels right. A thrill passes through me.

Lukas comes out of the bathroom and looks at me like I'm something good to eat. I check the clock. It's almost time to leave for work.

Thrill quickly turns into hesitation—I've never actually worn a full men's outfit. My jeans and T-shirts are ambiguous enough to suggest I just don't care much about my appearance. In these clothes, with my partially shaved hair and no makeup, I could pass for a man. Yet exhilarating as that is, I have no idea how everyone at work will react, and it's supposed to be a good day. Katherine is bringing me more information about Gertrude and Marta. And if I want to be on time, I have to go—now.

I hear the consignment shop salesman's condescending voice. *Going to a costume party, are we?* It would have been easier if he'd been an asshole, instead of some clueless old dude who can't imagine any reality outside his own. Maybe Jae wouldn't have stayed for the shoes. The clock is looking back at me like an animal baring its teeth.

Before I know what I'm doing, I've punched the mirror.

"Dammit." I grab my fist with my good hand. My knuckles sting. I've scraped the skin, but the mirror, as if to mock my fragility, is fine. It's not actually made of glass, so it only warped momentarily under the impact.

"What was that?" says Lukas. He's standing in the kitchen half dressed, eating a banana.

"Fuck." Frantically, I loosen the tie, unbutton the shirt.

"Dawn, what are you doing?"

I ignore him. Kicking off the shoes, I wrestle myself out of the clothes and leave them in a pile on the bed. I throw on a pair of jeans, a T-shirt, and a cardigan. "I have to go," I say.

Lukas kisses me goodbye. I grab my bag and step into my boots on my way out the door.

I'M LATE TO work. But the articles are sitting on my workbench.

With Katherine off at a meeting and Amina and Stacey toting a big box of scrap materials upstairs, I have a rare thirty seconds alone. Sitting on my stool, I thumb through the articles. The first is only two-and-a-half pages, and it focuses on how the Industrial Revolution changed publishing. The second, "The Changing Story of American Bookbinding in the Twentieth Century," is nine pages long and broken into five sections: "Hand Bookbinding," "From Craft to Commerce," "Five Pioneers," "Other Players," and "The Modern Binder."

Before I finish scanning the article, Amina and Stacey return, out of breath and giggling. Amina comes to see what I'm looking at.

"Are those the articles about the death of hand bookbinding?" She picks up a dry glue brush, runs her fingers through the bristles. "Wouldn't that be sad?"

I laugh. "It does sound sad. Fortunately, we three are saving it from certain doom."

Stacey mixes a bowl of glue. We all settle down to work. Between every step I complete on my book-patient, I pause to steal a glance at "The Changing Story of American Bookbinding." In the "Other Players" section, something catches my eye. When the American Book Bindery expanded in the late 1940s, Louis Satenstein partnered with the German binder Hermann Kleber, and the article has this to say about him:

> Kleber came from an artistic family and was given many opportunities to explore his chosen craft before he had to go into hiding during World War II. As a result, he encouraged creativity in his own family—his wife, Helga, daughter of Munich architect Otto Kempner, and their three children, all of whom assisted Kleber in his bindery from the time they were old enough to hold a glue brush.

It's not much, but two things draw my attention: Kleber is indeed German, and if his children used to help him in the bindery, then any one of them could have hidden a letter in a book. What if one of them was Gertrude?

I shoot a glance at Amina and Stacey to see if they're watching me, if they can sense what's going on inside my head. But they're both still focused on other things, Stacey lost to her earbuds, Amina measuring a piece of linen against the spine of a book and humming. I stand and announce I'm going to the bathroom. I don't have a plan, I just want to get out of the room, but when I get there and lock the door behind me, immediately I take out my phone and call Lukas. While it rings, I stare at myself in the mirror. In the pale fluorescent light of the bathroom my lips are almost white.

"What's up, babe?" he says.

My shoulders drop with relief. "Hey," I say. "You in front of a computer?"

"Yeah, I'm at work."

"Can you look something up for me?"

"Where are you?"

I look at the tiled walls, the smiley face some museum rebel has drawn in thick red marker below the toilet paper roll. "Also work."

"Don't you have a computer in the lab?" he says.

"Yeah, but everyone's there, and this is"—I'm afraid he'll tell me I'm being stupid—"It's about the book cover."

"Fine, shoot," he says.

"It's a name. Gertrude Kleber." I spell *Kleber* slowly to make sure he types it correctly.

He goes silent, but his keyboard clicks in my ear. Finally he says, "Just a few phone book results that you have to pay for if you want the full entry. Who is she?"

"How much?" I say.

More clicking.

"Not sure. It seems like you have to put in the info you're looking for first."

"Do they at least give you a general location?"

"One does. Looks like she's in Colorado. Why?"

"If it's who I'm hoping it is, she was the daughter of one of the bookbinders at the American Book Bindery." I close my eyes to concentrate. "But maybe Colorado would be too far. Try Marta Kleber."

A few more clicks and Lukas says, "Nothing. Sorry."

I sigh.

"It was a long shot, anyway."

A weight settles in my stomach. I draw breath, taste the chlorine in the air. "You're probably right."

"Besides, what are you planning to do if you find the person who wrote it? Give it back?"

I lean against the sink. "I haven't thought that far ahead." I look at myself in the mirror again. I almost don't recognize my face.

"I know you're excited," says Lukas.

"I'm not excited," I say. "I'm concerned." I don't know what I'm talking about. I just don't want Lukas to be right. "I mean, I've got to get back to the lab. Thanks for your help."

"No, Dawn, wait." He pauses. "I guess it's still *possible* you can track them down—Gertrude and Marta." He stresses *possible* so as not to sound unduly sincere.

"Yeah, and maybe I'm crazy."

"That goes without saying."

I laugh, but I'm too discouraged to play along with his teasing. "I have to go."

"Fine," says Lukas. "I just don't want you to get your hopes up."

I know he's trying, in his way, to apologize for not being supportive. He can't just say *I'm sorry*. "Still have to go," I say.

"Okay. See you later."

"Yeah, see you later." Before I hang up, I mouth *I love you* into the receiver.

DURING LUNCH, WHEN everyone's out, I do a quick Internet search myself. But I'm staring at the same results Lukas got—including the one for a Gertrude Kleber in Colorado. Digging deeper, however, I discover she's not even a real person, just some algorithm to get you to the page where they ask for your money. I can type *Marta Kleber* or any other name and get similar results, different cities. I head back to my workbench, surprised at the intensity of my disappointment. Even though I don't know what I'd do if I found Gertrude or Marta, I can't shake this feeling of urgency. I spend the afternoon trying to focus on work, and then I beg off with a stomachache an hour early to head to the main branch of the New York Public Library.

When I get off the subway in midtown, I weave through crowds and past a food cart, a man behind it yelling out the names of sandwiches like an auctioneer. After I get through the bag check at the main door of the library and the one upstairs at the General Research Division, I can no longer hear the street, just the quiet echoes of tourists' voices in the giant hallways and the shuffling of bags and feet.

I look up at the sky painted on the ceiling, bluer than the one outside. A sign above one of the doors reads, *A good Booke is the pretious life-blood of a mafter fpirit, imbalm'd and treafur'd up on purpofe to a life beyond life.* I stop and scribble the words into my sketchbook. Then I walk past two teenage girls staging photos of each other reading, toward one of the many computers. I load the library's catalog, typing

American Book-Stratford Press and *Kleber* into the search bar. Only one result. I fill out my slip and bring it to the reference librarian.

Fifteen minutes later, I'm holding a history of bookbinding in early twentieth-century America. I flip through slowly, until my eye catches a photograph with the word *Kleber* in the caption. Helga Kleber and the three Kleber children are huddled together on the sidewalk in front of a tall brick building—the American Book Bindery—the sun shining strong on their faces. I hold my breath. The child on the left is named Gertrude. She's a stocky girl of medium build, who stands in stark contrast to her much younger sister, all bonnet, skirt, and little boots. In fact, I have to look twice to make sure I haven't mistaken Gertrude for Tomas, the son, because she looks more like him in her bright white button-up, collared jacket, and short pants, her dark hair cropped close in a bob as short as a girl could probably get away with back then. She stands more like her brother too, one hand in her pocket, a casual lean, eyes that seem to say *I dare you.*

For a few moments I take her in, unable to pull my eyes away, unsure if I'm dreaming.

Then I scan the chapter for more information and land on the word *Holocaust* near the end. Kleber had made his career as a fine binder in Germany at the Bremer Presse, which was destroyed during the war, shortly after he and his family escaped to the United States. While antisemitic sentiment was escalating in 1938, a fellow craftsman named Vogt took pity on the Klebers and found them a place to stay in Switzerland until their US visas would come through. Sadly, it's a story that's become too familiar to me, especially after growing up hearing survivors talk to our congregation. So I pause to let the weight of it sink in.

Next there are two translated excerpts from a letter Kleber wrote after arriving in the States. The first details how he came to be employed at the American Book Bindery and his relationship with its Jewish owner. The second describes how he was made a partner at American Book-Stratford Press, but it also includes this:

> Sometimes I wonder if I did the right thing bringing my family here. Of course I'm grateful that we made it to the States, against all odds, but I can't help wondering if we'd be better off somewhere smaller than Manhattan. Here, the girls have me worried. I'm afraid the sense of freedom that Gertrude in particular feels in this city where anything goes has made her too fearless, that her taste for justice and liberty has grown too strong and she'll refuse to conform to any of our new society's expectations.

I think of the book cover again—the satisfaction on the face of the man in the mirror—Gertrude's words: *Lately I've dared to hope*.

I turn back a few pages and stare at the photograph again, then snap a close-up of Gertrude with my camera. I get up to photocopy the pages, and as I do, I look around to make sure I'm really in the library and that there are other people here who can see the same things I can. I've spent days imagining this girl, this possibly trans or gender-bending girl, trying to communicate with me from the past, trying to get me to follow her (his?) story, but I'm only now fully realizing how brave she must've been, how much she was risking. I look again at the photograph, at Gertrude—her easy posture, the challenge in her stare—and I know she's the one who wrote that letter on the back of a queer pulp book cover. And I'm going to find her.

‖SIGNAL

WHEN I GET home from the library, Lukas is still at work. I don't stop to take off my coat, just grab the leftovers from the fridge. Waiting for the computer to boot up, I shovel cold lo mein into my mouth, and within seconds I'm searching again for Gertrude Kleber. I get more specific, typing in phrases like *public records*, *employment*, and *address in New York*, but no matter what I try, I'm faced with the same useless results. I try banging on the side of the monitor, as if the information I want is merely stuck inside.

BY THE NEXT evening I've still had no luck. But now that I've found someone who could actually be the Gertrude who wrote the letter, I'm determined to keep looking. I only need to figure out what my other options are. Even Lukas is becoming invested, except he keeps trying to give me advice, and it's frustrating me. I don't want to start another argument with him and then sit around for the rest of the night feeling sorry for myself. Which is becoming our routine. So I get out of the apartment before he returns—to clear my head, maybe look at the pictures I've been taking, and, god forbid, make some art. I decide to go to the bindery where I used to intern, which is only a fifteen-minute walk. I still have a key in case I ever need to help out in "emergencies."

It's a mild spring evening. People walking with jackets hanging around waists and looking alive in their bodies. Exhilarated by the feeling of warm air on my bare arms, I'm more hopeful with every step. I've finally escaped an argument, if only for now. But anxiety starts to creep in too. Like, what if Lukas isn't there anymore when I get back? It's a fear I've had since childhood. When my mom was leaving the house, she used to tell me to count to sixty sixty times, and by the time I got to the end, she would return. It was a smart trick. I always got distracted before I made it through the first time.

Sweating and out of breath, I arrive at the bindery. After raising the gate and opening the front door, I set my bags down on a stool next to the workbench. I pull out my camera and scroll through pictures. The ice cream cone. The teeth. The wispy mustache. *UNITED WE STAND*. I like them, but they're not getting me anywhere just sitting on my camera. Zooming in on the details, with the image of Gertrude still fresh in my mind, finally I'm overcome by the desire to make something out of it all, get my hands on paper, begin folding and shaping it.

I pull out my sketchbook and map out a simple accordion book, then fill in some details, creating a backdrop of tall buildings, a bridge in the distance. In the foreground some shorter buildings, a bus, a billboard. I sit and stare at what I've drawn. It's a start, but it's too generic. Maybe it needs more dimension, like some pop-up elements. Or maybe the accordion is the wrong structure. Frustrated, I draw a big X over the sketch, drop my pencil next to it, and look around at all the tools and materials I once would've had a clear plan for.

I want to scream. I turn back to my sketchbook. On a clean page I write:

Street art. Intrusion or remaking the city?
Speaking from the shadows.
Peeking out from behind their masks.
What do they want?
Protection.
Protect freedom N◉W.

I look at the ◉ and wonder if it holds any special meaning. I drink the coffee that's gone cold in my travel mug and labor over the art that's forming in my head but refusing to reveal itself. *Remaking the city.* I think about how memory, especially of trauma, can split a whole city—a whole nation—in two: the place of before and the place of after, where fear becomes the collective emotion. Even as no one agrees on what to fear. No wonder I haven't been able to create anything meaningful since returning to New York. I don't know if I belong here anymore. If I ever did. I look down at my notebook, cross out the words, and tear out the page I've written on. Ball it up like a dirty napkin and toss it into the garbage. Then I gather my things, stand, and shove the stool back into place.

AFTER A GOOD night's sleep, I can't even remember why I was avoiding Lukas. Of course it would feel good to have his help looking for Gertrude. And maybe if I find what I'm looking for, I'll be able to stop pushing him away. I want to be stronger than we both think I am.

Over the course of the day, my determination increases. After all, I work in the research library of one of the world's biggest museums, and there's no better way to find anything than to ask a librarian. On my way out at the end of the day, I stop at the reference desk. After I summarize all the searches I've tried, being deliberately vague about who I'm looking for, my colleague Vika suggests searching real estate records, giving me a few URLs for databases in the tristate area.

Back home, I give it a go and almost can't believe it when it works. After everything else has failed, there she is. A person named Gertrude Kleber purchased a house on Philips Court in Mount Sinai, New York, in 1981. That's just a few hours east, on Long Island. Quickly my hands are back on the keyboard, entering her name and address. But the results are not much better than before—more of the same so-called public records that turn out to be private companies promising information for money. I'm about to call it quits when something new leaps out at me: *Mount Sinai School District*. I click. Gertrude's name is buried among a list of teachers, though it says she retired in 1999. I close my eyes to concentrate. If she retired at sixty-five, that would make her about sixty-nine now. Which means she would have been somewhere in the neighborhood of sixteen or seventeen when that letter was written.

Excited, I scrawl the district office's phone number on a piece of scrap paper. By then I'm sitting practically in the dark.

The evening sun has begun to fade and I haven't turned a light on. I look at the time on the monitor. 7:33 p.m. Way after-hours for the school district, but I don't want to give myself time to change my mind. Before I plan what to say, I click the light on and my fingers are dialing, my chest rising and falling. As the phone rings, my eyes trace a crack in the corner of the wall. At the top it breaks off into a half arrow, pointing up and away.

Although I don't expect a person to answer this late in the day, when a recording picks up, my stomach softens.

At the beep, I clear my throat and try to sound professional. "Hi, I'm a bookbinder writing an article for the *Grolier Club Gazette* on Hermann Kleber. I have reason to believe that Gertrude Kleber is his daughter, and I'm very interested in interviewing her for the article. I know she used to teach in your district. If there's some way you could put me in touch with her, I would greatly appreciate it." I leave my name and phone number and sit listening to the blood pound in my ears.

Standing, I pace the living room. It's Friday, so Gertrude probably won't receive my message until Monday morning, if the district passes it along to her at all. What if she doesn't return my call? What if she does? What will I say? *I have this very intimate thing you tried to hide. Can you tell me, a perfect stranger, all about it?*

Then I remember Lukas's extra tobacco in the desk drawer. I pull it out, grab a rolling paper, and fumble along until I have something resembling a cigarette.

I open the window and climb out onto the fire escape, next to Lukas's habanero pepper plant. As I suck in smoke and pick loose pieces of tobacco from my tongue, I try to imagine

Gertrude. Maybe she's home eating dinner. Would she be alone, or would Marta be at her side? I picture them, Gertrude tall and sturdy, Marta shorter and slighter, sitting across from each other at a small table, buttering their bread, catching up on the day.

I imagine her surprise at hearing her father's name in my message, learning that a bookbinder from the twenty-first century is interested in him. Will she return my call herself, or will someone from the school reach out? Maybe they'll give me her phone number. Or would they refuse me? Tell me she prefers not to be contacted?

So go my thoughts, around and around, as I watch the streetlights stagger on below, the messenger bags jostle on the sidewalk, and the night sky continue to fall.

‖PLAN

ONE MORNING, AFTER days have dragged by with no word from the school district—or Gertrude—I step out of the shower and Lukas comes into the bathroom holding a piece of paper. He hands it to me, trying not to smile.

"What's with you?" I say.

"Look."

Still dripping wet, I glance at it, expecting it to be a flyer for the show he's playing tonight with Pete. It's the first one in a while, and it's special to him because they're doing it as a benefit for the Brooklyn ASPCA. But the paper says *Gertrude* and has a phone number. It takes a second to register. "Wait," I say. "She called?"

Lukas nods. "Just now. And she said you can call her back this morning."

"Holy shit." A jolt of excitement launches me out of the

shower, and I run to my phone, still dripping wet. But as I pick it up, I see the time. "Shit. I have to leave for work. Damn."

Lukas steps out of my way, and I make a frantic attempt to brush my teeth and get dressed with time to spare. Thinking of his gig tonight, I throw on my new crocheted vintage dress. But when I'm finally ready, the clock says it's too late for a phone call. As I finish gathering my stuff, I shove Gertrude's phone number into my bag and then hightail it out of the apartment.

By the time I get to work, I can't concentrate on anything else. Amina's already busy, mixing paint to dye a piece of muslin. Stacey's at the ultrasonic welder, encapsulating the pages of a brittle manuscript in Mylar. Katherine's at a meeting, and besides, since I've told her I'm writing an article about Kleber, there's no reason I can't operate in the open. I walk over to the office phone that sits on her desk. My hands shake as I dial. The receiver presses against my ear. On the first ring, I almost hang up, but a deeper impulse overrides the fear. On the fourth ring, I'm preparing to get an answering machine, but a voice says, "Hello?" It's a soft voice and sounds younger than I expected.

Adrenaline forms my response. "Hi, my name is Dawn Levit. I'm returning a call from Gertrude Kleber about an article I'm writing for the *Grolier Club Gazette*." The phone cord is digging into my right hand. I look down and release the fist I've tightened around it.

"Yes, Ms. Levit, just a moment."

There's a long pause. Then a deeper voice on the other end of the line. "This is Gertrude." It's a confident voice, and I can't tell whether it has a German accent. I wait for her to say more, but this is all she offers.

I've rehearsed this moment in my head through the entire subway ride and the walk from the station to work. But now my words are rearranging themselves. "I was hoping I could interview you for the article," I say. "It's about your father. At least I wanted to ask if he was your father. His name is Hermann Kleber." I pause. "Sorry. He worked for American Book-Stratford Press, in the 1950s."

Gertrude says, "Yes, my father was Hermann Kleber, and he was a bookbinder there."

My mouth goes dry. "Thank you. Um, I said this to the person who answered the phone, but I'm a bookbinder too, and I'm really fascinated by the history of the press." I wince. I sound like an idiot, not a reporter.

"All right, what did you want to ask me?"

"Uh, now?" I say. Amina looks up at me and furrows her brow. I wave her off and try to seem calm. "Actually, I don't have time to interview you right now. I'm calling from work. But I see you're on Long Island. Is that right?"

"Yes."

"I'm just in the city. If you're free this week, I could come out there and take you to lunch."

"That's not necessary," she says. "I wouldn't want you to come all the way out here just to ask me a few questions."

"My parents are out there," I say. "I can visit them too." Another lie. I have no intention of seeing them.

"In that case, hold on. I need to clear it with Clare. My hospice nurse. She's threatening to come every day."

"Oh my gosh," I say. "I'm sorry. I didn't know."

"Of course you didn't. But don't sound so alarmed. I'm not dying yet, just putting you on hold."

I don't know whether to laugh at her joke. My hand grips the cord again. This changes everything. I should hang up and leave her in peace. But quickly she's back on the line.

"How about Wednesday next week? There are a few restaurants in Stony Brook, which would be close to the train. Do you like Thai food?"

"I do," I say.

"Why don't you come to Thai Palace, right on Route 25A. What time?"

"I don't know. Twelve thirty?" I say.

"Fine. See you then."

"Thank you. I appreciate it, but are you sure?" I say.

She's already hung up.

"What was that about?" Amina asks.

"The article," I explain. "Seems I found the binder's daughter." *And she's dying*, I want to add, but I don't.

"Cool. Big adventure to Long Island? Are you really going to see your parents?" She looks hopeful. She knows we're not really in touch, but I've never explained why.

"No."

Amina frowns. "So it's just an adventure, then?" She perks up a little, gives me a look like she knows I'm hiding something. This is the sort of thing I would usually invite her along for, but I've hardly even mentioned it.

Stacey comes over and sets down her stack of Mylar-encased pages. The crumbly old paper now plastic and shiny. "What's going on?" she says.

"Dawn has a secret," says Amina.

"I do not."

"What kind of secret?" says Stacey.

"Okay," I say. "I'm going to lunch. Who's coming?" *I can still change my mind about Gertrude*, I console myself. I can call back anytime and tell her never mind, the article was pulled.

"I'm coming." Amina threads her arm through mine.

THE STAFF CAFETERIA at the Met is a city of its own. Hundreds of people milling about with trays. Amina and I split in the entranceway—me toward the pizza, Amina toward the deli. After we secure our lunches, she leads me to one of the quieter tables off to the side. Which means she's planning to press me for information about Gertrude. We sit, the corners of our trays touching. She bites into her sandwich, a small, neat bite. I tear into my pizza, but it's too hot. I drop it back on my plate.

Amina laughs. "So, tell me about this mystery trip to Long Island."

"It's no big deal."

"It has to be a little exciting. Otherwise, why are you going?"

"Not really," I say. "Just a quick research trip." What I want to say is, *This isn't the fun kind of excitement. It's not fancy chocolate or a winning raffle ticket.* I want to say, *It feels like my sanity is on the edge of slipping, and for some reason I think a stranger can help me.*

Someone at the next table is talking about the Temple of Dendur, one of the exhibitions in the museum. It's the first time she's been in there and she was alone and swore she had a spiritual experience.

Amina is waiting for me to divulge more about Long Island. I say, "So, what's new with you? How's tap dancing?"

"Good," she says. "I mean, I'm still definitely a beginner,

but I really like the people. It's been a nice way to forget about dating for a while." She nods to herself. "Oh! Also, I spoke to my mother yesterday and guess what she said? She wants to come to the US for my recital. I just said, 'What?' Can you believe that?"

"Whoa, that's awesome," I say. "I can't wait to meet her."

And I can't. But at the mention of her visiting, I also find myself a little homesick. And jealous. Of Amina's confidence, her life alone on the Upper East Side, an ocean away from her family and somehow okay with that. This would only be the second time her mother has visited and, as far as I can tell, Amina's just adapted. She's been living in a foreign country where she once knew no one, and even though it doesn't quite feel like home, Dakar feels less and less like home to her too. I once asked her if she ever thought she'd go back, and she said not yet. Eventually she'll make up her mind, but for now, she's making the most of the moment.

She takes another bite of her sandwich. Then she pauses and says carefully, "You look blue."

I try to make light of it. "You sound like Katherine."

"I know. Sorry." Amina sips her drink. But then, with a mischievous look, she straightens up in her seat and, doing her best British accent, says, "Your face sends a signal to the world—and no one likes a sourpuss, so fake it till you make it."

"Ugh, gross," I say, but I can't help laughing. "That's way too close to reality."

Amina giggles. "Not as good as your impression."

Playing along, I clear my throat and pretend to wrap a shawl around my shoulders. "If a thing is worth doing, it's worth doing right. So, put your goddamn eggs into it, ladies."

Amina laughs so hard she has to wipe her eyes. When

she calms down, she says, "I don't think she's ever said 'god-damn,'" and that sets us both off again.

Eventually Amina's laugh trails off into something like a sigh. "Speaking of putting your eggs into it," she says. "Did you see her practice cake yesterday for the Center for Book Arts edible book exhibition?"

"Would've been hard not to. I mean, if you bring a giant cake to work, aren't your coworkers going to expect you to share it?"

"Right? I asked," Amina says. "She was taking it to a dinner with some friends after work. But wasn't it amazing? All those fine details?"

"Yeah, it was incredible. True Katherine style—eggs all in."

"Seriously. I'm glad you agree. Because at the end of the day I heard her on the phone with Richard, and it sounded like he was giving her a hard time about the fact that it was a cake, not technically an edible book. She just kept agreeing with him, and when I asked her about the exhibition this morning, she said she's too busy and had to drop out."

"Wow, that's shitty."

"I know. And I was surprised to see her give up so easily. Like, what's the deal? She talks back to everyone but her own husband?"

I think of the dynamic between my mom and dad. "Yeah, but sadly, I've seen it before. Not that I understand why people just give away their power to someone who's supposed to love them." Then I wonder if this is what I'm doing with Lukas.

Amina nods. "Maybe you're right. But it's jarring to see it with her. She's so outspoken."

"I know. For someone who doesn't censor herself, you'd think she'd have more confidence." It's surprising, but I'm actually feeling a little sad for her. "Makes me wonder what all that bluntness is covering up."

"Yeah," says Amina.

I pick at a piece of cheese that's hanging off my pizza. "Listen, let me know when that recital is too, okay?"

"Why? You coming?" She sounds surprised.

"Why wouldn't I?"

"I don't know. You just seem more distant lately or something."

Her words sting. I haven't been the best at making—or keeping—friends in recent years. And I don't want to lose her. "I'm coming to your recital," I say. "I promise."

She smiles.

Maybe I'm getting tired of the tough act. Or maybe I feel like I owe her because of all the times she's opened up to me. Whichever it is, I say, "Listen, can you keep a secret?" Then as soon as the words are out, I'm a schoolgirl—the schoolgirl I've never been but love turning into with Amina.

"Of course I can," she says.

I look around to make sure no one we know is close by. Then I move my chair toward her and tell her everything. How I found the cover of *Turn Her About*. How I'm pretending to write an article so that I can track down whoever wrote it. It's only after I tell her that Gertrude is dying that she breaks in to say, "How sad. Do you know why?" But then I don't leave it there, as I'd intended. I explain how Lukas doesn't understand what I think is so interesting and how we've been arguing ever since I found the book cover and that I don't know what to do

about it. Finally I stop talking, and she asks why we're arguing, and I say probably because I'm confused.

"About what?"

"I don't know. About who I am, I guess."

She's silent.

"Never mind. I don't know why I'm talking about it."

Amina fiddles with her sandwich. She says, "Is this about—
Are you a lesbian? Because if you are, I hope you know you
can tell me."

I feel like a slob, covered in sauce and pizza grease. Worried
I've made a mess of the dress I've worn for Lukas's gig, I wipe
the front. Nothing comes off on the napkin. "Not exactly.
That's kind of the problem." I pause while Amina looks at
me. Or the me she knows. The me I've always been at work:
Dawn the heterosexual female (Lukas calls me a professional
female). I'd thought it would be a good idea to use this job as a
chance to try on something closer to femininity again, at least
breaking up the jeans and T-shirts with dresses sometimes.
Since no one knew me, it meant another chance to be normal.
So that's how Amina has known me and how I've been trying
to keep it. Not wanting yet another person to change their
mind about me.

She doesn't look the least bit troubled. She says, "Just so I
understand, are you attracted to Lukas?"

"Yes."

"And he's a guy."

I look down at my plate. "Mostly," I say.

Amina regards me matter-of-factly. "And both of you like
this?"

"Seems like it."

"So what's the problem?"

"It's just that Lukas is attracted to the masculine things about me—but not so much the feminine."

I haven't told anyone this. I haven't even admitted it to myself. I feel like I've just made it real and am terrified that now I'll have to do something about it.

Amina says, "Sounds like he's the one that's confused."

‖HINGE

EVENING ERUPTS IN a hard rain, pounding sidewalks, flooding sewers, and battering umbrellas. As I head out to Parkside Bar for Lukas and Pete's gig, I take off my hood and let the sky soak my hair. I've been excited all day to hear what they've been up to.

The subway station smells of wet rat. It's hot and everyone's struggling to hold their dripping umbrellas away from everyone else, but there's nowhere without bodies. When I finally surface on the sidewalk downtown, the rain has calmed to a drizzle. I feel sticky all over, but I'm wearing shoes with heels and I let myself enjoy how they change the way I hold myself. The pavement coming up to meet me with every step, challenging me to keep my balance. The insides of my thighs rubbing together under my dress. I can already taste my drink. I want a thick lager in a cold glass.

I want Lukas.

When I arrive, he and Pete are onstage doing a sound check, Pete at the mic with his bass, all glasses and messy hair, Lukas behind his synths. It's a Thursday night, but it's still early, so the place is barely full.

I wave to them and walk to the bar, where I find Jae. He's with a woman, his hand resting on her back as he orders a glass of wine. I punch his shoulder.

He turns to me and smiles. "Hey, meet Lindsay," he says. "My coworker who thinks she doesn't like electronic music."

Lindsay says, "Ha ha," and swats his shoulder, a lock of short dark hair escaping from behind her ear.

"Nice," I say. "You've come to the right place."

Jae looks at me like he's sizing me up. He always looks at me that way when he has news. "What's up?" I say.

"Nothing. I just spoke to my sister. But we can talk later."

"Oh no, you can't do that. If there's something to share, let's have it."

"You have to promise you'll keep an open mind."

I raise my right hand. "Scout's honor."

He waves me even closer. "All right. My sister's been working with Frank Maresca, the director at Ricco/Maresca Gallery, and they're putting on a group exhibition about imagined cities. It's mostly emerging artists, with one or two exceptions. But one of them pulled out at the last minute, and Maresca needs to fill the spot. He asked Mi Sun if she knows of any other up-and-coming book artists . . . and she gave him your name."

I listen, but it's not sinking in.

"The show's in seven weeks or so, but I'm sure you could

get something together. I was thinking of something along the lines of that self-portrait you showed me, with the clown face, but, like, as a book—you know, something kind of surreal."

I'm stunned. "Wow. . . . Tell Mi Sun thanks for thinking of me. Truly. But I don't know if I could get something together that quickly. I'm not really even working on anything right now."

Jae smiles like I've just said something funny. "Dawn, this is not an opportunity you turn down. This could mean a career. Also, Mi Sun says you'll need to let her know by the morning because she knows plenty of artists who would die to take the spot. So get on it, yeah?" He punches my shoulder and goes back to Lindsay.

I'm still unsure of what exactly has just happened. A year ago I'd sent my portfolio—or at least the few pieces from college that I didn't hate—to the Miller Gallery, a hip "underground" art space on the Lower East Side of Manhattan, where Mi Sun knew one of the directors. Even with her recommendation, it took six months before I heard back from them to say they couldn't offer me representation. I know I need to say yes to this offer, but my classmates from college are already showing their work and starting to make names for themselves, and what have I been doing? Sitting in the basement of the Met's research library fixing other people's craftsmanship, unable to make anything new of my own. My so-called career already feels like one of those fragile pages I watched Stacey encase in Mylar—ready to crumble to dust if I don't do something to save it.

Pete's voice comes over the microphone, startling me. "We're Typo. Thanks for coming out. And don't forget that proceeds from every CD you buy will go to the Brooklyn ASPCA. So please give to the critters."

A low drone fills the space. I squeeze Jae's arm and move closer to the stage so I can be alone with my thoughts—and watch Lukas. His eyes are fixed on the keyboards in front of him, his fingers working knobs and swiping keys. As the music morphs into a spacey, pulsing rhythm, the light changes the color of his face from blue to green to red. He looks lost in a dream, his eyes mesmerized by sound.

As he and Pete play, the lounge continues to fill. Jae and Lindsay end up in a corner, taking advantage, it seems, of the need to put their faces close together in order to hear over the music. At some point, when she breaks away to use the bathroom, Jae comes over to me.

"She's cute," I yell.

He shrugs. "Yeah, but not sure how interested she is. She's already told me she needs to make it an early night, so. . . ." He downs the rest of his beer.

"Dude, give her a minute. How many times have you been out with her?"

"This is the first."

Lindsay emerges from the bathroom. Jae salutes at me. "Tell Lukas he was awesome and I owe him money for a CD. I'm going to head out after I get her into a cab. And I'm telling Mi Sun yes unless you text me before work tomorrow."

I kiss his cheek, then turn my attention back to Lukas, who's moving to the synth-pop beat he's coaxing out of a little machine next to him, his hands working with the rhythm. I love watching him get lost in his music, his body giving itself over in a way I've only seen it do when he's with me.

WHEN THEY FINISH playing, they pack up their gear and Pete heads out. Lukas wants to go too, but I want to dwell a little longer in the vision of him onstage. It's also the first time we've been out at a bar alone in a while, so I persuade him to stay and get another drink with me.

We're squeezed onto barstools when I tell him about Mi Sun and the show at Ricco/Maresca. By then, however, I've talked myself into it and out of it again. It would be impossible, I tell him, to create something new in less than two months that would be worthy of showing in my first exhibition. I'm counting on him to agree with me. But he says the same thing Jae did—this isn't something I can turn down.

"At some point I might have thought you were right," I say. "But be honest. Everything I've made over the last few years is crap."

Lukas is peeling the label from his beer. "And what if that's just an excuse?"

"For what?"

He releases the wet paper from the bottle and folds it in half. "For hiding at the Met."

I put my drink down and look at him. "You think my job at one of the biggest museums in the world is hiding?"

"Obviously it's an amazing job," he says. "But for you? You have to admit, spending your days fixing old books is not exactly the art career you had in mind."

I want to be angry, but my heart is too heavy. Lukas picked a crappy time for one of his rare moments of frankness. I had no idea he feels this way, sees me this way.

"You okay?" he says.

"Yeah, it's just . . ." Suddenly it's like I'm back at the airport, terrified to get on the plane. "Maybe you're right. I'm not an artist. I haven't made anything good since I finished school."

Lukas leans his elbows on the bar. "Don't do that. That's not what I said."

"Then tell me, what the fuck am I supposed to show? What have I been making that's good enough?"

"That's not for me to say."

"See? Because there's nothing."

"No, because you need to stop trying to force something out of yourself that you don't care about. Isn't it obvious? The theme is imagined cities, and you've been out scouting this city for, like, two years."

I grimace. "Looking at other people's art is not art."

"What if it is? I've seen the sketches you've been making. You've been trying to work something out. Maybe you need to go with that. Stop thinking about a plan and just start."

Pausing, I take in his face, his eyes. He looks sincere. "You really think so?" I say.

He nods.

I never imagined that Lukas might think my recent drawings are any good. At another time, it would feel amazing to hear him say that. I down the rest of my beer. Right now, however, I want to go home.

AS WE FALL asleep that night, I know he and Jae are right. I have to say yes to the gallery show. I can't imagine a life without art. Without it, the future stretches before me like a meaningless void. What would I do? Even if I decided to continue doing book conservation, in order to make a decent salary I would have to get a library degree, and going back to school for that is the last thing I want to do. There's nothing I can see myself doing except art or moving back home and listening to my parents say *I told you so* and working on their plan for my marriage to a Jewish doctor. I'm sure that would be a real two-for-one as far as they'd be concerned. Whenever I showed signs of deviating from the norm, my doctor-husband could treat me.

So this is my shot. I don't know when, or if, I'll ever get a chance like showing in Ricco/Maresca Gallery again—a place, as Jae said, that can launch my art career. If only I had something to show. If I can't make the deadline, I won't just be letting myself down, I'll be letting Jae and his sister down too.

Again I think of Gertrude and her hidden letter. I wonder if it's true that I've been hiding in a basement to avoid everything that art-making keeps asking me to confront. If it is, then I can't ignore the fact that it's from that hiding place that Gertrude's book cover has come. The question is: What does it mean? In less than a week I'm supposed to get on a train to meet her. I hope I find my answer.

‖ MOTION

AS THE TRAIN goes through a tunnel, I take out my camera and pull up the picture I took of Gertrude from the library book. For days I haven't been able to stop looking at her grainy stare, wondering if I'm imposing my own ideas on her because of the illustration on the cover of *Turn Her About*, if she meant to look as androgynous as she did or if she thought she was just being fashionable. Searching for the answer in her expression, I zoom in, but it only makes her face harder to read, like ink spreading under a drop of water. I stare at her eye until it becomes unrecognizable. A black bird. A faraway pond. A mistake that's been poorly erased.

The train rocks on the tracks, and I remember an article I saw this week about a queer Muslim woman in the Bronx who threw herself in front of a train days after getting attacked on her walk home from a nightclub. One more casualty of Bush's war. To think it just as easily could have been me or Jae if some psychopath had seen us coming out of Pyramid a few weeks ago. More and more, nothing feels safe.

I imagine what it would be like if we derailed. Would we slide into the street and come to a jerky stop, or would we crash and burst into flames? What if it happened while we were on a bridge? My mind has always worked like this, but it's getting more intense. I can't stop noticing the fragility of things, especially returning to a city that once felt indestructible but now is struggling to reassemble the broken pieces of itself. I can't stop thinking about how much we depend on everything to work the way it's supposed to for our very survival. Life is beginning to feel tenuous, survival an accident of chance.

I pick my head up and scan the train car. I've taken the day off work, and at midday on a Wednesday there are only a few other people. I look back out the window, at the backyards of little houses packed tightly together, the sad things people have left outside to die. Tires, weathered rope, kiddie pools stained with dirty water.

I think about imagined cities and curse The Project, which is the temporary name I've given to the artwork I finally committed to making for the gallery show. Even though all my attempts at art are still refusing to take shape. I open my sketchbook and try to conjure an image, to picture a city full of books instead of hate and tired old possessions. Then a city made out of books. I sketch what I see out the window, turning roofs into open books resting facedown on top of houses made of books. The leaves of trees now leaves of paper. Book-birds flapping their page-wings in the sky. It's terrible.

The train pulls into Jamaica Station.

Exiting onto the platform, I straighten my dress. A strong breeze blows by. A few cars down, a gay couple stands gripping each other's hands. The connecting train pulls in and a conductor yells for us to have our tickets ready.

I step into the fluorescent light of the car and make my way to a cold vinyl seat, where I close my eyes. As I get closer to Gertrude, I understand less and less why I think she can make anything better for me or why I've thought it would be okay to intrude on a dying woman's life. Besides, maybe I'm not prepared for what I'm bringing out of hiding. What if Marta rejected her? Or worse, what if she broke Gertrude's trust and told someone? Gertrude could've been beaten up or kicked out of school or sent away for conversion therapy. Maybe I should've left this alone. Maybe some things are better off hidden.

I try to give in to the train's gentle back and forth, the *click-click-click* of the conductor's hole puncher, the shuffle of his feet. Then I open my eyes and watch him punch my ticket.

THE TRAIN ARRIVES at Stony Brook at 12:06 p.m., my side of the platform a desert. I find the cab stand and ask for a ride to the restaurant where I'm supposed to meet Gertrude.

Fifteen minutes later, the driver delivers me to Thai Palace—a few minutes early, which I take as a sign that everything will go well. Opening my messenger bag, I check the inside pocket for the book cover. It's still there. Finally, I walk through the door.

The restaurant is bright and airy. From the host stand, I scan the dining room and see a woman sitting alone next to a window. She looks about Gertrude's age. She has short auburn hair and wears a salmon-colored blazer.

The host comes to greet me, a teenage girl in a short dress and wobbly heels. "Just one?" she says.

"Actually, I'm meeting someone. I think I see her."

The host turns to the dining room. "Yes, follow me please."

‖ GERTRUDE

GERTRUDE IS NOT what I had expected. I'd been imagining a Gertrude Stein type, sturdy, with gray hair cut close. Basically an older version of her photograph from the library book. This Gertrude wears eye shadow and blush, dyes her hair, wears tailored clothes. And except for how thin she is, she hardly looks like a person who's dying. But I remember my grandma, my father's mother, who'd been diagnosed with liver cancer when I was thirteen. One day she seemed fine and two weeks later had lost half her body weight. A few weeks after that, she was gone.

Gertrude fixes me with a penetrating look, her head tilted. A smile dashes across her face. "You must be Dawn." She stands awkwardly, steadying herself with one hand on the table, extending her other.

"Yes. Gertrude? Ms. Kleber? I'm sorry," I say, taking her hand.

"Have a seat." She lowers herself back into her chair.

I think I should help, but she doesn't seem like the kind of person who wants help.

She says, "Have a look at the menu, and then we'll talk."

I do as she says. I get the feeling most people do. She watches me while I read the menu. "If you like seafood, I recommend the panang curry."

"I'm vegetarian," I say.

"Oh." She looks at me sideways in a way I don't know how to decipher, her eyes never leaving my face. "You'll have to find something you like, then."

My cheeks burn. Now that I'm in front of her, I feel like a peeping Tom, like I've already looked into her underwear drawer and now I'm pressing her to give me a detailed list of its contents. What was I thinking—because I expected her to look more masculine, everything would be okay, I would deserve access to a dying woman's innermost secrets? What right do I have to step into the end of her life and muck everything up for her?

She points to the menu again. "It says they have tofu." Her voice carries a hint of disapproval.

I nod. The server appears and twists his watchband back and forth while he listens to us recite our choices. I ask for the panang curry with tofu.

With the ordering done, I finally have to perform the charade I've set up. Gertrude is still looking at me. She seems content with silence, whereas it's making me sweat. I force a smile and take out my notebook.

Gertrude sips her jasmine tea, coughs. "Okay, I'm here. Ask me your questions." She speaks firmly, emphasizing every word.

I pull my cardigan tighter across my chest, look down at my notes. After rereading the first question silently, I still don't know what it says. I reach for my water glass and take a sip. A drop falls onto the word *father*.

"Sorry, my mouth is just a little dry." I look at my notebook again, and this time the words come into focus. "I know we went over this on the phone, but I figured the first thing I should do is confirm that your father was Hermann Kleber, the German bookbinder working at American Book-Stratford Press."

"That's right," she says.

"Okay." I make a mark in my notebook that's meant to be a check but comes out more like a swirl. My brain is too distracted to send proper instructions to my hand. "Did you spend your childhood in Germany?" I say.

"I did. My earliest days, anyway." So far, Gertrude betrays no hint of emotion. Only a deep intensity.

I sip more water. "So the first thing I'm interested in hearing about is what you know of your father's experiences. Do you know when he started binding books?"

"Of course. I'm sure you can find that information in a news article somewhere, but if that's what you want me to tell you, I would say during the 1920s. He had an uncle, Fritz was his name if I'm remembering correctly. He worked as a bookbinder, and he invited my father into his shop to help out here and there with sewing or gluing. My father said he liked the odors—the glue and paper—that they were like no other odors he knew. And Uncle Fritz was quiet when he worked. He didn't make my father talk about school or home life or anything grown-ups usually went on about, so Papa enjoyed his time in the bindery with Uncle Fritz. The smells and the quiet—that's what he always talked about."

I'm surprised to hear Gertrude say so much. I take notes, and listening to her describe her father's experience, I begin to relax. I say, "I totally relate."

"How long have you been at it?" she says.

"Professionally, only about two years. So far."

"And you work at the Met?"

"I learned a lot during an internship there."

"Good for you," she says. "I never liked it—bookbinding. To me, the smells were too strange, the bindery too messy and dusty, the glue unpleasant to touch. And the work was so fussy. It kept my father away from us for many late nights. Ach." She waves her hand dismissively.

I'm confused. "I read in an article that you all—his children—worked in the bindery with him once you were old enough," I say. "What was it like to be around that all the time if you didn't like it?"

Gertrude laughs. A short, clipped laugh. "No, no," she says. "I never worked in the bindery. Father tried with me, but I was a stubborn one."

My heart sinks. "Never?" I try to keep my voice even. "Not even when you got older?"

"No, it wasn't *my thing*, as my students used to say." Gertrude smooths a small lock of hair. "I can tell you many things about my father. I even have memories of his hands flying across a piece of paper with a glue brush. But I can't tell you much that's specific about his techniques or his approach to binding books. I can only tell you what I thought while I watched him. The way he put his entire focus into what he was doing—whether it was measuring, cutting, or folding—was something he rarely did with us children. I used to think he loved the books more, even though I had no other reason to think so. My father was a good man. He was good to us. But he was distracted all the time. I suppose you couldn't blame him for wanting another world to disappear to in those years." Gertrude sips her tea. She seems to have gone off into her own world as well. "This probably isn't very helpful for your article," she says. "Tell me what else you want to know."

I'm afraid I'll give myself away if I keep pressing her, but after I've come all this way thinking I've found the author of the letter, I don't want to be wrong. I look down at my notebook, steel myself. "I'm sorry, I'm just curious—even with your father and siblings binding books, you never learned?"

"Of course I learned," she says. "But learning and doing are very different."

I swallow. I want to apologize, close my notebook, and go. But I've committed myself to this deception. I tell myself it will be over soon enough.

I read the next question from my notebook. Then the next, and the next. Gertrude tells me everything she knows about her father's time at Bremer Presse in Germany, which isn't much. Her family had already left the country before the press was destroyed by a bomb on July 13, 1944, but her father followed the fate of the press obsessively, tracking down as much information as he could through the little news he was able to find.

Finally, we finish our food and the waiter delivers the check. I reach for it, but Gertrude puts her hand out. "No, no," she says.

"But I invited you."

"Nonsense. Give it here." She grabs the other end and I let go. "I don't feel I was much help to you anyway," she says as she pulls a credit card from her wallet.

"No, this was great. Thank you."

She looks at me the same way Katherine does, a little curiosity, a little sympathy. I turn away. The waiter is twisting his watchband at the table next to us.

"Do you go to your parents' now?" she says.

I'd forgotten about that lie. An urge to cry forces a strange grunt out of my throat. I cough. "It turns out they're out of town this week." It's a lame excuse. But I don't care anymore. I just want to go.

"So you'll go back to the city?" Gertrude is still looking at me like she thinks I need something, which is only making me feel worse.

"Yeah, there's a train in about an hour."

"Come to my house, then," she says. "Clare brought bread this morning. We'll drink tea and have a slice."

It's not an invitation so much as an instruction. I don't know how to say no. I gather my things into my bag until I have nothing left to do. "Are you sure?"

By way of an answer, she stands and waits for me to do the same. She seems to have no patience for indecision or polite negotiations.

I stand and follow her out the front door. She walks with surprising steadiness.

A FEW MINUTES later, I'm trapped in the passenger seat of Gertrude's brown sedan. Watching traffic speed by on two-lane roads. Eventually she turns off the highway onto a small tree-lined street and everything goes quiet. Out of nowhere, she says, "You seem sad."

I can't help but laugh. "You sound like my boss."

She glances at me. "Maybe your boss is on to something."

I rub my lips together. "Maybe."

We reach a fork in the road, and she slows down and points to a dilapidated white church with boarded windows. "You see that? At the back of the driveway is a dirt road that leads to an old estate where Marilyn Monroe once lived. I've heard it's been divided into apartments and that people still live there. Could you imagine driving back there every day to get home? I don't think I would have the nerve in the dark."

"Wow, yeah," I say. But I find it intriguing. What would it be like to live in a place like that with Lukas—far away from everything, where even the way in isn't obvious? Maybe in a place like that we would be able to just be ourselves, like we were when we traveled together through Europe.

Gertrude turns off onto another quiet road and into the driveway of a yellow house, the small front yard of which is all garden.

"Welcome to chez moi." She opens the car door and pulls herself to standing. Without waiting for me, she heads to the house. As I catch up, she turns and points to the garden. "My protest against death."

I laugh awkwardly and follow her inside. The house is filled with equal parts sunlight and shadow, beautiful dark wood-work everywhere. I want to use the opportunity to dig a little deeper, ask about whether she'd ever fallen in love or gotten married. As we walk through the living room, I quickly scour photographs for clues. There's one of her with another woman, their arms around each other, but the woman looks much older. She could be Gertrude's mother. There isn't enough time to let my eyes land anywhere else.

I come at the question from another angle. "Do you have any kids?" I say.

Gertrude stops short. "Heavens, no. Unless you count the hundreds of kids I taught over the years. They were more than enough." We continue onward. Every room is full of books, even the kitchen, where we land. Gertrude gets to work heating up water in a teakettle. "And now for a slice. I call it tit bread," she says, holding up a rectangular loaf made of two square loaves joined together. At the top of each is a swirl. "You can see why."

I'm starting to like her very much. Despite her stern manner, she's full of these small, unexpected intimacies. But the more I like her, the more I regret the fake pretense I've used to get myself here. I watch her slice the bread, pull jam and butter from the fridge. As she works, she says, "I never asked you, what was it that made you interested in the American Book Bindery? And my father?"

My throat closes. But I've prepared for this question, so I begin to repeat the answer I've been practicing. "My boss showed me a fascinating article on the transition to mechanized binding, and when I learned that hand binding had a resurgence in the 1950s, it got me interested in the bookbinders working back then . . ." My voice trails off. Gertrude is watching me, the bread knife still in her hand.

She sets the knife down and puts the bread on plates, then carries them to the table. The teakettle hisses.

"Let me help." I stand and turn the heat off under the kettle, reach for the box of tea bags Gertrude has left out. "Please, sit down."

Annoyed, Gertrude waves my suggestion away, but she sits anyway.

With my hands busy and my back to her, I make a quick decision. I say, "Anyway, one day I was repairing a book at the Met, and I found something under the endpaper. It was a paperback book cover, with a personal handwritten letter on the back. I checked the book it was hiding in and saw that it was bound at American Book-Stratford Press, and it seemed like too big a coincidence to ignore. Like, I was meant to learn more about them. I thought I could track down the author of the note—as part of writing my article." I can't look at Gertrude. I open and close drawers, searching for a spoon to stir the tea with.

When I stop, the room is quiet.

"Interesting," she finally says. "What does this letter say?"

"I don't know," I lie. "It's in German." I hear Gertrude's feet move.

"I just realized I forgot to put out cheese." She goes to the refrigerator. I watch her back as she shuffles things around.

When she finally sits down, her demeanor has changed. She's no longer looking me in the eye. She clears her throat, says, "Where is this book cover now? Do you still have it?"

My breath quickens, the bread in my mouth turns to cement.

Gertrude slices cheese.

"Yeah," I say, my heart racing. Then I make another quick decision. I can't let this opportunity pass. Anxious that I'm about to expose her, I pull the cover of *Turn Her About* from my bag. But once the illustration sits between us, it feels like me who's been exposed, whose reflection is in the mirror.

It's only a second, but recognition lights up Gertrude's face, just long enough for me to catch it. I'm exhilarated and terrified. As I keep my eyes on the cover, on the small, imperfect type running across the top, a bird flies past the window and almost startles me out of my seat.

Gertrude touches the book cover, then pulls her hand away as if she's burned it. She mumbles to herself, "You think the past is the past." Then she says, "May I see it?"

I nod. She picks it up and brings it to the window, and I watch the Mylar sleeve make sunlight dance on the ceiling as she turns it over in her hands. In the natural light, she looks defenseless, every blemish visible that she's tried to erase with makeup.

She waves her hand across her face again, like she's shooing away whatever she's feeling. Then sets the book cover back on the table. Looks at my half-eaten bread, at me, sizing me up as if she's seeing me for the first time, while I resist the urge to cross my arms over my chest. "You should go," she says. "You have to get a train."

For once today, I force myself not to agree. "You didn't finish your tea, and there's a train every hour."

She looks back at my plate. Touches her hand to her chin.

I struggle through another bite of tit bread.

"You're Jewish, aren't you? Levit is a Jewish name?"

I say yes, grateful her attention has shifted away from the illustration.

"My father had a partner in Germany—another binder—who had the foresight to send us to safety. I remember that time as a blur, leaving what had been home, living in secret, traveling to the States, where everything was new and everyone spoke a strange language. It was only years later that I understood how all of my father's distractions were really the result of his singular focus, to keep us safe. All the secret plotting and coordinating it must have taken to get us out of Germany, being forced to give up the job and home he'd built to start over somewhere completely foreign, and then to have to make it feel like home for his family. How could someone let their guard down after a thing like that? Every little thing he did, he had to keep our safety in mind. So it didn't leave much time for warmth. But when he showed that side of himself, it was clear how much he loved us."

"That must have been very hard," I say. "I can't imagine." Although I don't know where she's going with this.

"Nor should you have to." Gertrude catches me with a diagnostic look. "Those first years in New York, I knew I was supposed to be happy, or at least grateful. But I was also a child and couldn't figure out how I fit in. It took me awhile to understand that what was different about me was something more than my language. In fact, there were many Germans in our community who had escaped during the war, like us. We had our own small Germany in New York. There was even one girl at school whom I developed a close friendship with. That was Marta. I'll never forget her last name, Brahm, like the composer but without the 's' at the end. She was the prettiest—and most stubborn—girl I'd ever known. Nice strong eyebrows, a bold face." Gertrude fixes her gaze on me. "I imagine you have some idea of what I'm talking about."

I shift in my seat.

"I had never seen anything like it, that perfection," she says. "So there I was, sixteen and knowing I was supposed to like boys, but I never had. I'd never liked anyone that way until Marta. You can imagine my confusion. I had no idea what it meant. Not yet."

As Gertrude takes me into her confidence, I'm a bit stunned. And eager to finally hear her story. But something about her tone suggests these memories trouble her.

"I'm sorry," she says. "I don't need to tell you about this."

"It's okay," I say. "I'm interested."

"The point is, one day I was in a five-and-dime buying a pack of gum, and something on the rack near the counter caught my eye. It was a small paperback book, and it had a picture of two women on the cover—in bed. Of course, only one was lying down and the other was sitting on the edge, but it had a romantic quality to it, if you catch my drift. And the title, *Spring Fire* or some such thing, suggested I was right. I wanted to open it right there but even touching it would be unthinkable, so I paid for my gum and left it behind. The whole night I couldn't stop picturing it. So the next day I borrowed my mother's wide-brim hat—I must have looked ridiculous—and went back with the sole purpose of purchasing that book. My hands shook like leaves and I never once looked at that poor cashier, but you can bet I did it."

I smile. "And I'm guessing it was worth it?"

"It was." She brushes her hair away from her face with her fingers. "I haven't spoken about those days in a very long time. You know, it's remarkable how much you can block out."

"Why do you need to block it out?"

She cuts another piece of bread. "Ach, I was young and stupid." She lays a slice of cheese on the bread, lining it up perfectly, then sits and studies her food. Her mind seems to have gone off somewhere unpleasant. She laughs cheerlessly. Then she stands again and goes to another cabinet. "It's three o'clock. I hope you don't mind if I take a bit of whiskey. Would you like a glass, or are you too young for that? I have a hard time telling anyone's age anymore."

"Yes, please," I say, as if she were offering me a sugar cube for my tea.

She pours two glasses, neat, and hands me one. "Cheers," she says, taking a sip. "That'll do."

But her mood isn't lifting. "Anyway, as you might already guess, it was that book that helped me identify what made me different. Of course there were still feelings I didn't know how to admit or explain to myself, like why I preferred pants to skirts or short hair to long, like the butch characters in the story." Gertrude gives me another knowing look and I stop myself from caving in.

"What mattered was, I was figuring it out. Even though the book was utterly tragic in its depiction of lesbian life, it unlocked something inside me and I needed to know more. Well, after I read it a few times, I wanted another one, and I began to see others like it everywhere—newsstands, drugstores, all over. So one day when my mother asked me to pick something up at the drugstore, I went all the way across town where no one would recognize me. I must have walked fifty blocks. Again, with shaking hands I brought a novel to the cashier and looked away as I paid. But before I left, she told me to check the bag for a special coupon, and she winked. I couldn't believe it. As I walked out, she said, 'I hope you'll come again soon.' I shivered the whole way home and then went straight to my bedroom that I shared with my younger sister, which thank goodness was empty, and hid the book under my mattress. The 'coupon' was a small slip of paper with a name and phone number on it."

"Oh my god, no way," I say.

She nods. I raise my glass and we clink. At least for the moment, her mood has brightened.

"It took me forever to work up the nerve, but I did call eventually, and the young woman—Grace was her name—explained she was part of a group that got together to talk and swap books like the one I had purchased. If I was interested, I should meet them at Hinchey's Soda Fountain the following Saturday. You can bet I was."

I finish my whiskey.

"It was like fate, the way that fell into my lap. Though later I came to understand this was how so many of us found each other. Especially those of us who were too young to go to the bars." She raises her glass again and gestures toward the book cover. "So you can appreciate the irony that this should bring you to me."

I almost can't believe it and want to say something about fate myself, about how I've been obsessed with this coincidence for weeks. And I've just about worked up the nerve to say it when I look back at Gertrude and see the weight that's returned to her expression. She's looking at the book cover now like it's an unwelcome guest.

After a moment she says, "Though I have to admit, I have no idea how this ended up in your museum's book."

I want to ask what she means. If she didn't hide it, then who did? But she picks up the book cover and makes a sound like *tsk-tsk*. She says, "'I do not need to see the kiln to know this pot has been through fire.'" Then she leaves the room with it, returning empty-handed—and a little bit lighter for its absence. "That's the Jewish poet Roald Hoffmann. He was actually more of a chemist, but his writing is wonderful. Do you know his work?"

I shake my head.

She sits and looks out the window across the room. "I've never told this to anyone," she says. "But you seem like someone with secrets."

Suddenly my chair is too small.

"You see, back then we were 'sick,' according to the psychologists, and 'criminals,' according to the law. No one was eager to make themselves known. So although those novels said horrible things about us, they gave us something we needed more—a way to connect. And good or not, they taught us so much about ourselves. But I was afraid if I kept bringing them home, someone would find them, so after a little while I got the idea to use the bindery to help us hide. I snuck the girls in after hours so we could replace the covers of the pulps with rejects from other projects, to make it look like we were studying the natural sciences or reading Tolstoy. Clever, yes?"

I smile, even more impressed by her than I'd anticipated, but if I'm reading her mood correctly, she's still filled with as much regret as nostalgia. I wonder why. "I thought you said you hated bookbinding—never did it," I say softly.

Her face settles into a guilty, almost sad, smile. "What can I say? When you're used to covering things up, it becomes a reflex." She pours herself more whiskey. "Actually, the girls had so much fun, we decided to take things a step further. Since those pulp novels painted such a dire picture of our futures, we pledged to write our own stories. They weren't quite novels, but they expressed the joyful lives we wished we could live. And once a month, we snuck them into the bindery to turn them into slim little paperbacks."

"That's incredible," I say. "Do you still have any of them?"

Gertrude ignores my question. "At first we shared them only among ourselves, but Grace had a bigger vision. She'd discovered an actual lesbian organization in California called the Daughters of Bilitis. Somehow she'd gotten hold of one of their newsletters and wanted us to have our own club with our own newsletter. But we didn't have much news to share as a group of girls who were only just discovering who we were. So one day I got the idea that we should share our fictional stories instead."

My spine straightens. Sensing I'm about to learn something important, I scoot my chair closer. "How?"

Gertrude seems encouraged by my eagerness. "So as not to give ourselves away, we came up with a plan that I believe my students would have called book-bombing. We bound as many copies as we could type or handwrite and took them to drugstores, anywhere you could find the novels. We'd put our stories right behind, or tuck them into their pages, hoping people would find them and take them. We even came up with a name and a motto, if you can believe it. We were the Sapphic Warriors, and the first page of every one of our books said 'Live openly, love fully.'"

"That's amazing," I say. I can't believe how fierce she had

been, how much wilder her story is than anything I'd imagined. "Did anyone ever find one?"

But suddenly she stands, steadying herself against the table. Within seconds her face has completely closed off. "All right," she says. "That's enough babbling from an old lady. It's time to get you on a train."

Before I have a chance to protest, Gertrude is shuffling toward her coat, gathering her things, the table still full of dishes. The conversation seems to be over. Startled by this turn, I stand and walk after her. "Let me help. Please."

"Suit yourself." She allows me to help her into her coat but then makes straight for the door. Producing a pack of Marlboros from her pocket, she steps outside.

For a moment I look out the window, trying to figure out what to do as the sun dodges behind a cloud. A tall patch of wildflowers lumbers around in the wind, hunched over as if looking for something that's fallen on the ground. Next to it is another garden plot, smaller than the one in the front but bursting with color. Gertrude's words come back to me. *My protest against death.* I wonder what's spooked her about having all those memories stirred up.

When I finish clearing the table, she's still outside, waiting to take me away from here. The sun, however, has decided to show itself again. As Gertrude rounds a corner toward the car, I lose sight of her, but her shadow stretches halfway across the yard.

‖ BACKWARD

BEFORE I KNOW it, I'm on the platform, waiting for the train to take me home to Lukas and Jae and the Met. Gertrude has driven the whole way without talking and barely acknowledges me as I step out of her car. The tension is bewildering. I want to ask so many questions. What happened with Marta? What, if anything, has Gertrude discovered about her own gender? And what did she mean when she said she had no idea how her letter got bound into *Building Beauty*? But clearly there was something she didn't want to talk about, or even remember. I wonder if the Sapphic Warriors were found out or, worse, if one of them gave the group away. Could it even have been Marta? A feeling of dread spreads through my chest. Half of me is eager to go back and press her for more, but the other half wants to run as far away as I can.

Maybe it's simply that it was too hard for her to think back to that time, to remember all that joy and comradery she felt as she was discovering who she was—only to inevitably come up against a world that would hate her and her friends. Just as I have my own painful memories I've been trying to stuff back down. Like everything that happened with Alice, and then afterward, when I got to college and thought it would help me cope if I chose a side. When I threw myself into my own warped versions of masculinity. At the diner, ashing my cigarettes in my coffee and drinking it. At parties, trying to pass as male in order to fool straight girls into kissing me. I'm ashamed when I think about it now, but back then as far as I was concerned, my crass behavior had become a matter of survival. To my parents and straight friends from home, I'd turned into a freak, and that became all they were willing to see. And to the queer community at Purchase, whose acceptance I craved like a drug, it felt like anyone whose sexuality was ambiguous posed a threat. They seemed to harbor a deep distrust of bisexuals because we might just be using lesbians to experiment, as I heard way too often. And even if we weren't, eventually we would take refuge in hetero relationships, so what was the point? Bi people were muddying the waters, so I got the hint and closed off that part of myself. And I couldn't imagine anyone would welcome me with open arms if I showed up in the LGBTQ lounge in a dress. It was like even the smallest deviation from what was expected foreshadowed some kind of betrayal. When I graduated and met Lukas, I felt free from all that. Free to start over.

Now I miss him something awful and want to be home,

lying against him. I want to apologize to Gertrude for stirring a pot I shouldn't have. For the first time since I was a teenager writing in my diary, I have a strong desire to pray.

Dear God, I used to write. *Dear God*, I prayed on the page, laying my feelings bare to a God I didn't believe in, because I had nowhere else to put them.

Like Gertrude and her secret publishing society, I filled pages with poems full of my most secret desires. Railing against everything my body was and wasn't. Against injustice and desire. Who else could I tell but the lines on the paper? My notebook was sacred, and it hid under my bed where no one could find it.

Dear God. Today I kissed a girl. Her name is Alice, and she smells like shea butter. Her skin is the softest skin, and her mouth is small and wet. I can't explain what it was like except to say that, finally, something fit in the space between my arms.

Dear God. Dear Diary. Hear me. I go to sleep a girl, dream a boy's dreams, and wake as neither. I shower, eat, and dress myself in armor so the kids at school will look at me like I'm one person. But I can't see what they see. Please help me.

Dear God, I wrote every day. *Dear God. Please. Please show yourself. Please, if you exist, I need to know.*

PART II *Preservation*

‖FLYLEAF

IT'S BEEN A few days since I met Gertrude, and I'm heading into the weekend by catching up with Lukas and Jae at Mars Bar in the East Village. When I arrive, they're sitting together at a dark little table in the window, pints in front of them. Lukas has taken out his new phone and is showing it to Jae, the easier texting or whatever.

I grab a beer at the bar and then join them, leaning into Lukas and kissing his cheek. He stiffens, as if it's not okay in front of Jae. So I lean toward Jae and kiss his cheek too, as if to say *No big deal.* Jae wipes it off and onto Lukas, who looks down sheepishly.

"I'm going to get another drink," Lukas says before I can even open my mouth to tell Jae about Gertrude.

As he walks away, Jae says, "Sister-friend, before you tell me how things went with your meeting, I need you to promise me something. I scored an interview with this CPA uptown for an internship, and I'm going to need someone to go over practice questions with me."

I laugh.

"Nah, I'm serious," he says. "You know how much work has sucked lately."

"Yeah, but what the fuck? You're going from publishing to accounting?"

"How else am I supposed to get out of this shit town? In case you haven't noticed, publishing barely pays the rent."

"You're leaving?" I say. "Where are you going?"

Lukas returns with two pints and squeezes back into his seat between us. I watch him set a glass in front of Jae, his eyes shy. His hands look restless. I want them on me.

I'd been looking forward to this evening, updating Jae on Gertrude, blowing off steam with him and Lukas. But sometimes when Lukas drinks he can't help but break his own rule and get flirty in public—with guys. I can't help but notice it's been happening more often. And Jae seems to get a kick out of amusing him. I swallow.

I say, "Jae wants to be a businessman."

"No shit," says Lukas. "Since when?"

"Yeah, since when?" I say.

Jae presses his glass against Lukas's arm. "What's wrong with that?"

"It's just . . . I don't know, it's not *you*." I try to make a joke: "You'll have to shower."

Lukas smiles.

"I'm not going to be that kind of businessman," says Jae.

"He wants to leave town," I say.

"Where are you going?" Lukas is almost done with his second beer already. "Not too far?"

I roll my eyes. Jae shifts in his seat, drinks. "I don't know. I'm not going anywhere anytime soon. Just looking down the road, imagining an easier future. Moving somewhere I can have a family someday. You know. The American Dream."

"The American Dream," Lukas repeats. He holds up his glass and clinks with Jae.

Since when does Jae want the American Dream? Since when does Lukas toast to it? None of this makes sense. "You're not serious," I say.

Jae nods.

"Then how come you never told me?"

"You never asked." He sets his beer down, averts his eyes. "Besides, I knew this is how you'd react." He punches my arm jokingly, but his comment doesn't feel like a joke.

I try to brush it off. "You're always trying to subvert the system—not join it," I say.

"Who says I'm joining it? I'm going to subvert it from the inside."

I take in his face. So gentle and earnest. "Of course I'll help you," I say. "Just stick around for a little while."

Lukas laughs.

"What's so funny?" I say.

"Jae in a ranch house, standing over a hot stove in an apron."

"Dude, that's not funny," says Jae. "I'd make a hot housewife."

Lukas's face flushes. "True," he says. He stands. "I need another one."

I've just finished my first, but he doesn't offer to get me one, so I hand him my glass—a bit too roughly. Looking like a dog who got caught doing something naughty, he takes it with him. Just then I notice two guys by the bar staring at us. They look like they don't belong at Mars Bar. An American flag waves across the chest of one of their T-shirts.

I take Lukas's seat, next to Jae. "Sorry, Lukas doesn't usually drink this much."

"Nah, he's kind of funny when he's drunk."

"That's one way to put it." I've become irritated. I keep one eye on Lukas and the guys at the bar.

Lukas returns with our beers and trips as he sits down, which makes him and Jae burst out laughing. I've had enough. I get up to go to the bathroom. The American Flag and his friend are still looking at Lukas and Jae, who are too drunk to realize they're sitting closer together than they should be.

I'm not in the mood for any shit, and my drink is making me bolder than I should be. As I pass them, I say, "You have a problem with my friends?"

"No," says the Flag. He looks me up and down. "No problem."

"Good."

But when I get to the bathroom, I'm shaking. The room is a dark, rancid hole covered in graffiti and who-knows-what, like the rest of the bar. It's hard to make out what anything says, but my eye lands on one phrase: *harass each other—run.* I pee quickly and head back, ready to make up an excuse about why Lukas and I have to leave.

But the guys from the bar are standing at our table. It seems like they're trying to joke around, but Lukas and Jae look more uncomfortable than amused.

"Hey," I say, and try to move around them to my seat, but one of them holds his arm in front of me.

"What's the rush?" he says. "I'm trying to get to know your friends, especially seeing as how this one blew a fucking kiss at me." He gestures to Lukas.

I push the arm that's blocking me out of the way and sit down. Then the guy grabs my bag from the floor and says, "This yours?"

"Look, dude," says Jae. "We're good over here, all right?"

"Oh, that's reassuring," says the guy, turning to his friend. "Because I wasn't sure, with them ignoring us and all. Were you sure?"

The American Flag says, "No. I don't know if he's being sincere."

"What the hell is going on?" I say.

"These guys just have nothing better to do," says Jae.

"Oh, *we* have nothing better to do?" says the guy who blocked my way. "You and this fairy are sitting here blowing kisses at us, and *we* have nothing better to do?"

"Fuck off," I say, trying to grab my bag, but he pulls it away and opens it, making a show of going through it like he's trying to intimidate me. Jae and Lukas look like they're about to intervene, but then the guy laughs, pulls out a piece of paper, and drops my bag to the floor. "Well, now it all makes sense," he says, shoving the photocopied picture of Gertrude too close to my face. "This dyke your mother?"

The bartender comes over—a scrawny goth punk—and

says to the Flag, "Whatever this is, you need to take it some-where else." Then he hightails it back to the bar and the Flag and his friend look at each other like they can't believe how offended they are.

I snatch the paper and jam it back in my bag. "Fuck this," I say. "Let's get out of here." Lukas and Jae follow as I push past the friend, who laughs again, a loud, childish sound. I don't breathe until all three of us are out the door. From the sidewalk, I think I can still hear them laughing.

Jae lights a cigarette, his hand unsteady. "Fucking ass-holes," he says.

Lukas finishes rolling one and leans toward Jae for a light.

We start walking, but within a block, the guys from the bar are behind us. The Flag says, "You're lucky I don't hit women, even ones that look like men."

"Bite me," I say.

"Come on," says Jae. He takes my hand.

After that, time seems to warp. When Jae hits the ground, all I understand is the back of his head where it doesn't belong, framed by pavement. It takes what feels like a few minutes, but is probably only seconds, for me to understand that the guy has punched Jae in the face. I've never seen that before. It didn't sound like it does in the movies. There was no neat *crack*, just the disgusting thud of flesh pounding on flesh, a horrible grunting and panting. Then Jae on the ground, face-down, not moving.

My first thought is that he's playing dead, trying to get the guys to lose interest in him. But while I'm figuring it out, the friend pins Lukas's arms behind his back. Lukas is kicking and jerking around. He spits his cigarette onto the man's arm, and as the guy swears, Lukas pulls his own arm free and lands a punch on the side of the guy's head. I hear a loud, high-pitched scream, and before I can even look around, someone says, "Shut her the fuck up." Then the friend comes at me, going straight for my stomach, and the screaming stops. Pain shoots up my side.

The Flag is kicking Jae, who still isn't moving. But it's more like he's trying to see if Jae is awake. He doesn't appear to be.

"Fuck," says the guy. "Fuck, fuck, we gotta go."

The friend has Lukas in a headlock.

"We gotta go," the Flag says again. "Come on. Leave him alone." He turns to me. "We were just fucking around," he says. "You remember that. It's not my fault your friend can't take a punch."

I try to respond. I want to grab them and hold them there so I can call the police. But I'm frozen. And my stomach hurts. Lukas might be crying.

"Dawn," he says. "Dawn." He's pointing to Jae.

"Oh my god," I say. I kneel down next to him. When I touch his back, his head moves. It might be the first time I've breathed. And then I can't stop. And then I'm saying his name. "Jae. Jae. *Jae.*"

Finally, he pushes himself up, opens his eyes. Lukas helps him roll onto his back and slides his jacket under his head. People pass on the sidewalk as if we aren't there. As far as they're probably concerned, there's nothing to see but someone who's drunk too much and fallen down, and we're helping, so there's no need to intervene.

"What?" Jae says. He touches his head, his eyes barely open. "What happened?"

"One of those guys had a mean left hook," I say.

"What?"

"Why don't you call the police?" I say.

"Fuck no," says Lukas.

"Dawn," says Jae. "What are you talking about?" He's trying to sit up. "Shit. I don't feel too good."

"Take it easy," I say. "Oh god, I'm sorry."

"What happened?" Jae says again.

"One of those idiots punched you. Just give it a minute."

"I really don't feel good."

I turn to Lukas. "We should call an ambulance."

"No," says Jae. "I just need to sit up."

Lukas ignores me. He helps Jae up. Jae doubles over and puts his head in his hands.

"What's the last thing you remember?" says Lukas.

Jae doesn't answer.

"All right, call fucking 911," I say.

"Wait," says Jae.

I stand. My body feels like some weird alien thing. Except for the pain on the right side of my stomach, which makes it hard to move too fast.

Jae says, "I remember we were in the bar and some guys were calling us fags and then we left and they followed us outside."

"Do you remember getting hit?" says Lukas.

"No."

"He needs to get to a fucking hospital," I say.

Jae is still doubled over. Lukas is kneeling in front him. A couple walks toward us. They look about our age.

"Are they okay?" says the woman.

"Yeah, my friend just tripped and fell," I say. It hurts to stand.

The woman shrugs her shoulders, looks at her boyfriend. His face says, *We tried.*

The woman says, "You're sure?"

I nod and they keep walking. They whisper to each other, and the woman looks back at us before they round the corner.

Lukas tries to help Jae stand upright. He steadies him against a wall and holds on to his shoulders for a moment, until Jae frees himself and hunches back over, leaning his hands on his thighs.

"Fuck this. I'm calling an ambulance right now," I say.

"Dawn," says Lukas. "Don't worry. Just give him a minute."

"Oh, like I should take advice from you? It's your fucking fault he got hit in the first place."

Lukas doesn't respond. He's keeping his hand on the wall next to Jae, ready to catch him if he starts to fall.

Jae says, "Can you hail a cab? I want to get home."

Lukas looks at me. "Dawn, keep an eye on him?"

"God. What the fuck?" I say.

"We can go with him."

"I don't know how to treat a concussion. Do you?"

"You need to chill out," says Lukas. "Getting an ambulance would mean reporting this to the police, and in case you haven't noticed, the police aren't exactly our friends, especially not these days."

"Fine, then you go with him. I'm not going to sit around and wait for him to lose consciousness again. Next time it could be too late to take him to a hospital."

"That's not going to happen."

Lukas looks pale and fragile. I need him to know what to do, want to believe that he's right. But I don't trust him. I take out my phone and call 911, but as soon as I start talking, he grabs the phone from me and slams it shut.

"You're fucking kidding me," I say.

"Dawn, he's right. No police," says Jae.

Lukas is frozen with my phone in his hand. He looks scared, like he knows he's gone too far, but he doesn't say anything.

I grab the phone from him, sending a sharp pain through my right side. "You know what? Since you're doing so great, I'll make sure you two lovebirds get a cab, and then I'll get a train home."

Jae holds his head. Lukas doesn't argue. But the thing about Lukas is that he doesn't know how to ask me to stay even if he wants me to.

‖ PRAYER

AFTER JAE AND Lukas get into a cab, the world is still vibrating and the pain in my ribs hasn't subsided, so I try to walk it off. I hope I made the right decision letting them go. I hope Jae is all right.

As I walk, the pain gets worse, however, instead of better. I keep looking over my shoulder to make sure no one's following me as I search for a place where I can sit down. Everything's crowded. Too dark or too bright. I stop and lean against a wall to try to calm my mind, put pressure on my side and breathe as deeply as I can until it hurts. None of the usual things are helping. I wish I knew what I needed. Then I remember seeing a big Jewish star with a sign that said *Reform Congregation* on my way to Mars Bar.

I hadn't given Judaism much thought in a long time until I discovered Gertrude. I haven't observed any of the holidays for years and haven't set foot in a temple for even longer. It's a Friday evening, which when I was young would have meant Shabbat services and then dinner at my grandparents' house, with candles and challah and wine that I was allowed to sip after my grandfather recited the blessing. Suddenly I'm missing the sense of comfort that comes with something familiar. Maybe I'm looking for God, or maybe just for the feeling I used to get when my grandfather hummed "If I Were a Rich Man" while he held my hands and walked me around the kitchen, my feet on top of his.

The truth is, I've never been so scared. I can't stop shivering. I need a small connection to something much bigger than myself. I turn around.

THE NARROW SANCTUARY of Temple Israel feels like Noah's ark, a sea of blue carpet with dark wooden walls, punctuated by long stained glass windows. The service has already begun. I sit in the back and take in the rows that stretch in front of me, the different-colored yarmulkes on the men's heads. And a few of the women's.

I close my eyes and listen to the rabbi, his easy way of switching back and forth from English to Hebrew. He's young and eager to please and has a soothing voice. I try to pay attention to the words as I'm flooded with an unexpected homesickness for a part of myself I didn't know I've missed. The sweet smells, the sound of Hebrew, the glow of the eternal flame, the gentle jingling of the *keter* as the Torah is brought out of the ark, the cantor's sway as her voice rises in song. It's all so familiar and unfamiliar at the same time. This is what I've come for. Even the feeling of the bible-thin pages of the siddur between my fingers as I try and fail to follow along is like a homecoming.

I wipe tears from my eyes and page through the book, looking for blessings I recognize, testing myself to see if I can still decipher any Hebrew, when a Shabbat meditation makes me pause. It begins:

> This is an hour of change.
> Within it we stand uncertain on the border of light.
> Shall we draw back or cross over?
> Where shall our hearts turn?
> Shall we draw back, my brother, my sister,
> or cross over?

As the rabbi delivers his sermon, I keep flipping back to the meditation, looking at the prayers and passages around it, hoping for something that might shed light on what it's referring to. When he concludes, he asks us to call out names of anyone we know who's in need of healing—physical, spiritual, or emotional—so that we can hold them in our thoughts during the *Mi Shebeirach*. I stand with some effort and whisper to God to watch over Gertrude in her final days, however many she has, and to make sure Jae's okay. Then I'm afraid I've blasphemed because I don't believe in God.

I sit back down and listen to the final blessings, over the challah and wine. I keep prodding my side to see if it's any better. It's not. Then I slip out of the sanctuary. I return my siddur in the lobby and head for the door. But I stop short. I probably won't be back anytime soon, if ever, so I grab the same siddur I'd put away with the others and walk back into the sanctuary.

I pretend to look at the stained glass while I wait for the rabbi to finish shaking hands and wishing everyone Shabbat shalom.

When the room finally empties, I approach him, keeping some distance between us so he won't smell the alcohol on me. "Shabbat shalom, Rabbi." I straighten my dress.

The air tastes sweet and yeasty from the challah. My mouth waters. He returns my greeting and says he doesn't remember seeing me here before. Up close, I can see he's a little older than I thought, but probably not by much. He has crooked front teeth that make it seem like he's smiling all the time.

"I hope we've made you feel welcome," he says. "What brings you to Shabbat service on this spring evening?"

I want to say, *I was hoping God would prove me wrong and show me He exists. That He would tell me why I found that letter. Why it came along and awoke some hope in me, just so the world could punish me for it. Why my closest friend had to get hurt tonight. Why all of a sudden it feels like I have to stuff myself into a tiny little box in order to be with the person I love most.* I want to say, *I disturbed the peace of a dying woman to satisfy my own selfish curiosity.* I want to say, *I'm a coward and maybe I'm looking for a way to take everything back, to forget about what I've seen and reset things to the way they were before. But I don't know how to live with myself if I do.* Instead I say, "I guess I wanted to see if there was still a connection, if I might find some meaning that would inspire me to return to a temple."

"And?" He leans back a little.

"If I'm being honest, I don't think so."

He bows his head.

"But you gave a wonderful sermon," I say.

He laughs. "It's okay. Your relationship with God, or Judaism, is a personal one."

"I do have a question about something in the prayer book. I was wondering if you could tell me what it means." I've used my finger to mark the page. I show him, trying to keep my face steady as I hold my side with my other hand.

"Are you all right?" he says.

I nod. If I try to speak I'll start crying or something.

He looks like he wants to say more, but he lets it go, and I'm grateful for that small mercy. He says, "Yes, that's a great meditation. A friend of mine wrote a wonderful sermon inspired by it, based on the story of Abraham and Lot—do you know it?"

I shake my head.

"When God came to Abraham to tell him that he planned to destroy the sin-filled city of Sodom, Abraham was faced with an hour of change. As God's most faithful believer, he had a tough choice—let the people of Sodom perish, including his nephew Lot, or stand up to the God he followed unconditionally. And Abraham didn't hesitate. He crossed over, beseeching God, 'Shall not the judge of all the earth deal justly?' In other words, surely there must be some people in Sodom and Gomorrah who aren't sinners. How can you strike down whole cities if there are even a few good people who deserve to live?

"Meanwhile, even as visitors came to warn Lot of the danger, he lingered in Sodom. Now, there are many different opinions about why Lot didn't spur into action: some say he was trying to preserve his wealth, others that he was paralyzed by fear or he was simply in shock. But the point is this: We can all relate to Lot. We all know what it is to want to protect what we have, to fear that we don't have the strength within us to act when faced with a difficult hour of change. But we also know the courage of Abraham. As Jews, we can learn from his example how to recognize a call to justice, and how to find the inner strength to meet that call. And, I would argue, that is the highest calling of our people.

"But the beautiful thing about this story, perhaps the most beautiful thing, is that there aren't just two choices—to be like Abraham or to be like Lot. Because it was a visitor that ultimately saved Lot. The Torah tells us that this visitor seized Lot and his family by the hand and led them out of the city. So our third choice is to be like the visitor, to recognize when the people in our lives need a hand, when, for one reason or another, they can't cross on their own. Then we have an opportunity to help them get there." He puts his hand into his pocket. "Gorgeous, right?"

"Yeah, thank you," I say.

"To give another example from our more recent past, our congregation has been wrestling with what our role should be in the aftermath of 9/11, asking ourselves, 'What is our responsibility as Jews—who suffered greatly during the Holocaust, who relied on our non-Jewish brothers and sisters to break the law and risk their lives in order to hide us and fight against the Nazis?'"

He takes his hand from his pocket and straightens his yarmulke. "But I could go on." He smiles. "I hope I've answered your question about the meditation."

"You have." I want to tell him how lost I feel, but I can't find the words. "Thanks again for the service."

He puts his hand on my shoulder and I flinch. He pulls it back. I must seem like a mess.

"I hope we'll see you again," he says. "You're always welcome."

A FEW MINUTES later I'm outside, returned to my familiar city. But the sun has set and the energy on the street feels different, like everyone is moving too quickly. I want to slow them down, want to slow time down. I want more time to figure out who I am—Lot, Abraham, or the visitor—and who I want to be.

> *Where shall our hearts turn?*
> *Shall we draw back, my brother, my sister,*
> *or cross over?*

‖NIGHT

LUKAS DOESN'T COME home all night. I wake several times and check my phone, but there's nothing.

Finally, when it's barely light out, I hear the front door open. Lukas's heavy footsteps, his bag hitting the floor. Then the bed lurches beneath me as he falls into it, sending a sharp pain through my side. He lies on top of the covers, reeking of cigarettes, coffee, and alcohol.

"Jae's all right," he says. He doesn't ask about me.

He rolls onto his side. I pretend to be asleep.

LATER THAT MORNING we wake separately. We use the bathroom, wash, and eat our breakfasts in shifts. Lukas says he has to get to work early and leaves before eleven.

After he walks out the door, as if on cue, the sky goes gray and starts to rain.

I'm too scared to rock the boat any further but wish I had the nerve. I'm wanting. Wanting Lukas to come back. Wanting to feel whole. Wanting to be a kid again in my bed at home. Wanting things I don't have words for.

I call Jae to apologize for putting him in harm's way, and for leaving him, but he doesn't answer his phone. I think about apologizing to Gertrude for lying and then stirring up such complicated memories, but if I'm being honest, I want to talk to her again because I want the rest of her story, the parts she held back.

The wind picks up outside. A flock of small birds flies past the window, and every tree on the street bows in their direction.

‖TISSUE

I DON'T HEAR from Jae for hours. When he finally texts me back on Saturday evening, he says he's been too dizzy to look at his phone. I'm furious at Lukas for telling me he was okay. This doesn't sound okay. Somehow, I persuade Jae to postpone his CPA interview so that I can take him to a doctor. He doesn't resist as much as I expected, and I worry that he's scared. That there's a reason to be.

Come Monday morning, we sit in a claustrophobic waiting room stuffed with dusty brown chairs and a coffee table littered with old magazines.

I'm wearing a dress and lipstick, but it's only a costume, not who I am today. The past couple of days, I've been afraid to wear anything that could make me more of a target. But I'm also guessing that the doctor will have more sympathy for Jae, will give him the best medical care, if he hasn't made any life choices that would attract trouble. I don't want to give them any reason to blame him—or me—for what's happened.

But I do blame myself. Jae wouldn't have gotten attacked if he wasn't hanging out with us queers. If I hadn't started with those assholes. And if I hadn't been carrying around a photo of a complete stranger just because she looks genderqueer. I've been used to getting strange looks myself, but this is different. Now I don't feel like my friends or I are safe anywhere. And every time I move the wrong way, the pain in my ribs reminds me. Sitting in the doctor's office with Jae, looking at the scrapes and bruises still fresh on his face, that fear keeps intruding, the same way disturbing, nonsensical images repeat in your dreams when you have a fever.

To focus on something else, I pull out my camera and scroll through images, landing on the photo of young Gertrude. Maybe it's creepy of me to even have this, but I need to understand her confidence. I've been wondering so much about the Sapphic Warriors—especially that name they chose. How as teenagers, they already understood that just to be themselves would require a fighting spirit, and they were ready and willing to join the fight. At least they had been—until whatever it was that made Gertrude cut off her story. It makes me wonder whether her makeup, her outfit, is all really her choice now or if there are things she's still been too afraid to show. At her house, she seemed to have more to say about her gender, but it's possible that was only my imagination. That I've been wasting my time trying to understand her. Maybe in the end most of us simply lose the fight.

"I can't believe you made me cancel my interview for this, bro," Jae says. I look up from my camera, and he seems like he's trying to smile. But his eyes look unfocused.

"Sorry," I say. And then because I can't help it, I add, "What the hell was all that about wanting to work for a CPA, anyway?"

"I don't know, dude," says Jae. "I just want to try something different. See if it's worth it."

"Sorry, I don't get it." I cross my legs, pull my dress over my knees. Everything feels too tight.

"Why do you assume that working for a CPA somehow goes against who I am? It's just a job. We work because it pays money. So if I have to work, and especially if my coworkers are going to treat me like shit, I want a job that's going to pay more."

"All right," I say. "No need to get bent out of shape."

Jae cracks his knuckles and looks away. "Anyway, this guy seems like he's on the right side. He's trying to get more people to invest in socially responsible industry."

"Aha! I knew there was something you weren't telling me." For a moment I revel in my victory, but then the walls begin to close in, and I wonder if it's possible to pass out while sitting down.

Jae touches the big scab on his head. I watch him, waiting to see if his face will drain of color like it did when he first tried to sit up after getting punched. I don't realize how close my face is to his until he leans away from me.

"Chill out," he says. "You're freaking me out."

"Sorry." I poke through the pile of newspapers on the side table. There's an article about the urgency of going to war against terror and one about the Dixie Chicks posing nude on the cover of *Entertainment Weekly*. I pick up a magazine with Julia Roberts on the cover. It says *World's Most Beautiful Woman*, but at first I misread it as *World's Most Joyful Woman*.

I say, "So what's the grand plan after you get the job and the wife and move out to Long Island?"

"What are you talking about?"

"I mean, will it be the whole thing—two kids, two bathrooms, two cars? Or something else? Like, you'll be artists, you'll travel the world, and you'll keep an apartment in New York?"

"You're giving this way more thought than I am." Jae touches his head again.

I grip the armrest.

A nurse enters the waiting room and calls his name.

"That's you," I say, offering him my hand. He stands, ignoring it, and walks in front of me. I follow, my steps heavy, my feet wishing for engineer boots instead of heels.

The nurse stops us in the middle of the hallway, at a nook with a chair, and instructs Jae to sit. Her name tag says "Roxanne."

"You're here for a head injury, is that correct?" she says.

Jae nods, and she takes his vitals without saying another word. Finally, she signals for him to follow her farther down the hall. It's as if they've made a silent pact to use as few words as possible.

Roxanne brings us to a small room with a brown examination table and matching stool. There's a chair in the corner, where I sit and stare at the wall, which is lined with cabinets and posters. One has an American flag and the Towers ghosted in the background and says "Do not suffer in silence. Reach out." And next to that is a poster about diabetes.

Roxanne fills out a few things on Jae's chart. "Dr. Mink will be in to see you shortly." As she closes the door behind her, I feel like she's locking us in.

Jae sits on the examination table.

"Dawn," he says. "You okay?"

My right leg is bouncing up and down really fast. I stop it.

He picks up a battered issue of *People* magazine and flips through the pages, then closes his eyes like they need a rest and puts the magazine down. "I hate doctors," he says. "It doesn't seem right that you need someone else to tell you what's going on inside your own body. Not to mention you have to pay them for it."

"Yeah, it kind of sucks when you put it like that. But it's okay. You probably just have a mild concussion or something. No big deal, I promise." I try to sound reassuring.

"Thanks. Your professional opinion as a bookbinder really eases my mind." Jae picks up the magazine again. "You haven't even seen anyone about your own bruise," he says. "What if you have a broken rib or something?"

I look at the diabetes poster, start counting how many times the word *you* appears. When I get to number four, there's a knock on the door and Dr. Mink enters—a small woman with thick eyebrows. She introduces herself and shakes Jae's hand, a heavy charm bracelet dangling out from her lab coat sleeve. It looks like a gift from a child.

"I'm guessing you're Jae," she says.

He nods.

"Can you tell me why you're here, Jae?" She looks at his chart.

"I just told the nurse," he says.

"I'd like to hear it from you please, Jae." Dr. Mink seems to make a point of saying his name, like it's a tactic she's learned to improve bedside manner.

"I have a head injury."

Dr. Mink looks at him attentively, waiting for him to continue.

"And I guess I've been feeling a little dizzy and having trouble concentrating."

"When did you injure yourself?" she says.

Jae keeps offering only bits and pieces at a time, Dr. Mink patiently encouraging him to elaborate. Eventually, she examines him, looking closely at his bruises, listening to his heart and breathing, shining a light in his eyes and ears. She asks him to follow her fingers with his eyes.

"How many am I holding up?" she says.

Jae puts his hand to his head.

"Does looking at my fingers hurt your head?"

"Two," says Jae.

Dr. Mink looks at me, then back at Jae. "So, what happened? Were you in a fight?"

My stomach contracts. I look back at the diabetes poster. I need to get up but I'm afraid it would look weird, so I force myself to stay in the chair.

"Nah, it was just some asshole in a bar that punched me."

"Really? Why would someone punch you?" Dr. Mink is leaning him back on the table, wedging a pillow under his head.

"I don't know. He thought I was gay."

"I see." Dr. Mink opens the button of Jae's jeans and feels around his stomach. Once she's satisfied, she helps him sit up, which doesn't look like it agrees with him.

"When you got punched, how hard was the impact, on a scale of one to ten, one being the least painful, ten being the most?"

"I don't know. I don't even remember getting hit."

"I see," says Dr. Mink again. For the first time, she appears to be concerned. Then she seems to think of something and turns toward me. "Were you there when this happened?"

My mouth goes dry. I say yes but it comes out as a whisper.

"Could you tell how hard the impact might have been?"

I remember the sound, the thud, and the ground drops away for a second. "It all happened so fast. But it sounded hard. And then he fell facedown on the sidewalk."

"Facedown," she repeats. "Thank you. Is there a police report?"

"No." I think I should explain, but I don't know what to say and, fortunately, she doesn't ask.

In fact, she doesn't ask many more questions. On the one hand, I'm relieved not to have to answer anything else about "the incident." But as I sit silently while she finishes examining Jae, my anxiety turns into anger. She seems to be taking it as a matter of course that someone would attack Jae for being gay—or looking it. I detect no outrage on her face, or even surprise. Only a clinical interest in the mechanics that led to his injury so that she can form a diagnosis.

I cross my arms and sit forward in my chair, my gaze toward the door. The floor in front of it is dirty, the molding chipped and scuffed. "Excuse me," I say. "The whole thing was also pretty terrifying."

Dr. Mink looks up from her charts. "I'm sure it was," she says, and turns back to Jae. I hate her poor attempts at sincerity.

"What I mean is, it's possible that Jae's symptoms are from more than just the injury, right? Couldn't it be some kind of post-traumatic stress disorder?"

Dr. Mink is looking at his eyes again. She doesn't answer.

I say, "So?"

Dr. Mink sits on the stool and rolls a few inches backward so that she can address both Jae and me. "I understand that you and Jae experienced a trauma, but I'm here right now to evaluate his physical injury." Her hand goes to Jae's knee. She says, "Jae, there's no need to be alarmed, but I'd like to run one or two more tests."

"Really? Have you considered that his mental state might be affecting how his body is responding to the injury?" An edge has crept into my voice.

"My concern," says Dr. Mink, who's now addressing only Jae, "which right now is only a concern—is meningitis, so we'll want to act quickly. The first step will be a blood test to see if that's what we're dealing with. Unfortunately, we don't have a lab in the office, so I'm going to send you to a facility on Twenty-First Street. June at reception will give you the address and the forms you'll need to bring." Here Dr. Mink turns to me. "If possible, I'd urge you to accompany him right after you leave here. As I said, there's no cause for alarm, but if this is meningitis, early detection will go a long way." She turns back to Jae, whose face has lost expression. She explains that meningitis is an infection that sometimes results from a brain injury, and it would most likely clear up with antibiotics. When she's done, she says, "Do you have any questions?"

Jae shakes his head.

This new information has come so fast, I've barely processed it as we're heading out the door. In the hallway, Dr. Mink wishes us luck and tells Jae that she'll call him as soon as the results come in from the lab, which will be sometime today or tomorrow. Then she tells me that June at reception can give me some names if I feel like either of us need to talk to someone. The subtext I understand as *I'm not your therapist.*

Within minutes, we've been handed a bundle of papers by June and spit outside, the street suddenly a foreign land. We retreat to opposite sides of the doorway and call our bosses to say we won't be in for the rest of the day. Then finally it's just Jae and me.

"Tell me how you're doing," I say.

"Whatever, it sounds like no big deal. Just some antibiotics or something."

"You sure?"

Jae points to my bag. "You got a cigarette?"

"I don't know if that's the best idea."

"Dude, it's not lung cancer." Jae holds out his hand.

I fish out a cigarette and look at the paper with the lab's address. "This is too far to walk. We should grab a bite and catch a train." I head east, toward Sixth Avenue, and Jae falls into step with me.

"Just do me a favor," he says. "Try not to argue with anyone at the lab."

"What does that mean?"

"It means you didn't need to question Dr. Mink like that. She was just doing her job."

"Really? Her job is to help you get better. She was failing to consider a big part of the problem, so I asked her about it."

"Dawn, not everyone is out to get you, all right? Dr. Mink was trying to help."

"Is it helping when someone tells you they were attacked and all you want to know is the size of the fist?"

"Look, I get it. But you have to stop assuming everyone's a piece of shit."

Says the straight guy who can flirt with a man when it's fun for him, blissfully unaware of the danger, who can waltz into a men's clothing store and buy a pair of shoes for his queer friend no problem, I think. But I don't say it. What I do say is "I don't assume that."

"Good."

I stop walking and dig another cigarette out of my purse. My tights are chafing the insides of my thighs and I'm sweating inside my bra, the damn underwire cutting into my bruised ribs.

Jae has stopped too and is waiting for me a few paces ahead. When I catch up with him, he runs his hand through his hair in an exasperated kind of way, which I haven't seen him do before. He says, "Look, it's just not always a fucking fight."

He's never talked to me like this. But of course this is different. He's scared. And even though I'm still pissed at Dr. Mink, I'm also scared for him. I take his hand. "Hey, I'm sorry," I say. "All right? I know this is fucked up, but it's going to be all right. I'm here for whatever you need, okay? I'm sorry."

Jae's face softens. He takes a drag from his cigarette and

exhales slowly, a thin stream of smoke toward the sidewalk that disperses into nothing before it hits the ground. "Forget it," he says. "It doesn't matter."

I put my arm around him and try to make him laugh. "Let's just get you to this lab and we can talk about what a shitty person I am afterward."

He runs his hands through his hair again. I reach for his cigarette and light mine with it.

‖SENSE

THE NEXT MORNING as I'm gluing a spine in the lab, Jae calls, and I answer expecting good news. But he tells me his test results are positive. Dr. Mink was right about meningitis.

"Dude, fuck."

"She has me taking this bomb of an antibiotic. I just started it and it's making me puke."

"I'm so sorry. What can I do for you?"

Jae doesn't say anything.

"Are you taking probiotics? That might help."

"I can't talk or I might puke again."

There's a *click* and the line goes quiet.

Now I'm really worried about him. And I feel like I've cursed us somehow. I know what Lukas says about coincidences, but ever since I found the book cover it feels like my world has been crumbling around me. First I've been making things harder with Lukas, now my best friend is hurt. With a jolt, I realize that I haven't even thought about The Project in days. Jae gives me this amazing chance to show my work, and I'm failing at that too.

I think of the rabbi's story about Lot and Abraham. The visitor. I have to figure out who I am.

THAT NIGHT, WHEN I leave the library, the sun is hanging low in the sky and not a cloud can be seen. I want to check in on Jae, but when I texted him, he said he needed to rest. And it suddenly feels important to get back to The Project, to make good on it for him. There's an idea that's been hanging around, gnawing at me, but that won't come into focus: to make an enormous book out of drawings or photographs of New York City buildings, subways, and bridges, then find street artists to cover it in graffiti. I imagine it bound as an accordion so that the book opens up into one large mash-up of the city skyline, completely plastered in art. The problem is I don't know where to start. I don't know any street artists—at least not anymore—and even if I found them, I don't know exactly what I want them to do or whether they would be interested in creating "public" art on a paper replica of New York.

But I need to start. I make my way to a downtown 6 train to go scouting. When I emerge from the station, I scan the street and nothing immediately catches my eye, so I look for a small side street, someplace out of view where an artist could spend time. As I walk, I find a series of small faces with x's for eyes, spray-painted on news boxes; a wall full of intricate, colorful lettering; and a painting of a tree with roots in the shape of the Twin Towers. I snap a photo of the tree and then a block later I walk right into a swirl of reds and purples. In the center of a big mural, a woman holds her rose-colored lover mid-dip, kissing her on the mouth. With a wave of excitement, I lift my camera, capturing the two women in the viewfinder, imagining them as Gertrude and Marta, finally together in the light of day. But as I zoom in, a sharper image begins to emerge. The hair that's been piled atop the first woman's head now a bowler hat. Her violet dress a long men's coat. These are not two women kissing, but a man and a woman.

My excitement fades, but I zoom in closer on what's visible of the man's face, studying him, and I decide that he's been made to look feminine. Sentenced to inhabit two genders. I snap a few close-ups of the kissing couple and zoom out to get a shot of the whole piece, so big it co-opts my entire field of vision. As I stand submerged in this world where colors blend together and maleness has lost its boundaries, for a rare moment I feel both sides of myself come together—I'm the man and his lover.

Bringing up Gertrude's picture on my camera, I imagine her again as she is today—in her salmon blazer, offering me tit bread and tea, at her kitchen window, holding a small piece of her past in the sunlight—and I consider once more whether I've misread her. But here, in front of this mural, I don't think so.

I lift my camera and shoot the patterns the buildings make against one another and the sky, signs and lampposts, a trio of pigeons perched on a window ledge. I can almost see the book I'll make out of New York, what surprises I could stash between its covers. Focusing back on the image of the kiss, I try to remember which artists were prominent while Gertrude and her friends were running around 1950s New York, wondering if I can draw inspiration from them too. If memory serves, it was the abstract expressionists, with their massive canvases and experimental materials, their emphasis on process over product, and their insistence on making themselves known in an authentic way. I make a mental note to look into them more deeply.

Then I zoom in on the lower-right corner of the kiss, where there's a tag. *B-FLY*. I lower my camera and review the photos. When I'm satisfied I've gotten what I wanted, I set off for the closest train to Brooklyn.

THE SUBWAY LURCHES forward, and I hold my side. It's been throbbing all afternoon. I probably should see a doctor, but I haven't thrown up or run a fever, and also I don't have someone for primary care. I've avoided doctors since all the ones my parents made me see when they were trying to fix me. During my senior year of high school, my mother insisted she'd found someone "perfect," a chiropractor that specialized in something called applied kinesiology. According to my mother, she'd healed a coworker from a disease that no regular doctor could diagnose.

When I'd changed into the hospital gown, the chiropractor—her name was Sheila—entered the exam room with a box full of small, clear plastic vials holding pills and rocks. She asked me to hold a few of these mysteries in front of different parts of myself—my navel, my heart, the space between my eyes. As I held them with one hand, I had to extend the opposite arm, and Sheila pressed down hard on it to see how well I could resist her pressure. The result of all this "testing" was that Sheila pronounced me allergic to corn.

"It's not a big deal," she said, turning out the overhead lights and switching on a small lamp on the desk in the corner. "Just a minor allergy, but we can't go any further until we take care of it. It's blocking your energy."

"I didn't think you could cure allergies."

"Trust me. Go with it and you'll see." She pulled a white binder from the shelf above her desk and slid out a color wheel. She opened a drawer and produced a pair of green glasses. "Please put these on."

I put them on.

Sheila referenced the binder again. Then she pulled a few of her vials out. "Good. Hold still, but don't close your eyes."

I held still.

Sheila waved several vials over me with one hand while flashing a small light at my face with the other. Then she stopped abruptly and set an empty hand on my belly. We were both quiet. Sheila because she seemed to be listening for something. Me because I was afraid we'd have to start again if I made any noise.

Sheila broke the silence first. "Do you feel that?"

"What?" I whispered.

"Your belly button. It's radiating heat. Here." She took my hand and held it about an inch above my navel. "Can you feel it?"

I could. I said, "What does it mean?"

She said, "I don't know." Then, seeming to lose interest in it, she turned on the lights and declared my corn allergy cured.

She asked me to sit up and came to stand next to me. "So, why have you come here?" she said. "I've spoken to your mother, but I want to hear from you."

"I don't know. I guess I've been depressed."

"And how do you think I can help you with that?"

"Aren't you supposed to tell me?" I said.

"I could tell you several ways that I treat depression," said Sheila, "but every person is different, and I believe you're the expert on what you need."

"No offense," I said, "but my mother was the one who said I needed to come here, so I really don't know."

"I see." Sheila put her hand on the examination table, next to my leg. She looked like she was trying to think of the right words. She said, "Would you say you're comfortable in your skin?"

I sighed. "I had a feeling this was coming."

"What?"

"My mom thinks I'm confused about whether I'm a girl or a guy. She was hoping you'd cure me of that."

"What do you think?" said Sheila.

"I think I don't need anyone's help," I said. "So if I'm cured of the corn allergy, can I go?"

"You're free to go anytime." Sheila looked at me as if she were trying to read my thoughts. "Can I just tell you something interesting before you go?"

I didn't answer. But I didn't leave either.

"Do you know about anglerfish—how they mate?" she said.

"No."

"Anglerfish are bottom dwellers. They live way in the depths of the ocean, where there's no light and very little nutrients. The males are much smaller than the females, so in order to survive, as they swim along, they attach themselves by the mouth to a female. After a little while they begin to merge with her, even losing their eyes and starting to see out of her eyes. Eventually, they become one with the female, and the only thing that remains is their testicles, which leave a permanent bump on the female's body."

I said, "Okay, that's not true."

"Scout's honor," said Sheila.

"Then it's gross."

"What's gross about it?" Sheila said.

"I don't know. It's just gross."

"Maybe it wouldn't seem so gross if the merge were complete." Sheila handed me my clothes from the chair in the corner. "Please leave the gown in the bin next to the door. If you want to make another appointment, Michelle can help you at the front desk. Otherwise, it was very nice to meet you, Dawn." She touched my knee comfortingly. Then she stepped out of the room.

The subway stops, and as the doors slide open, the tangled mess of coats and bags elbowing their way off the train become the tangled mess elbowing their way on. I step aside to make room and think about the irony in my mom sending me to Sheila. She'd wanted to fix me but, instead, without knowing it, she'd sent me to someone who encouraged me. I don't think she realized that, either way, there was no way for her to win. I certainly didn't realize the same was true for me.

‖EMERGENCY

WHEN I GET home, I'm surprised to find the light blinking on the answering machine for our landline. It's Gertrude. She wants to know how the article is coming. Could I give her an update on when it might come out? "I'm not going to be around forever," she says. "Ach, it doesn't matter. I only have so many words left in me. I should save a few of them."

Of course. What an idiot I've been. Not once since I came up with this plan have I considered that I'll have to actually write an article—or at least pretend to. Maybe I can tell her the newsletter has turned it down. But she might still want to see a draft. I pour myself a glass of wine and sit down to think. The worst part is that I sought Gertrude out because I thought I needed something from her, but now she seems to need something from me. And of course she does. I've opened a door that she sealed shut a long time ago, so it makes sense she would be looking to me for—what? What is she hoping my article will do for her before she dies? Whatever it is, I now owe it to her. Again I think of Marta. But this time wondering if she's alive somewhere, if it would be possible to track her down to put her back in touch with Gertrude. I go to the computer and run some searches online, but I get nothing. Maybe I can ask Gertrude for something more about her next time we speak to make my search easier. Then again, would Gertrude even want that?

Unsatisfied, I change my search terms, typing in *1950s, United States,* and *gay paranoia.* One of the first things that comes up is an article on something called the Lavender Scare. As I read, I can't understand how it is that until now I've never heard of it. Thousands of people had been fired from federal government jobs for being gay or even suspected of it—and then left with a permanent tag on their records so that they couldn't be hired anywhere else in the country. And even more chilling was how they got caught. The police followed "suspects" on the street outside their homes and staked out public restrooms. Together with the military, they secretly photographed gay bars and sent pictures to the FBI. And then none of the people they caught were even allowed to speak or testify at their own hearings. My stomach turns. I want to know more. The article is brief, so I look for others, but I only find one and it's more of the same.

I try to put it out of my mind, but the next day at work I'm still thinking about it. I can't understand how something on this scale hasn't become common knowledge, and I'm frustrated with how little I've learned. So on my lunch hour I go to the nearest branch of the public library, but I only manage to unearth one journal article. As it turns out, homosexuality was criminalized even before the Lavender Scare, but the Red

Scare exacerbated people's fear. Gay people were framed as "moral weaklings" who had a "sociopathic personality disturbance." The fact that no one would choose to be homosexual served as proof that that they were easy to manipulate, leaving them only one dangerous step away from being recruited by communists.

I look up at the shelves and shelves of books and feel the same anger I felt at Dr. Mink's office. Where are all the stories about this? Where's the outrage over people's privacy being violated and lives destroyed? A chill settles on the back of my neck.

ON MY WAY back to the museum, I call Jae to check in. The antibiotic is still making him sick, so he's home from work. He tells me I'm projecting, that I don't want to look at all the things I'm repressing so instead I'm obsessing over Gertrude and Marta.

I tell him of course I'm projecting but who cares. And suddenly I realize what my imagined city can be. "Holy shit, that's it," I say. "If you were here, I'd kiss your damn cheek."

"What are you talking about?" he says.

"You just solved my problem—the focus for my artist book."

"Really?" His voice perks up a bit. "What was my brilliant idea?"

"The theme is imagined cities. You said I'm repressing things and I've been thinking: What kind of a city would it be where no one had to do that, where no one had to hide who they were?"

"Wow, great question. What are you imagining?"

"It's a little hazy, but maybe I can get some street artists to fill my paper city with queer bodies. Beautiful ones."

"Okay, but Dawn, that city already exists. You just have to decide if you're willing to go."

"Oh, you're a poet now?"

"Meningitis, baby. Makes you wiser."

"Don't joke like that," I say. "You have to respect the illness so it doesn't have cause to show you who's boss."

Jae sighs. "You don't really believe that."

"Just take care of yourself. Please." I glance at my watch. "I have to get back to work before Katherine thinks I jumped ship, but I'm going food shopping later, so let me know if you need anything and I'll stop by on my way home."

"Nah, I'm good. But the interview prep."

"I know. I have time to help you practice."

"What? Just like that? No wisecracks?"

"You want to push me?"

Jae laughs.

"See you later," I say.

I hang up and climb the steps to the front door of the Met, with each step, my tights slipping down a little and pulling my underwear with them. Actually, it's Lukas's underwear. I've worn it under my dress, hoping it would be enough. It's not. Immediately I begin to second-guess my idea for The Project. Because, of course, it would mean revealing myself to Katherine and everyone else in the library.

IT'S ONLY TWO hours later when I get a call from Lukas. Jae is in the emergency room. He vomited three times, passed out, and woke with a fever.

Like the jealous dick I'm becoming, I say, "And he called you?"

Lukas's phone makes a scratchy sound like he's moved it away. "Do you want to come over here or not?"

"Of course I do." Katherine is eyeing me from her desk.

"I'm out of tobacco," says Lukas. "Get me some on the way?"

"Fine." I hang up before the reality of what's happening settles in. I just talked to Jae, and it was the first time since the incident that he sounded like his old self. It doesn't seem real that two hours later he could be in the emergency room.

Katherine is watching me again. I touch my hip, checking for the outline of Lukas's underwear as I tell her I have to go see Jae.

WALKING DOWN THE hospital corridor, I relieve the pain in my side by giving some of my weight to the railing on the wall. The lights are surprisingly dim, but I can still see the grunge at the edges of the floor. I go to Emergency first, people everywhere. They tell me Jae's been admitted. He's in the intensive care unit. I pass the maternity wing, gynecology, a nurses' station. The staff walks around purposefully, picking up folders and setting them down. And I'm removed from it all, as if watching them on television. Then I come to Jae's room. Lukas is hovering just inside the doorway, a privacy curtain on the other side of Jae's bed making the space claustrophobic.

Jae's sitting on the bed. They have him hooked up to an IV and a heart monitor. He looks even skinnier than usual and all of the non-washing is finally showing itself. Still, when he sees me, he gives me that half smile, and Lukas gestures toward me with his head. A polite hello.

"You look like hell," I say, sitting at the foot of the bed.

"It's good to see you too," says Jae.

"Why is it so dark in here?"

"My eyes are sensitive."

"Where are the doctors? They're just leaving you with needles in your arms?"

"Looks like it." He leans his head back.

"For real though, what's going on?" Sitting down, I'm eye-level with Lukas's arm.

"They're just running some tests," says Jae. But I can tell he's scared. He touches his head, like I'd seen him do at Dr. Mink's office.

"What are they looking for?"

"Meningitis. Or something worse." He looks at Lukas. "Dude, you got any cigarettes?"

Lukas laughs nervously. His arm bounces against his stomach.

A nurse knocks on the door and hurries in, a stocky guy with curly hair. "Excuse me," he says. "Time to get your vitals." As he walks around Lukas to check the IV bag, he says, "Okay, friends, visiting hours are over in five minutes, but you're welcome to come back this evening or tomorrow between ten thirty and eleven thirty." He sticks a thermometer in Jae's ear.

Lukas steps away from the bed and leans on the opposite wall. "Dawn," he says, and he gestures toward the hallway with his head.

"Just a minute," I say, and turn to the nurse. "Can you tell me why you're keeping Jae overnight?"

"I'm just making the rounds. I'm sorry, I haven't spoken to Mr. Kwon's doctor."

"You have his chart there, don't you?"

"Yes, ma'am, but Dr. Mink will know better what treatment she has in mind."

"Can't you just give us a general idea?"

"Listen, ma'am—"

"My name is Dawn," I say, my face getting hot.

"Dawn, I know this is stressful, but Dr. Mink will be in shortly, and she can answer all of Mr. Kwon's questions."

Jae is shaking his head as if to stop me from escalating things.

"If you'll excuse me," says the nurse, and he walks out of the room.

I move to follow him and Lukas grabs me by the arm. "What are you doing?"

"Trying to get some answers," I say. "Is that guy incompetent or just an asshole?"

"Calm down."

I want to say, *Don't tell me to calm down*, but he's right. It's not the time to be starting arguments. I pull my arm away and go back to the bed. "Dude," I say to Jae, "you really need someone here to advocate for you."

"My mom and sister are on their way." Jae forces a smile. "I don't know about advocating, but I'm sure they'll be on the doctor's case all night."

"Good," I say.

Jae closes his eyes. The heart monitor beeps rhythmically. The line at the bottom a little city skyline. I remember the pouch of tobacco I've picked up for Lukas and feel inside my bag to make sure it's there, as if doing this small thing for him is going to erase the tension between us. Out of the corner of my eye, I see him step out the door.

Jae is leaning sideways, the neck of his hospital gown falling down one shoulder.

"You need rest," I say. I want to stay and make sure he's all right, but I'm worried Lukas will leave without me, and I can't handle the thought of another night waiting for him to come home. "Promise me you'll get a good night's sleep. I'm coming back in the morning and I want to know what you need so I can bring it with me. Text if you think of anything. In fact, text as soon as you know anything."

Jae salutes. He's trying to be funny but he looks terrified. I hug him and shoot a quick glance into the hallway to check if Lukas is still there. If he is, I can't see him. I hate how desperate I feel.

As I stand to go, he appears in the doorway, and I let out breath.

"Hey, feel better," he says to Jae.

Jae holds out his fist. Lukas comes over and fist-bumps with him. I squeeze his hand and follow Lukas out of the room. We walk down the hall and step into an elevator. The doors close and I think I can't breathe. Lukas is tapping his foot, playing with the flap on his bag. I still have his tobacco, but I don't say anything. I'm waiting for him to ask for it. When we get out of the elevator, we walk past the cafeteria. A stuffed animal display in the gift shop window makes me think about my childhood bedroom, and I'm filled with a deep longing for the comfort that thought should bring me. Lukas is walking in front of me. He always ends up getting ahead of me because of his long legs, even when he doesn't mean to.

"Lukas, stop," I say. "Slow down."

We're almost at the door. He sighs, turns around but doesn't look at me. I worry I'm going to cry so I bite my lip. My phone buzzes. Katherine. *Hope everything is ok.* Then, *U coming back this afternoon?*

I want to smash my phone.

"We going?" says Lukas.

People are being pushed by in wheelchairs, others asking for loved ones at the front desk, and I stand lamely in the middle of it and start to cry.

Lukas unwinds himself from his messenger bag and drops it to the floor, still holding the strap in one hand. "What's wrong?" It seems to be all anybody asks anymore.

"I'm just tired," I say.

He's quiet.

"And why the hell did Jae call you instead of me?"

"This is about Jae?"

"No," I say. "Not like that."

Lukas squats next to his messenger bag. Gravity too much for him. "Listen," he says, "there is nothing going on between me and Jae. If there were, I would tell you."

"It's not that," I say. I want to say, *I'm just worried about him and scared that my stupid curiosity is the reason why everything's falling apart.* I say, "It's like the more I try to understand myself, the more I risk losing the people I care about, and I'm tired of not telling you how I feel because I'm afraid of your answer."

A nurse in Sesame Street scrubs walks by. She spots Lukas squatting on the ground and comes over. "Can I help you?" she says to him in a voice that sounds like she's talking to a child, even though I'm the one who's crying.

Lukas stands. "No, thanks."

The nurse regards both of us, turns a practiced compassionate face toward me, and moves on.

Lukas can't look at me. "We should probably talk somewhere else," he says. He reaches for his bag, revealing the fading black-and-blue mark on his wrist, the one small injury he managed to escape with while Jae is in the hospital and I've been struggling with bruised ribs. It would be a great metaphor if it wasn't so sad.

"Fine, yeah."

We head outside, and the sun is so bright it hurts my eyes to look at the sidewalk.

Lukas says, "I have to go back to work." He scrunches up his face apologetically.

"Yeah, of course, me too," I say.

"I'll walk you to the train."

We walk in silence. From time to time, I let Lukas get ahead of me. I imagine stopping on the sidewalk and just letting him go, right out of my life without his even realizing it.

We get to the subway station and he kisses me.

My heart aches. I say, "So I guess we'll talk later."

Lukas looks toward the stairway leading down to the train. "It's just—I only have a few minutes."

"I know, I know."

188 || JENNIFER SAVRAN KELLY

He looks like he's in pain. Like it hurts to go but it would hurt more to stay. "See you later," he says, and he leaves me at the top of the stairs.

As soon as he goes, I change my mind about work and, with greater determination and certainty than I've felt in a while, cross the street to get the downtown train. I need to salvage at least *one* thing, and I still have over a month before the gallery show. I pull out my phone and text Katherine. *Jae ok. Getting things from his apt. Back at work tomorrow. Tx.*

The train comes right away, leaving me no time to reconsider. I sit in the almost-empty car and set my bag on the seat next to me. There's a new sketchbook inside. I take it out and open to the first page, stare at it for a while, then write, *Imagined city: full of beautiful, nonnormative bodies.* Then I write one more word. *Alice.*

‖ALICE

I GET OFF the train at York Street, as I'd done weeks ago, to look for street art. But this time with purpose. To make something go right today.

It's unseasonably hot, and New York smells like a sewer. As I walk, all I notice are a few forgotten "Have you seen?" ads, weathered and faded, like nothing more than the ghosts of people's pain. How many of the missing were never found? How many people are still hoping to learn what happened to their loved ones? Approaching the bridge, I put my hands to my ears, as if to block out the sound of my own thoughts. In a moment of weakness, I dig out my phone and call my parents. I know it will make me feel worse, but hope is its own piti- ful animal. After four rings, the machine picks up. My mom's voice. "Hi, it's Fran and Doug. Leave a message and we'll call you back." During the beep I hang up. They've taken me off the message. Fran and Doug. It should be no big deal. I've been living away from home for six years, but last time I called, whenever that was, my name was still on the message.

I keep walking until I'm standing in the archway by the bridge where I'd found the genderless face demanding (begging?), *Protect freedom N*●*W*. It's still there. I lean against the wall and study it, until two guys in baseball caps come through. They're talking to each other, not even looking at me, but I clutch my bag and dig my keys out in case I need to use them. Then I walk outside into the sunshine, where people can at least witness me being murdered.

As the baseball caps walk out of my field of vision, I duck under the bridge by the water and mix with the crowd. Finding an open seat on a bench, I give the pain in my side a rest and watch a group of kids pass a basketball back and forth, shooting hoops into imaginary baskets. Their bodies are lean and nimble and seem to bring them a lot of joy, and watching them makes everything seem so uncomplicated. I tell myself it's time to stop wandering the streets and make a real start on The Project.

Alice and I haven't talked since high school, but the fact that I stumbled across her small rainbow eyes has to be more than another coincidence. I take my phone out and flip it open and shut a few times, then dial her old number.

"Hello?" says a woman's voice.

I open my sketchbook and doodle. "Hello. I'm a high school friend of Alice's. I was wondering if you could give me her phone number." I pause. "My name's Dawn."

"Oh, hi, Dawn. Of course." Her voice is friendly. "I'm sure Alice will be happy to hear from you." She recites the number.

I thank her, hang up, and read it a few times. Pacing by the water, I look around to make sure no one's watching, then take a coin out of my wallet and throw it into the East River. I text the number from Alice's mom. *Hi, it's Dawn from SVA. Long time no speak. If u don't still hate me, I could use yr help w an art project.*

Tucking my phone into my bag, I think about how memory distorts what we think we know about people and how I have no idea what to expect from Alice now, if anything. But I guess that's why we need memories in the first place. We rely on them to keep us tethered to life when reality keeps changing on us. That's probably why I keep thinking about my parents, hoping they'll revert back to the mom and dad who once seemed to love me unconditionally. I miss the mom who taught me that no matter how bad a day gets, there's always a reset button somewhere within reach.

I want to get back to Brooklyn, grab some veggies at the bodega near the subway, and cook a nice dinner for Lukas. A reset button for both of us to start the day over. As I head back to the train, my phone vibrates. I take it out of my bag and hold it against my chest before flipping it open. *Whoa, long time. Of course I don't hate you. Give a ring whenever.* My body buzzes with energy. I pick up my pace and, for the first time in weeks, can't stop smiling. I start to dial but change my mind. It would look desperate. Perhaps I should wait a day or two. I can't believe she still has me under the same spell.

I try to calm down by focusing on my surroundings, but instead I start reliving my outbursts in front of Jae and Lukas at the hospital. Then I console myself that I just need to apologize to both of them as soon as possible, and once I get help from Alice and begin working on The Project, I'll start to feel better. Whatever's blocking me from making art is driving me crazy. So if I can get past this hump, everything else will straighten itself out.

I pass a small group of protesters on their way somewhere, holding signs. *No Blood for Oil. Drop Bush, Not Bombs.* They smile as if recognizing me as a kindred spirit, and I take this momentary sense of belonging to mean I'm on the right track. Then I see an antique shop and step inside to look for a gift for Jae. Once, when I'd gotten food poisoning, as a get-well gift he gave me a fake tarantula in a little plastic boat. The side of the boat said *It is not the ship so much as the skillful sailing that assures the prosperous voyage.* He told me that when you put two unexpected things together, it creates humor, and humor is good for healing, so he hoped I liked it.

In the toy section of the antique store, I find a tiny rocking chair and a stuffed owl in an apron that's the perfect size to fit in the chair. I want to go back to the hospital but figure his mom and sister should be arriving around now.

BACK IN BROOKLYN, I find a perfect eggplant and some spinach and peppers. As I'm boiling water for pasta, my phone buzzes again. Lukas. *Need 2 work late. Have dinner w/o me. xx.* I look at my watch and my heart grows heavy. So much for the reset. I stuff the food in the fridge, sit at the table, and punch it as hard as I can. I stand and pace, rubbing my temples, feeling sorry for myself.

Then I pick up my phone and call Alice.

"Dawn Levit," she says. A voice that floods me with remembering. "Wow."

I nod, as if she can hear me.

"How are you, stranger?" She sounds more confident than she used to.

"I'm fine." My hand hurts from punching the table. I open and close my fingers. "Thanks for responding, you know, to my text. How are you?"

"Good. I'm glad you found me."

"Yeah." After a long pause, I explain why I've called and tell her about The Project, and she says it sounds cool and asks if I'm still in New York. I say yeah, I came back after college, and is she still here too? She is.

"We should grab a coffee sometime," she says. "I'd love to see your work."

"That would be nice." I open the kitchen cabinet above the cutting board and pull out an old bottle of red wine. "I'm in Brooklyn, but I work in the city." I pour myself a glass and drain half of it.

"I'm in Williamsburg," she says.

I say I'm in Park Slope, but still, Brooklyn, what a coincidence. I take another long sip of wine. She says she'll reach out to some street artists she knows and get back to me. I say I can't wait, and we hang up.

According to the clock, only fifteen minutes have passed since Lukas's text.

"All right, enough of this," I say to the empty apartment. I drain the wine, leave the pot of water to cool on the stove, and head out the door.

ONE SUBWAY RIDE and countless blocks of walking later, I arrive at Cubbyhole, a dyke dive in the West Village, where I hesitate before I open the door, remembering what the dude at Pyramid Club said to me about wandering into the wrong bar, especially since I'm still pushing myself to dress more femme. It's been a couple of years since I've felt at home around other queers. As long as I can't choose a side, I don't belong anywhere. But tonight I guess I need to be someplace where the queer part of me can breathe again. I step inside, pass by people primping, drinking, howling with laughter, and sit at the bar, rainbow streamers and pinwheels dangling above my head like thought bubbles.

The bartender smiles. "You just missed happy hour."

"Figures," I say.

She laughs. "What'll it be?"

I order a lager and check my pockets for cash. The bartender sets my beer down. "Are you new in town?"

"Sort of," I say.

"I'm Beth."

"Dawn," I say. "Pleasure."

Beth winks. There's a trio of older, soft-butch women sitting at the other end of the bar. "Hey," she says. "You going to let my friend Dawn here drink alone?"

"Nah, that's not necessary," I say, but the women call me over. I wave.

One of them pats the seat next to her. "Come on. We don't bite."

Settling into small talk, I learn their names and what they do, answer their questions about bookbinding. *How'd you learn that? Aren't paper books expected to go the way of the dinosaur? And then, the inevitable. Do you have a girlfriend? No? A pretty thing like you—come on. Then let me buy you another.*

Suddenly I can barely taste my drink. The feeling of it moving around my mouth too complicated, every flavor wrong.

My vision blurs. My body is failing me again. "I'm good, thanks," I say.

"Suit yourself."

I try to relax, but then I get the feeling that everyone in the bar is trying to manage more than they can handle—balancing too many glasses, tripping over their chairs. Without planning to, I stand, leaving my half-drunk beer and a tip for Beth.

"Hey, you okay?" comes a voice. It's one of the women.

"Yeah, I just have to go."

"Already?"

"I was just stopping in on my way home," I say.

"You'll have to come back again, then."

"For sure," I say. I put my hand over my heart to make sure it's still beating while I walk out the door.

AS I RIDE the train back to Brooklyn, my body begins to return to me. Slowly, the world comes back into focus, though I still don't like what I see. Jae injured, in the hospital. Lukas, and how he always seems to escape unharmed, or maybe avoids getting involved in the first place. It scares me how, so quickly, I've become afraid of him. Ever since the night we got attacked, I've been tiptoeing around him, really starting to fear his indifference to my female self, the self I now believe I need to keep me safe. When I left for the train station this morning, I put my arms around him and kissed him on the mouth, but he squirmed away, blaming the hot coffee in his hands.

Come back, I wanted to say.

AS SOON AS I get home, I peel off my dress, tights, and bra and look at myself in the mirror. The purple bruise an ugly flower below my breast, Lukas's underwear tight around my hips. I sit and contemplate the little owl in the rocking chair, wondering if Jae will like it, and my phone buzzes. Alice. *Nice to hear from you today. Talk soon.* Cradling the phone in my palm, I decide to make her wait for a reply.

To pass the time, I grab my camera and scroll to the photo of Gertrude, hoping it will inspire me to work on The Project. And as I take in her bold gaze yet again, I realize there is one possible way to get more answers about her: the book. *Turn Her About.* Perhaps her message for Marta went beyond the illustration on the cover. Maybe there was more to be said by the novel itself. Pulling the chair up to the desk, I boot up the computer and find a used copy on eBay for forty-five dollars. It has a different cover, but the author is the same. All the description offers is "Early homosexual novel dealing with a woman's tormented struggle against her guilt over her unnatural desires!"

It has to be the one. I click. Now all that's left to do is wait.

Settling on the futon, I draw a rough picture of Gertrude standing on her back porch in the sunlight, a cigarette in her hand. Underneath I write, *G*, then, *Protest against death.*

‖INVITATION

LUKAS DOESN'T COME home until eleven o'clock, when I'm getting ready for bed. So much for talking after work. Pete had asked him to see *Confidence* and then they went out for a beer. Now he's drunk and playing damsel in distress, resting the back of his hand against his forehead, asking for help getting out of his clothes. He lies on the futon and makes me promise I won't take advantage of his altered state. It's meant to be flirty, but I don't know how to keep doing this with him—giving in to such intense desire without knowing where it's going. I leave him on the futon and sit in the kitchen to work on The Project. He dozes off, but ten minutes later he's up, walking around in his underwear. He finds the wine and pours himself a glass.

Crossing his legs and drawing his hair behind his ear, he says, "Have a drink with me?"

I want to. "Not now," I say.

"What are you doing?" He leans over my pile of folded paper.

"I need to concentrate. I'm working on the idea for my gallery show." Tearing a sheet out of my sketchbook, I mark off nine equal sections with my spring divider. Then I fold it into an accordion, making a rough mock-up to test my idea.

Lukas goes back to the futon. He takes out his tobacco and sets it on his lap. A few minutes later he's passed out again.

IN THE MORNING I get a text from Jae. Dr. Mink said the intravenous antibiotic is working, but they're planning to keep him in intensive care for another day or two to monitor his progress. I'm so relieved I almost cry, but I'm not ready to celebrate until he's clear of the infection. I write back, *Don't fuck this up. I'll be there in an hour to make sure.*

Lukas is still asleep when I leave.

I've been thinking I need to finally get back to Gertrude to confess I won't be writing an article, so on my way to the subway I call. Dialing her number, I count the doorways I pass while I wait for her to pick up. She answers on four.

"Hello, this is Gertrude." Her voice rings loud in my ear. I move the phone a few inches away.

"Hi, Ms. Kleber, it's Dawn Levit returning your call."

After a few awkward pleasantries, I'm practically out of breath, which happens easily since my injury. I lift the mouthpiece up toward the top of my head to mask my heavy breathing.

"How's your article coming?" she says.

This is the moment I've gone out of my way to plan, determined to tell the truth. But now that I have her on the phone, I double down on the lie. I can't give up on the chance to get more information about the Brahm family. It might help me track down Marta. Which I tell myself would be just as meaningful as writing an article. "I'm still working on the outline, so it's in a pretty rough state," I say.

"Sounds like a good start. Do you have everything you need?"

"I think so. Except for one thing." If I can locate the neighborhood where Gertrude lived, I might be able to find the right Brahms. "Can you tell me where you lived when you got to the States, what neighborhood?"

"Of course, we lived in Washington Heights. There were so many German Jews there, they called it Frankfurt-on-Hudson."

"Perfect. Thank you."

"Another thing," she says. "I found a few photographs of my father's and I thought you might find them interesting—to publish with the article. I was going to mail them, but it would be safer if you came here to get them—if you have the time. There aren't many, and they're all I have."

I freeze. I can't believe she's inviting me back to her home. "Of course," I say.

She coughs, but I soon realize the cough is actually laughter. "Can you believe? I went through some old things after you left, and I found one of those old pulp novels I'd put a new cover on. It was that very first one I bought. Disguised it as a Shakespeare play."

I hold my breath.

"Oh my, I was a bold one," she says. "I guess I couldn't let them all go—even though I knew it was dangerous. You know, I realize I never even considered what my parents thought about all that time I spent reading and writing. I suppose they must have thought it a little strange. Ach." This time she coughs. "All right," she says. "If you need anything else, give a call. And you'll call to let me know when you can come out to get the photos."

"Yes," I say. "I'll do that."

"You'll keep me updated, then?"

"I will, Ms. Kleber."

"And you'll call me Gertrude."

"If you say so." My heart is racing. I have an invitation to see her again. I have her old neighborhood and the hope that it can lead me to more information about the Brahms.

After a moment, Gertrude says, "I had the funniest fortune cookie this week. It said 'It can't rain all the time.' What do you think of that?" Before I answer, she coughs again and tries to clear her throat, but it's taking considerable effort.

"Are you okay?" I say.

"Yes, yes, we'll talk soon," she manages. She hangs up.

I approach the subway, my head spinning. As I descend into the station, mingling with the bodies and the grit, I picture Gertrude hiding her books, getting rid of them all except the one she couldn't bear to part with. And now I understand a little more about the extent of the danger she'd put herself in. Because of the Lavender Scare, if her secret had gotten out, it's possible she would never even have become a teacher. I wonder what happened to all those people the government tried not only to criminalize but to erase through their undercover surveillance, blind memos, and secret hearings. Not to mention all those who escaped government erasure but hid their own truth out of fear. The thought makes me sick. Gertrude may be dying, but if there's anything I can do about it, she won't be erased.

‖PATIENCE

BY THE TIME I get to Jae's room, I'm winded from carrying the care package I've assembled for him: clothes from his apartment, the owl in the rocking chair, and a couple of corn muffins I picked up on the way. He's sitting in bed, fidgeting with a Rubik's cube, which makes me nervous, like it will overtax his brain. As I'm about to ask who gave it to him, I notice a woman sitting in a chair next to the bed, reading a magazine.

"Hey," Jae says. "You look like you just ran a marathon."

The woman in the chair turns to me. She has Jae's face, at least around the mouth and jaw, and bleached hair down to her shoulders.

Jae says, "This is my sister, Mi Sun."

Mi Sun holds out her hand.

I take it, though I'm in no mood to meet anyone, let

alone someone to whom I still owe a piece of unfinished art. "Hey, sorry, I didn't know you were here. Should I come back?"

"Oh, no," she says.

"This is Dawn," says Jae.

Recognition lights up Mi Sun's face. "Dawn, nice to finally meet you. I feel like you're family."

"Same here," I say. "And I hope you got my note. Thanks again for the opportunity at Ricco/Maresca."

"Oh, my pleasure!"

I smile. Then I catch sight of the Rubik's cube in Jae's hands again and something about the way he's holding it, or not holding it tightly enough, brings on a wave of nausea. Suddenly I'm anxious. Unexpectedly meeting Mi Sun puts The Project in a whole new light—makes it a real, living thing that people are actually going to see. If a little flirtation between men and a picture of Gertrude were enough to provoke some assholes in a bar, enough to put Jae in the hospital, then what would a big colorful book full of queer bodies do? And who would pay the price for that? *Maybe there's such a thing as being too fearless,* I think. Maybe this isn't the right time for The Project. Maybe it isn't worth it.

Then again, I shouldn't even be thinking about this right now. I present my care package to Jae. He takes out the owl, and it's good to see joy on his face for real.

"Two unexpected things," he says, examining it with care. "Come here."

I move closer to the bed. He punches my arm. "Thanks, sister-friend. I love it."

He pulls out the clothes and the muffins and sets them on

the table next to him. Mi Sun goes to the bathroom. With the room suddenly quieter, Jae seems to sink back into his bed.

"Still warm," I say, pointing to the muffins. My stomach hasn't settled down. I tell myself to get a grip. I just need food and I'll be fine. "Aren't you going to try one?"

He closes his eyes. He looks like he's expended all his energy on the owl. "Maybe later."

"You need to keep your strength up."

He opens his eyes only long enough to roll them at me.

For a moment I sit quietly, trying to think of something that will perk him up. "Any word about how the protest went?"

He shakes his head.

"Well, as soon as you get out of here, I'll help you make signs for the next one."

Nothing. I stare at him, feeling useless, and notice his pillow is crooked, so I get up and lift his head to straighten it.

He flinches. "Ah. You startled me."

"I'm sorry," I say. "Just trying to help."

He lets out a breath. "I know. It's all right, but sit down. You seem so nervous."

I look away, afraid he can tell how scared I am for him.

Mi Sun comes out of the bathroom. "A nurse came by a little while ago. She said Jae's still responding well to the antibiotic."

"Good," I say.

"Stop talking about me like I'm not here," Jae says. His eyes are still closed.

"You're supposed to be resting." Mi Sun looks from him

to me. "So, bookbinding. That's cool. How did you get into that?"

"Art school." It seems like the simplest answer, even though it's not true. I force myself to sound friendly.

Her eyes are kind, but there's a question in her look that I can't decipher.

I avoid her gaze, put my hand on Jae's arm.

He flinches again. "Dawn, what did I just say?"

I pull my hand back.

Mi Sun says, "Don't mind him. He's been grumpy all morning. Anyway, I could use some water. I'll be right back." She gets up and leaves Jae and me alone again.

"I'm sorry," Jae says. "It's just the incessant poking and prodding, even in the middle of the night when I'm trying to sleep. If it's not a nurse coming in to give me meds or check my vitals, it's some machine beeping."

"Ugh. At least they're taking good care of you though."

"Yeah, maybe. Or they're putting on a good show." Jae swallows.

"What makes you say that?"

"Nothing. I'm just ready to get out of here, you know?"

"Don't worry. You will. It sounds like they're happy with how things are going."

He crosses his arms. "For the moment. If nothing else goes wrong."

I start to reach out to touch him again but stop myself. "Well, at the very least, I can help you pass the time. And I promise no more poking and prodding." I put my hands behind my back.

But Jae still looks serious. With his head leaning against his pillow, he says, "You know I love seeing you, right? So you can relax a little and stop trying to make up for what happened like it was somehow your fault."

The nausea returns. I put a hand on the table next to me to steady myself.

He says, "People can just be assholes."

"I know," I say. Then see Jae falling to the pavement. "And that's exactly why we need to be careful."

He seems to be considering what to say next. There's a new pity in the way he looks at me. "Do you really think I don't know that?" he says. "I mean, how do you think I feel when people shout at me on the street to go back to Iraq, back to Al-Qaeda, calling me Saddam Hussein? Never mind that I look absolutely nothing like an Iraqi. Our country has declared war on evil, right? A fucking idea. So everyone wants a target, and when you have yellow or brown skin, you get to be the target. You know what I'm saying?"

For the first time, I avoid his gaze. "Of course. I'm not an idiot," I say.

"And I'm not trying to make you feel bad, but sometimes I wish you would understand I'm not as naive as you seem to think. I'm just trying to be your friend." He sighs. "And you make it damn tiring sometimes."

His words are a punch in the gut. They're childhood words. Words that shouldn't carry weight anymore but somehow carry double. And after what he'd said at the bar about keeping his career plans from me and how he reacted outside Dr. Mink's office, I can't help but wonder how long he's been harboring such awful feelings about me.

"Wow," I say. "Sorry to give you such a great impression.

Sorry I can't try to help without you thinking my only motivation is to clear my conscience."

Jae runs his fingers through his hair. "Of course you can. You've just done enough for now. Like, the muffins and the clothes are awesome, but you don't have to bring me things or fix my pillow." He sinks back into the bed like our conversation has taken too much out of him. "The only thing I really need right now is rest."

I look at the owl in the rocking chair, then at Jae. I don't know if he's truly mad at me or just exhausted, but I hate that everything I try to do to make this better only makes it worse. I hate that he's still sick. How terrified he looks. All of it.

Mi Sun walks back in with a water bottle and her phone to her ear. When she hangs up she says, "Mom. She'll be back tomorrow."

I feel like I should go away. I practically jump out of my chair.

Jae shakes his head. He looks sad, or maybe hopeless. It's an expression I don't see on him often. "I'm sorry. I have to go," I say. "I need to eat something."

"It was nice to meet you," says Mi Sun.

"You too." I fist-bump with Jae, carefully, and step into the hallway.

Outside his room, I look through my bag for a cigarette even though I don't have any. It looks like the nurse at the nurses' station is holding one, but it's just a pen. I step into a full elevator. When the doors close, I pretend to keep searching my bag so I don't have to look at anyone. I'm feeling small and insignificant, like Jae said at the Empire State Building. Only it's not empowering. It sucks. Maybe he's right about me. I've been too wrapped up in my own problems to be a good friend to anyone.

But I don't know how to turn off my feelings like a faucet. It's one thing to try to figure out how to get comfortable in my own skin but entirely different to watch it affecting the people around me. It's hard to know where my responsibility ends.

Once again, I want to know what strength felt like for Gertrude, what it meant for her to actually have to hide, first in Germany, where her life was at stake and she was too young to understand, and then here, when she could be legally punished in countless ways for who she was—a godless, twisted sex pervert—when there were absolutely zero laws to protect people like her, like us, from harm. I wonder if Marta was hiding too, if Gertrude had been right to look for some message in her smile. Surely I owe it to people like them to find a voice to express what they couldn't, especially now. And the only way I've ever known how to do that is through art. If only I could coax a fully formed vision of The Project out of my head—one that feels decent enough to show in this exhibition.

But as I step into the subway to head for work, I'm already losing confidence. Am I really obligated to risk the safety of the people I care most about in order to try to create a better world? And is it even possible to make a dent in so much hatred with one piece of art?

Then again, maybe I was right when I told Lukas that change takes time. So maybe this one artwork is not the whole point. Maybe the important thing is simply to have a voice.

Shall we draw back, my brother, my sister,
or cross over?

‖HANDS

I ARRIVE AT work as everyone's getting back from lunch. For the rest of the day I avoid Katherine's gaze. When she asks me how Jae or The Project are doing, I shrug. When she asks me what's wrong, I say only that I have a lot to do and want to make up for the time I've lost visiting Jae in the hospital. "Fair enough," she says, and goes back to whatever she was doing on the computer.

Amina spends most of the afternoon doing housekeeping—cooking wheat paste, ordering supplies, and cleaning her side of the workbench. Every so often she comes to show me some treasure she's found in her tool drawer. A bone clasp, an antique button she thought she lost. Once, when Katherine is out of the room, she asks tentatively how I'm doing. She says I look tired. I mumble something about needing a break from people asking me if I'm tired, and she says, "Fine," and goes back to resetting the items on top of her half of the bench. I hate when I get this way, when I know I'm being a jerk and can't stop myself. I hate it even more with Amina, who's never anything but patient with me. After I first started at the Met, as a volunteer, it was her generosity that got me this job. I'd only taken a few workshops and interned with the binder in Brooklyn for a year—barely enough experience to even set foot in this lab. Amina and I hit it off right away, and when a full-time opportunity opened up, she offered to stay after hours a few nights a week to train me and give me a chance to build a small portfolio of conservation work. She promised it was a selfish move because she wanted me around and said I could pay her back in beers, so every night that we stayed late, I took her out afterward. We'd drink Guinness and sing '80s songs, and Amina would tell me about her childhood in Dakar. She said sometimes being this far away felt a bit like being lost, but that sometimes being lost is an opportunity.

All I want now is to get lost somewhere. Lost in the books I'm repairing, in each one's history, which I can feel in the tone and texture of its pages, in the well-intentioned but clumsy repairs that have been attempted by previous owners, in the weight of the boards and the brittleness of the sewing thread. This is where I belong, my hands on a book, feeling my way through its secrets and needs, repairing its wounds so that it can be what it was meant to be—a thing of beauty, an offering, an unquestioning companion. I paste a strip of Japanese tissue over a small tear and realize it's been awhile since I've come up for air. Stretching my arms over my head, I see Amina watching me.

"I'm sorry for snapping at you," I say. "It's just—there doesn't seem to be anything anyone can do for Jae. But thanks for offering to help."

"Thanks," she says. "I'm sorry too. About your friend."

I want to tell her how grateful I am for her, but I get back to work.

Amina does too, and then she pauses. "I was noticing earlier that you use your hands like tools. You do such small, precise work with your fingers."

I look down at my hands, the veins and knobby knuckles. For a weird moment they look like they're no longer part of me. "I don't know," I say.

"It's true. I don't know how you do it."

"I guess I need to feel what I'm doing. It's the only way I can tell if it's right."

"I'm envious." Amina picks up one of her brushes and dips it into her paste bowl. She looks like she's thinking about whether to say something else but decides against it.

I leave to go to the bathroom. On my way, I check my phone and find a text from Alice. *Got names. They want more info. Do you have a model or something you can show me?* Even with everything that's going on, at the thought of seeing her, my pulse quickens. I wonder what she looks like now and what she would think of me after so many years.

Then in the bathroom, as I wash my hands, the ache in my side reminds me I haven't fully healed, and all of a sudden I can't feel myself. As if I've left my body and am hovering a few feet above. I look in the mirror and feel like I'm watching myself look at my reflection. And all I keep thinking is *That isn't you.* It repeats in my mind like a warning. *That isn't you.*

It isn't you. I splash water on my face and mop it with a paper towel, avoiding the mirror as I leave the bathroom. When I get back to the lab, my hands are shaking, and it magnifies the sensation that they're no longer mine. A wave of nausea comes over me and I'm sure I've forgotten how to inhale.

"Are you feeling sick?" Amina's voice comes from far away, but she's standing next to me, her hand on my shoulder. I push it off.

"I don't know." Even my voice sounds like someone else's.

"You're scaring me. Should I call 911?"

"Give me a minute." My mouth has gone dry. "Maybe I need water."

Amina runs to the water cooler and back with a cup. I drink.

"Is that better?" she says.

"A little." Things go in and out of focus. "I think I need air. I need to go for a walk."

"I'm coming with you."

"No," I say.

I set the cup down and head out. Amina follows, and I'm too scared and confused to argue. We take the elevator up to the first floor and walk through the library, then out the museum's main entrance on Eighty-Second Street. Walking is the only thing that feels normal, so I keep doing it. After a few blocks, Amina asks me again how I am. Finally I stop and turn to look at her. We're still wearing our aprons. The top of a ruler is sticking out of her pocket. I want to touch it to make sure it's real.

"I think I'm doing better," I say. The nausea has subsided at least.

Amina feels my forehead. "No fever."

"Thanks, Mom."

She laughs. Her voice is starting to sound normal again.

I draw a deep breath. "We should probably head back, huh?"

She looks at me with serious concern. "You've been holding your side. Is something wrong?"

"I'm fine now."

She doesn't press me. I want to put my hand on her shoulder, put my arms around her and ask her to stay with me, but we're in the middle of the sidewalk. The only place that makes sense to go is back to the lab. Tucking my hands safely into the pockets of my apron, I turn around. Amina walks close at my side, our shoulders sometimes brushing each other. She has a story for every other place we pass on our way back to the Met. She's been on a blind date in one of the restaurants. She bought her first cell phone in one of the stores. And the other week, she walked more than twenty blocks down this avenue to take her friend from Senegal to Krispy Kreme. I enjoy hearing her talk, the way she pauses to get words right, the way she laughs when she likes the sound of a phrase or a particular memory. Her hands are like butterflies. Her energy infectious. But the more comfort I draw from walking close to her, the more I think about Jae—how he'd gotten attacked while hanging out with me and Lukas, with my picture of Gertrude in my bag, even though I'd been wearing a dress, even though I'd felt like my most feminine self. I start to feel exposed, like Amina shouldn't be seen outside with me, especially not walking shoulder to shoulder. Pretending to straighten my skirt, I move away.

BY THE TIME I've finished work, everyone has gone but Amina, who's lingered longer than usual. She makes sure I'm well enough to get home by myself before she leaves, and then even though I'm mostly feeling better, once I'm alone, I'm scared that whatever happened will happen again. As I gather my things, I take a moment to also collect my thoughts. I need to get my head straight. Maybe the way to begin is to apologize to Jae for being a shitty friend. Before I head out, I fish my phone out of my bag to call him, but as I dial, doubt takes over. He probably doesn't want to hear from me yet. So I consider calling Lukas to smooth things over with him, but he's still at work, so that will have to wait too. Dropping my phone on my bench, I feel like I'm getting nowhere—trapped in a cage of my own making.

Perhaps the easiest place to start would be coming clean to Gertrude. At this point, even if I do want to write the article, I have no idea how. So I might as well confess and get it over with. If it doesn't make me feel better, at least it will take something off my plate.

I check the time on my phone. Five thirty. She could be eating dinner, but I dial her number, taking advantage of my determination.

She picks up on the first ring. "Hello?"

"Hi, it's Dawn Levit," I say.

"Hello, Dawn. This is Clare, Gertrude's nurse. Are you a friend of hers?"

When I respond, it sounds like my tongue is clicking against the roof of my mouth. "Sort of. I'm calling about an article I'm writing."

"Ah yes, Dawn," says Clare. "She mentioned you'd be coming by for some photographs. If you're planning to—well, I don't want to speak out of turn, but it would make sense to come soon. Can I take a message for her?"

I wanted to come clean and tell you that I lied about writing an article because I wanted to meet you. But everything else I've told you is true. I promise. "That's all right," I say. I clear my throat. "Why don't I try again in the morning?"

"Sure. Let's hope she's feeling well enough to talk then."

When I hang up, I'm more confused than before. This morning, she didn't sound that bad, but now it seems her time is running out. I think of her pouring whiskey at her kitchen counter, standing in the sunlight in her garden. It still doesn't seem possible she's dying, at least not so quickly. I'm no longer sure telling her the truth is the best idea. The only thing I can face—the only thing that still feels safe—is books. I can't wait anymore, not for Alice or the street artists. I have to start building The Project.

I stay in the lab and get to work, gathering paper, tools, and markers that I'll need to create a full-size mock-up of the binding. Once I have everything laid out on my workbench, I imagine Gertrude as a teenager, daring to picture a better world for herself, as I concentrate on the book I want to make—the story I want to tell. Closing my eyes, I run my fingers over the smooth surface of the paper, the slick expanse full of possibility. As if the book is inside waiting to reveal itself and all I have to do is peel back the layers, just as I had when I found Gertrude's book cover under the endpapers of the architecture book. To find the shape of this book is only a matter of cutting away the excess, letting the paper bend and move as it wants in order to tell its story, bring me into its world. I hold it up to my face and breathe in its earthy, fibrous odor.

Finally something is shifting, an urgency rising in me, as I imagine my paper city in front of me, filled with graffiti, colors, and words. Again I think about the abstract expressionists, how they reached their height at the same time as anti-communist and anti-gay paranoia were spinning out of control and any hint of subversion could make a person suspect. They used abstraction to express the idea of freedom, to convey their authentic selves. But I have no desire to be abstract. My hands reach for a thick black marker and feel their way through line drawings of iconic buildings—the Empire State, the Twin Towers, Grand Central Station—storefronts, elevated trains, and buses. I cut them all out and shuffle them around until I'm satisfied with my mash-up of New York City, so big it's taking up almost the whole length of the workbench. Then I fold each element to bring this new city into three dimensions—buses and cabs in front, elevated trains and buildings behind. On the Twin Towers in the center, I sketch the kissing purple-and-red couple, one of them on each tower so that they will forever be about to kiss. I imagine them again as Gertrude and Marta. Then, without thinking, I sketch the same face onto both of them, and afterward realize that it looks like my face.

I pull double-sided tape from my drawer and attach the tallest pieces together into one long horizontal strip, then fold the whole strip into an accordion. With the other, shorter half, I do the same. Picking up the taller half again, I cut a horizontal opening through the middle, one very long rectangle that runs from one end to the other. And then I insert the shorter accordion into the opening so that stores and cabs and buses weave in and out of the taller buildings, as if the city is being run right through with itself. It gives the impression of chaos and motion, and feels, finally, like a good start. I step back and examine it, unaware of how long I've been here. The lab has no windows to offer me a sense of time.

I check my phone. It's been over two hours. I'm hungry and a bit delirious and grateful for a text from Lukas that says *Indian or Middle Eastern tonight?*

Sitting on my stool, I stare at my paper city and the mess all around it, which I still have to clean up. Then I hear humming in the hallway. Katherine. As if getting caught at something, quickly I straighten my workbench.

She walks in holding a large bag and stops when she notices me. "Hello there. I didn't expect to find anyone still here." She looks at my workbench, regarding my book mock-up with curiosity. "What's that?" As she sets her things down, she keeps her eyes on The Project.

"Just something I'm trying to work out," I say.

Katherine laughs. "It looks quite untidy, but I like it. Is it for the show?"

My face flushes. I don't want to reveal anything about it to her. "It's just an idea I got from a friend," I say. "I was feeling inspired." I remember the kissing couple that has my face and quickly fold up the accordion.

Katherine goes back to her own things, pulling a green box from her bag. "I'm glad to hear it. That's good for you," she says.

I keep cleaning.

"I hope you're not leaving on my account." She opens the green box on her bench and inspects its contents, which I can't see.

"No, I was done." I return my tools to my drawer and pull a few sheets of newsprint from the shelf in the back of the lab so I can I wrap my folded accordions together. When everything's secure, I grab my jacket and say good night.

Katherine looks up from her work and smiles. It's a warm smile. "Getting some supper?"

I have a feeling I sometimes get when I'm alone with her—that she's almost being motherly. I want to go to her and unload everything that's hurting, as if she might take me in her arms and hush me while I cry.

Instead, I say, "Yeah."

"Have a good night," she says, back to her work. "I can't wait to see your book when it's finished."

I nod and walk out, trying not to hunch despite the twinge in my side. The sound of her humming follows me to the elevator.

WHILE I WAIT for the train, I look again at the text Alice sent earlier. The girl who didn't want me to be a boy—my savior from the boy who doesn't want me to be a girl. I know no good can come from seeing her, but I don't care. I write back. *Sure. Meet for coffee next Tues after work? 5:30?* Almost immediately my phone buzzes. *Sounds good. CU soon.*

‖PROOF

A FEW DAYS later, I find a small package in our mailbox. It's the perfect size for a paperback book, so I run up the four flights of stairs and tear open the envelope. On the cover of *Turn Her About*, two women look wistfully into the distance. I flip through the pages, so excited it worries me. What if it turns out to be a whole lot of nothing? But unable to hold back, I make straight for the futon.

A few pages in, my heart skips a beat—already I feel like I'm being given more clues about Gertrude. At least it seems that she had been questioning her gender identity as much as her sexuality:

> With everything in my being I wanted to see Susie that night. But as I stood there looking at my reflection in the dark window, holding a drink in my hand,

I knew it would be ghastly to expose my terrible world of darkness to someone so innocent. What if she were to see me as I long to see myself, strong and angular, hard and solid? Would it break her to know how deep my sickness truly goes? Would she run away screaming? Would she lose all sense of decency and sanity, as I have? Or would it bring us so far toward wrong that it would make us right? A proper man and woman. Like her and that two-bit husband of hers. But damn that man! A real man would recognize what he's got, would work hard every day to keep her. Like I would. Yes, together Susie and I would be better than those two ever could. More committed. Deeper in love. Our two bodies becoming as one.

No, I reprimanded myself, as my heart raced and my face flushed. I swallowed a sip of Scotch, too big, too fast. I mustn't let myself think such horrid things. Instead, I thought, there has to be some friendly way to be near her without giving myself away, without enticing her into madness. But do I dare? And could I imagine sharing nothing more than friendship with her? No! That idea was simply suffocating and made me want to die on the spot.

It would be absurd if it weren't so tragic.

I read for almost two hours—until my stomach begs for food. If nothing else, I can see why Gertrude and her friends wanted to write their own stories. Even though I'd known the queer pulps weren't permitted happy endings, I had no idea how downright awful they made gay life out to be. Abusive relationships, double-crossing between lovers who've been caught together, drug addiction, suicide. And that's just this one story.

THE NEXT MORNING, as the sunlight starts to show itself and I lie next to Lukas unable to sleep, I replay the tragedies upon tragedies in *Turn Her About*. I wish I could read the stories of the Sapphic Warriors, to see the bright lives they'd imagined for themselves. Which makes me wonder if Gertrude was being truthful when she said she doesn't have any, or if it's another thing she's holding back. But I guess it wouldn't matter. She has no reason to trust me, and besides, I don't even know if she's still alive. With that thought, my hesitation over telling her the truth transforms into fear. If I have anything to say to her, I should really do it soon.

Then it occurs to me that I can be more articulate—and honest—in a letter. And once I've thought of it, it seems obvious. In fact, the more I think about it, the better the idea seems, until the urgency to write it makes sleep impossible. So as not to wake Lukas, I go to the bathroom and sit on the toilet with my notebook. I draft a letter in which I tell Gertrude about my father and the porch and my mother unlocking the handcuffs. I write about how they both warned me of the danger of being seen and about my struggles to understand my own gender identity, and I tell her I'm sorry for seeking her out but not sorry to have met her. Despite myself, I lie one last time and say the article will be coming out soon (in my mind it's postponed until after she dies) and that I hope it will bring her peace and closure.

I cross it all out. I try again:

Dear Gertrude,

    I had no right to seek you out, to lie to you, hoping to use your story to understand my own. But that's what I did. And I apologize. There is no article because I was never writing one.

The words keep getting away from me. Discouraged, I throw the pen, and it leaves a mark on the wall like cut flesh.

PART III *Endpapers*

‖ICE CREAM

OUTSIDE THE ICE cream place where I'm supposed to meet Alice (she wanted dessert instead of coffee), I open my portfolio and check my book mock-up for the five hundredth time to make sure I've removed the half-written unmailed letters to Gertrude that I've been drafting for days. For the five hundredth time, I reassure myself I have. I push the door open and Alice comes right over to hug me. As she pulls away, she shrugs a little, tucking her hair behind her ear like she used to do, though it was much shorter back then. The gesture is practically the only thing about her I recognize.

"I can't believe it's really you," she says, gripping her phone. "You look amazing."

I take stock of my T-shirt and jeans, my lack of makeup. Alice has on a light-colored lipstick and maybe even mascara.

"It's really me," I say. I don't push my hair out of my eyes.

"How long has it been? Like, six, seven years?"

"Sounds about right. You look different. You know, good though."

She laughs, tucks her hair behind her ear. "Thanks."

I take in her face. She holds my gaze.

"So, ice cream?" she says.

We walk to the counter, where a flurry of hands and knives are pouring cream and chopping brownies and cookies. A woman mixes our ice cream and scoops it into perfect balls. Then we sit and catch each other up on our lives. Alice isn't the person I've remembered. The Alice sitting in front of me has longish blond hair and wears tight, stylish clothes. This Alice, as it turns out, has already achieved a fair amount of success. In addition to continuing with street art, she's about to publish her second graphic novel, about life as a lesbian in college in the South. She tells me about all of her good and bad reviews, her DIY book tours, and the novel she's thinking about writing.

"Tell me about the rainbow eyes," I say. "I saw them downtown a few weeks ago with your 'DYC' tag and I've been wondering about them."

"Oh yeah, the eyes," she says. "About a year ago, some friends and I were looking for ways to use art to respond to the Patriot Act, and we came up with the idea of incorporating eyes into our work—at first it was a sort of warning, you know, the artist as witness to corruption, but then over time that idea evolved into us seeing them as a form of countersurveillance. Like, I'm watching everyone back with my queer eye."

"That's awesome. I sort of got the feeling like it was a

friendly form of surveillance, a way of seeing people who might otherwise feel invisible or something."

"Wow, I never thought of it exactly that way, but I like that. Thanks."

Finally she reaches for my portfolio, which has been on the floor leaning against my legs. She pulls out the mock-up and sets it on the table. Even closed, it takes up practically the whole thing. Then she flips through it, taking her time with each page, looking at it from different angles and running her hands over the paper.

"What is this?" she says. "It's so smooth."

"It's a Fabriano vellum."

"It would be amazing for inking my drawings."

"I'll send you a link," I say, enjoying a small rush over being able to impress her, even just a little.

She marvels over the materials and mechanics of the accordion book, which can be flipped through like a codex or opened up into one long page. When she gets to the towers in the center with the image of the kiss, she pauses. "I like this," she says.

Eventually, after we've long since finished our ice cream, Alice suggests we take a walk. We wander the West Village, and when it's starting to seem like our time is winding down, I ask her if she wants to get some real food.

We find a place on a corner that's part diner and part bar. I order for both of us, and when we're settled together in the little booth, I pull out my camera to show her the street art I've been photographing. She scrolls, slowly, until she lands on the picture of Gertrude as a young teenager.

"Who's this? Family?" she says.

I'd forgotten it was mixed in with those photos. I don't want to think about Gertrude. After working so hard to find her, for the past few days I've been feeling as if I'm merely towing her around like a heavy weight. I've failed to finish the letter I was so determined to write, or to even call her back. I'm too ashamed to explain any of it to Alice. Not to mention how crazy it sounds. "No, not family," I say. "Just something I found in my research."

Alice is focused on Gertrude, mirroring the energy in her gaze. "Interesting. I can see why you were drawn to her."

I drink, try to act like it's no big deal, but I don't like how Alice is sizing her up.

She finishes scrolling through my pictures, but when she comes to the end, she returns to Gertrude. "There's really something about her, isn't there?"

"I guess." I reach for my camera.

Alice pulls it back. "One second. I'm just thinking about something." She zooms in on Gertrude's face. "What would you think about me using this? I've been experimenting with paste-ups and she would be amazing."

I hold out my hand, hoping my face isn't as red as it feels. "Sorry," I say. I'm surprised at how agitated it makes me to hear someone talk about Gertrude like she's not a real person.

Unfazed, Alice hands me my camera. "No problem, I get it. It spoke to you—it's your image."

I sip my lager as I make the camera disappear into my pocket.

"Anyway," she says, drawing out the word. "Those are

cool photos. You've got a really great eye. So I have to ask—why aren't you doing the artwork for The Project yourself?"

Her question brings me back. "It seems like a better idea to have multiple styles, like real graffiti in a real city."

"I can see that," she says. "But it's your work."

"It's still my work. It's just collaborative. I mean, street art basically began in Latino and Black communities. So without those voices, it wouldn't really make any sense, right?"

"Good point," says Alice. "But are they all supposed to be saying the same thing?"

I haven't thought that far ahead. "I guess I'll find out."

"I like to have more control over my work."

"Control?" I say. "There's an interesting concept."

Alice tilts her head. "What's that supposed to mean?"

I take a swig of my lager. I think about saying, *The way you had the control in our relationship?* I say, "Nothing."

She rolls her eyes, but she's smiling.

"What?" I say.

"It's just—you're so mysterious sometimes." She nudges me gently with her elbow. "I guess some things don't change."

"Yeah." I take another swig. Then another, and another.

"I have an idea," she says. "I've got lots of supplies in my studio. How about you and I get started together, lay in some groundwork so you'll have something more fleshed out that we can show some artists to persuade them to get involved. And if they're game, we can swap the pages around, everyone adding to the work that's been done by you and the others. It's still a collaboration, but it would feel more like your artwork."

I think for a minute, taking in what she said about working together. Maybe she's on to something. Maybe I am partially using the other artists as a crutch because I can't make anything myself. But I'm not sure if her idea would be a remedy for my stubborn block or a means to expose me as an impostor. Either way, at this point I have nothing more to lose. Also, the lager is endowing me with confidence. "Okay," I say. "You're on."

We clink glasses and Alice shifts closer to me in the booth. Her face is next to mine. "Tell me more about Lukas."

My head spins. "Whatever, it's not serious."

"I wouldn't have predicted you'd go for a guy."

"Yeah?"

"Well, you just seemed so hardcore. And even now." Her cheeks flush. "With the whole look."

I put my elbow on the table, rest my head in my hand, look at her. "Yeah? How do I look?"

She squirms a little. She's still smiling. "Come on, you know what I mean."

I keep my eyes on her.

"Fine," she says. "Kind of like a guy. But a hot guy. Whatever, it's confusing." She looks away.

"A hot guy?" I say.

Alice raises her eyebrows.

"I see. And you think because I look like a guy, I wouldn't want to date a guy?"

"Well, no, but . . ."

"But," I say, and finish my drink. "But. But what?"

"All right, forget it," she says.

"I don't think so."

I can feel the heat from our thighs pushing against each other. With an unsteady hand, I reach for her face and tuck her hair behind her ear.

"Oh no," she says. And then before I can ask her what's wrong, her lips are on mine.

IT'S LATE. I don't know how long we've been sitting in the bar/diner, making out. They've dimmed the lights. The crowd has changed to a younger, drunker one. I'm exhausted and tipsy and Radiohead's "Let Down" is playing.

Alice hums along as she pulls out her wallet. "I guess it's time."

"Does it have to be?"

She looks at her phone. "Yeah."

"How about I see you home? You know, for your protection." I slide my hand between her thighs. She squirms again, this time away from me.

"I can't." She takes my hand, moves it away gently but keeps holding it. The gesture has an air of preparation. Of the first step in breaking unpleasant news. Scooting back a few inches, she looks into my eyes.

"You have a girlfriend," I say.

She nods. "I'm so sorry."

"Right."

"I lost my head."

"Whatever," I say. "It's fine."

"No, it's not. Really, I'm sorry."

"It's time to settle up." I slide out of the booth.

"Let me get half."

I ignore her and walk up to the register.

I think about letting her off the hook. Telling her that I've been an asshole too because I've been misleading her. That I am, in fact, serious about Lukas. That I've let my desperation get the better of me because I'm afraid he and I are growing apart. That it felt nice to confuse someone in a way that excited them for once. But that's not how it goes. Instead, I stand with her in the dark on the corner, waiting for her to hail a cab, barely saying anything. And when she takes my hand and says, "It was really good to see you," I just nod and let her get in the cab thinking she's the only one who's been an asshole.

‖LUKAS

IT'S NOT UNTIL I collapse into the back seat of a cab that what I've done sinks in. All this time, I've assumed that monogamy isn't important to Lukas, but his words keep haunting me as I stare out the window at the lights speeding by. Monogamy only means something when it happens on its own, because neither person wants to be with anyone else. Well, Lukas hasn't been with anyone else. It's turned out that I'm the one who's willing.

I get home at midnight and find him waiting for me with a bottle of wine. He kisses me and says, "You smell different. Like a hippie. Is that patchouli?"

I bring my arm to my nose. It smells like Alice, sweet and spicy. Fear and shame flush through me, but I say, "It's Alice. I met her for ice cream. Then we went to a bar and she kissed me."

"Oh." Lukas sits back in his chair. He's at the table, looking like a boss sitting at a desk, like I have to come into his office to face him about something I've done wrong. It's an odd sensation because it's never occurred to me that he could be jealous. But I can see the effort it takes him to keep his face steady, and I feel bad. I don't want to hurt him, not like this, anyway.

"It was no big deal," I say.

"I didn't say it was."

"Then don't be mad."

"I'm not."

Lukas pours two glasses of wine. I pick one up, put the glass to my lips, hold a sip in my mouth. I've already drunk two or three beers—I can't remember. I put the glass down. Lukas pulls me onto his lap.

"Was she a good kisser?" he says.

"Don't."

"I'm just curious."

"Yeah." I look at his face, his eyes, the lock of hair that's crossing his right eyebrow. I wish it didn't hurt so much. I've always had to fight so hard to be someone he could love and I'm running out of fight. And now, suddenly, it's clearer than it's ever been. I don't belong to him the way he belongs to me.

He puts his hand on my face, next to my mouth, and kisses me.

I pull away and open my eyes. I want to memorize every contour of his face, the strange scar just under his hairline that looks like a small white slip of someone's pen. A dash. An unfinished thought. I want to remember it all because I have a strange, nagging feeling this can't last.

In bed, we take our time with each other's bodies. Like on our first night together, we hold each other with a kind of desperation. Now I lie staring at the ceiling, looking for shapes in the textured paint, wondering if Lukas is asleep, but not wanting to break the spell our silence has created.

I WAKE MAYBE an hour later to a flickering light. The television. My brain. Lukas sleeping with the sheet bunched in his fist, his fist against his chest. In my head, names move round and round like they're on a merry-go-round. Lukas. Alice. Jae. Gertrude. When I stop at one, around they go again. I sit, rub my eyes, shake sleep from my arm, and climb out of bed to turn off the TV. A nauseous yellow light seeps through the window from the street below, the same color as the taste in my mouth. Sulfur. I stand in the middle of the small rug, my mind working like a broken calculator, trying to put everything that's been going on between Lukas and me through some complicated calculation, as if all the things we've said and haven't said could add up to something that will make sense—an answer, solid and testable.

I sit at the kitchen table and pick up my phone. There's a text from Jae. Finally. But not the one I'd been hoping for. Ever since my last visit, his texts have been short and evasive. I've been trying him for two days, asking what's going on and when I can visit. All he's written now is *Meningitis is stubborn. Need rest. Thanks.* I don't know what to make of it or how worried I should be, so I type, *Anything new, or just tired? xo.*

There's also a text from Alice. *Are we OK? Still want to help with your book.* As if there's a *we. Of course,* I write back. Because I need a friend. And I need to make this book. As much as I was talking up The Project to Alice, it still taunts me as nothing more than a general idea of an artwork, one I'm afraid I won't have enough time to see through by the deadline. I haven't even thought of a title. If I can't finish it, it will be my first truly public failure—and the first time I've let Jae down on this scale, since his sister put her trust in me. I have to hope that Alice is at least being more honest about her connections to these street artists than she is about her love life. I write again, *Do you still think we have enough time? (show's in abt 4 wks)*. Then I pull up the photo of Gertrude. Mindlessly, I grab a pencil from the table and a piece of junk mail and write the word *time* on the envelope. *Time. Ti me. Tie me. Try me. Try. Me.*

Creeping quietly past the futon, I go to the computer and boot it up, then run a search for Jackson Pollock. I've been trying to understand why the abstract expressionists thought abstraction was the key to directness, but when Pollock's *Autumn Rhythm (Number 30)* loads on the screen, all I feel is a vague sense of entrapment. Depending on how I look at it, it's either nothing more than a big mess or it's a large, menacing web holding fast to a dove furiously flapping its wings, to a woman with her arms and legs splayed, and to a man trying in vain to climb out. After a few minutes I lose interest. I click on Rothko's *No. 13*, a field of red and white on yellow. It gives me nothing.

Leaving the abstractionists behind, I look up a few of my favorite street artists, and right away I'm drawn in by graffiti that has color and motion and purpose. EGR's *Pound*—a strong brown woman jump-kicking over the letters *EGR*.

Prisco's *Graffopoly*—a graffiti-based version of Monopoly, with *Mi Tierra Represento* written in the square on top and the Statue of Liberty squatting to roll dice on the right. Lokiss's *TV Screen*, which at first glance looks abstract, but quickly reveals itself to be two screaming faces caught in a wild entanglement of cars, cameras, planes, and weapons. The messages are unmistakable. My vision for The Project isn't perfectly clear yet, but street art is definitely the right direction.

AT SIX IN the morning I get back into bed. The sun is just starting to come up, but I have an hour before I have to wake for work. Gently, I free the sheet from Lukas's fist. He rolls toward me and puts his arm over my shoulder.

When the alarm goes off, he gets up and makes us coffee, then leaves a cup on the table for me and climbs outside to smoke. I get dressed and follow him. The two of us fill the fire escape. I hold my hand out for a drag. Drawing smoke deep into my lungs, I watch a couple of birds stir up the morning sky over the buildings across the street.

Lukas inhales the steam from his cup. I'm not used to seeing him look so sad.

"I love you," I say.

He says nothing.

I lean over and kiss him on the cheek. I can tell he wants to be alone. As I climb back through the window to get ready for work, my heart is heavy. I wonder if there's a way to make up for kissing Alice.

But an hour later, as I step into the street and walk to the subway, I take everything in with new eyes. What if I have been right all along and Lukas just doesn't want to commit? If rather than ruining things between us, I'm beginning to free myself from that fear? As I do each simple task—taking out my MetroCard and swiping it through the turnstile, easing myself through the crowded train, and staking my claim on a tiny piece of a pole—this is what I tell myself, and at least for a few moments I enjoy a sense of calm.

‖DAWN

BY THE TIME I get to the museum, I have texts from Jae and Alice. Finally, a week after Jae was admitted, he says the infection seems to be gone for real and they're moving him into a new room to monitor him. Relief washes over me. *Good news, bro <3*, I type. *So you're up for a visit?*

I stand outside the lab to wait for a response, and open Alice's text: *Yeah, there's time. Can you come by my studio tonight?*

Drawing a deep breath, I write, *Yeah. Til soon.*

THE REST OF the day drags by. Jae finally writes back during lunch and I still can't get a read on his response. *Hope not to be here long enough for a visit.* Does that mean he's feeling hopeful about getting released or that he's putting me off? I want to ask him to clarify what the doctor said, but I'm afraid to push him, so I let it rest. For now. At least I'll be working on The Project tonight, so that's one thing I can reassure myself I'm doing for him.

WHEN EVENING FINALLY comes, I meet Alice at her studio, which she shares with three other artists, but she promised me they wouldn't be there. She has all the supplies ready to go. Paint and airbrushes, markers, card stock for cutting stencils, and a box full of tiny "riches" she's been collecting from the streets of New York: coins and marbles, dice, PEZ dispensers, doll parts. "You never know," she says, opening a drawer and pulling out a small box of her rainbow eyes. "Also, I was thinking of using some of these, if that's okay."

"I'd love that," I say.

"Cool. First I'll show you how to use the airbrushes and then you can go to it. Good?"

In the tightness of the space, our shoulders brush against each other. Alice smirks, and I step back, raise my hands—*I promise I'm not going to kiss you.* We both laugh, let the tension out.

Alice gives me a quick lesson on how to fill the brushes and how to control where the paint goes. Then it's my turn.

"Have at it," she says. "I'll wait to see what you're doing and work off that." She turns away from me, toward her box of riches, and pulls them out, begins arranging them in a tiny still life.

I stare at the paper, hoping something will come to me.

After a few beats she says, "Are you going to use that photo from the other night? The one of the girl?"

My shoulders tense. "I don't know."

"Cause I've been thinking about her and it gave me an

idea. What if you did something similar to Warhol's *Marilyn Monroe*, but instead of painting her, you use the photo itself, and instead of hyperfeminizing it with colorful makeup, you paint bright geometric shapes over different parts of her face—like, as a way to disrupt typical perceptions of masculine and feminine? We could have it turn up throughout the book, as a nod to pop art repetition."

I consider this as she describes it. It's an interesting concept, but the thought of using Gertrude's face in my artwork feels wrong. "It sounds cool," I say, "but I really don't want to use that photo." I sigh, roughly pushing my hair out of my eyes.

"Sorry," she says. "Looks like I hit a nerve."

I busy myself with trying to figure out the airbrush. "It's just . . . she's a real person. Someone I know."

"Oh. Can I at least ask who she is, then?"

She moves her hair out of the way to take a sip of her soda and holds it in place while she drinks. Something about it—an awkwardness in her movements—makes her look like a kid, like she's vulnerable, the way she often came across back in high school. It confused me how she could shrug shyly one minute and disarm you with her truth telling the next. It was one of the things that gave her so much power over me. I longed to be brought into her orbit of strength even as I desired to protect her. I feel the old pull and it makes me want to explain why I'm being so defensive. And hearing that she's still thinking about Gertrude, I hazard a guess that she might understand my fascination too.

"Fine, here's the deal," I say before I lose my nerve. Her face perks up and she rests her chin on her hand like she's settling in for a good story, and then I tell her the whole thing—including where it cut off, the mystery still to be solved, and how complicated it's all gotten because of my lie about the article.

Alice has been listening closely, but I can't tell if her expression is shock or disbelief. She shakes her head like she's trying to process it all. "Dawn Levit," she finally says, reaching for my arm. "Holy hell."

"I know. Weird, right?"

"'Weird' doesn't even begin to cover it. But you absolutely have to find out the rest. I mean, aren't you dying to know why Gertrude ended your conversation like that? And what happened with Marta?"

"It's pretty much all I think about, yeah."

"So what are you waiting for? Call her back. Go see her."

"I will. At least, when I figure out what to say. But once she knows I've been lying, she won't want to talk to me anyway."

"Obviously it's your call, but dude, you can't give up now. From the way you described it, you seem to have formed a nice connection. And this is our history. It's always good to honor that."

I don't answer. I'm not sure the way I've gone about things counts as honoring Gertrude. Still though, I'm surprised at how familiar it feels to be with Alice after all this time, how easy it was to share Gertrude's story with her—even if she seems a little disappointed with me. After a few minutes, she turns back around and says, "You're not going to call her, are you?"

"Don't worry. I'll figure it out."

"All right. But if you learn anything more, please promise you'll tell me."

"Of course," I say, but as I speak the words, I hope it's not another promise I can't keep.

Alice has become thoughtful. "Anyway," she says. "I do see how using her photo could feel like you're exploiting her."

I nod. But I'm starting to lose patience with all my failed attempts at this book. "Yeah, if only I could come up with a better idea." I try to make it sound like a joke. I don't want to be frustrated.

"Just get started," Alice says. "You'll work it out. You've always been amazing. You have such a unique way of expressing yourself."

I laugh. "There's a bit of irony."

"What does that mean?"

This time I don't hold back. "You have to admit, you didn't always like how I expressed myself back in high school."

"Oh my god. Dawn, we were kids, figuring things out. I had my own fears and shit to deal with."

"Seriously? At sixteen, you knew who you were better than anyone I'd ever met."

Alice shakes her head. "There's the irony. That's what I thought about you." She fidgets with the pencil in her hand.

I let this new information sink in as I pick up a blank piece of card stock, and she goes back to her work. Then I close my eyes and think of Gertrude and the book cover. How without meaning to or knowing it, she changed her own story—transformed it into something that would take on a life of its own decades in the future. And then an idea comes to me, and I pick up a pair of scissors and begin to cut.

When I'm ready to paint, I lay the first stencil onto the front of the Empire State Building, at the base. A small tribute to Jae. After some doing with the airbrush, I fill in the image with black paint, then lay out the second stencil and go at it with more paint, and then the next, and the next, getting the hang of it a little more each time. When I finally finish, I'm pleased with the result. A woman's full black silhouette stands tall on the wall, a bright red heart on her chest. Behind her, in a V formation, are more female silhouettes with hearts on their chests, like a small, queer army of love. And in the background, in classic graffiti-style lettering, I spray-paint *Sapphic Warriors*.

Alice comes over to peek. "Wow," she says, her golden hair closing like a curtain over her profile. I resist the urge to reach out and tuck it behind her ear.

Then her case of rainbow eyes catches my attention again, and this time it makes me think of the ◉ in *Protect freedom N*◉*W*. I pull out my camera and scroll to the image.

"Are you familiar with this artist?" I say.

Alice looks up as if I've brought her back from somewhere else. She takes the camera from me and grins. "Oh yeah, that's my friend Ray's work. That symbol is part of the eye project. How cool you found it. Where's that piece?"

"Down by the Brooklyn Bridge," I say. "I've been wondering about it."

"Man, I can't believe I didn't think of it before, but I should totally ask Ray to work with us."

My heart speeds up at the idea of having a trans artist—at least that's what I assume—working on The Project. I wonder if it would make me feel even more like a fraud. "Sure," I say, trying to keep my face even. "That would be cool."

Then Alice and I go back to our developing canvases, our little pieces of New York City, and continue to imagine.

❚SIGHT

IN THE MORNING I wake to Lukas sitting in bed with pancakes.

"On a school day?" I say, pushing myself up next to him. He hands me the plate, and I bite into a sweet, warm strawberry.

He's trying not to smile, but he leans against me while I eat, then puts his arm around me and lets his warm hand rest on my shoulder.

I don't say anything. For one morning, I want to stay lost under the weight of him, full of strawberries and syrup. And make it last for as long as I can.

BUT EVENTUALLY I have to go to work. The whole way there, the sweet taste lingers in my mouth, slowly weakening my resolve. I tell myself that if I can just be patient with him, it might all work out. Then my phone buzzes with a text from Jae, breaking my reverie. He's lost vision in his left eye. *Hopefully just temporary.*

Fuck, I write. *Coming by this morning.* I don't give him a chance to protest, hoping once he sees me, he'll be glad for my company. A week is a long fucking time to be in the hospital, and every time he makes progress, he takes a step backward.

THE HOSPITAL LOBBY is full of people coming and going, flapping around like confused pigeons. I make my way to the elevator and find Jae's new room on the third floor. He's sitting in a chair by the window, reading. It's a much nicer room, with a small couch along the wall and a big window. And he isn't hooked up to machines anymore.

"Moving on up," I say.

Jae raises his eyes from his book. *Moby-Dick.* "Somehow I've never read this." He closes it. "And since I can't fucking see it, I still don't know what all the fuss is about." He smiles, but there's nothing behind it. His face is wan.

"Yeah, I'm sorry about your vision. That sucks," I say.

Instead of coming back at me with one of his usual jokes, like *At least I don't have to see your ugly mug at full strength,* he's quiet. He looks sad, anxious, not quite here. I look away— to a metal bar over the bed, with a chain hanging about six inches down. At the end of the chain is a triangular bar like the ones you use at the gym to lift weights. "What's the deal with that?" I say. "You working out?"

Jae shrugs.

I sit in a chair in the corner, facing him. I don't know what to do with my hands, so I try to tuck them in my pockets, but they won't fit because I'm sitting. I fold them on my lap. "How are you holding up?" I say. "They planning to let you out of here soon?"

Jae sets his book down. "That's what they tell me. They're just waiting to make sure the infection's really gone this time."

"What about your eyesight?"

"They don't know. It may come back, it may not."

"For real?" I look at the framed print on the wall across the room. A bouquet of white flowers. Beneath it is a red plastic disposal bin. *Biohazard.* I remember Jae's face when we pulled him from the pavement. The scratch above his eye. The guy in the American-flag shirt. *It's not my fault your friend can't take a punch.* I want to say, *Look at you.* I want to say, *You're fucking blind in one eye and it's my fault.* I say, "What can I do?"

Jae grimaces. "For starters, you can stop asking. There's clearly nothing anyone can do. After all this time, the doctors are still telling me things can be unpredictable with head injuries. They treat one thing and another pops up. Today's menu is blindness and mood swings. So tell me something else. What's new with you?" He sits up taller, leans forward like he's trying to look interested.

My hands go for my pockets again, and they still don't fit. "Nothing," I say. "I'm just sorry."

His eyes well with tears and I realize I've never seen him cry before. "Please stop feeling sorry for me. I don't think I can take that right now." He wipes his eyes and then picks up *Moby-Dick* and tosses it onto the bed.

I rack my brain for something to distract him, feeling

terrible that after all the times he's known exactly how to make me feel better, I'm drawing a blank. I want to offer him a hug, but I'm afraid it might upset him more.

I say, "I think I have to end things with Lukas, but I'm scared."

"Really? Why?" At the mention of drama, Jae seems to come around. He sits up a little taller, anyway, like he's finally interested in something.

"The usual crap. It's weird how the thing that makes you fall in love with someone can be the same thing that drives you apart."

"Did something happen?"

My throat closes. I stand and walk over to the triangular bar, use it to pull myself onto the bed.

"I'm sorry," says Jae. His thin frame is insubstantial under his gray T-shirt.

I wonder if he's sorry for me and Lukas or for being depressed. And I realize maybe I shouldn't be bringing up anything sad. "You know what? I actually don't want to talk about it. You don't need to worry about my sorry problems either." I watch him for a moment while my thoughts flounder around. "You know last month when you took me to the top of the Empire State?"

He nods, but he looks disengaged again.

"You made me understand that my fear of heights was just perception, that if you look at something from an exaggerated angle, it can change the way you see it—and also the way you feel it."

"Dawn, if this is about me, remember I took you there because my fucking coworker was annoying me. I think that's a little different than losing my eyesight."

I recoil from his sudden annoyance. But if things were reversed, he wouldn't give up on me. So I try something else. "Fine," I say. "You win. You can just sit here and be miserable all alone without finishing *Moby-Dick*."

"What?" says Jae.

"You know, just give up."

"What are you doing?"

"Being your friend. Someone has to push you out of this bed."

"What do you think I've been trying to do this whole time? If you're my friend, you'll change the subject."

"Then tell me what to say. Do I need to remind you of the people rooting for you? People who care about you?"

"Seriously, bro, I need you to stop."

"Why? So you can keep sitting here feeling sorry for yourself instead of getting up and—"

"What? And what? I can't fucking see. What am I supposed to be doing?"

Every response I can think of sounds selfish. *Get up and leave here. With me.*

Just then a face appears in the doorway, looking at me, surprised. It takes my brain a minute to notice the body it's attached to, a woman's body in a brown pantsuit, holding a brown bag, blending into the brown shadows of the hallway.

"Ma, this is Dawn," says Jae.

His mother sets the bag on the table next to the bed and reaches for my hand, smiling. "Dawn, nice to meet you." She has a German accent, thicker than I'd have imagined.

"Mom's here to make sure I'm eating properly while I'm in the hospital. Before she tries to steal me away from the city," says Jae.

Ignoring him, his mother pulls a container out of the bag. "Do you want some time with your friend?"

Before Jae can answer, I hop up. "No need. I have to get back to work. But it's nice to meet you. How long are you in town for?"

"I told the doctor I'm not going anywhere until they get to the bottom of this and release him into my care."

"I'm not going back to Montclair, Mom," Jae says. His eyes are closed, and he sounds frustrated.

"Of course you are." She turns to me. "He's been fighting me all morning even though he knows it's the best thing. Wouldn't your parents want you home too, if something were wrong?" She looks at me, waiting for my response.

"Welcome to my life," says Jae.

I try to read his face to see if part of him is really considering leaving New York. But this colorless outline of a person isn't Jae.

Maybe his mother is right that it would be the best thing for him to be home, to be taken care of, but I wish I could grab his hand and pull him out into the street, where we could get falafel and duck into a little used bookstore and pretend none of this happened.

As his mother sets the hospital bed tray for his lunch, I say, "I really do have to go. But we'll talk later. Text me? Please?"

"Later," says Jae.

As I walk out the door, his mother says, "It was nice to meet you."

I pass the nurses' station, where someone, a patient, is leaning over the desk, as if waiting for help, as if he can't stand on his own but also can't call out for attention. I think I should stop and see what he needs, but everything inside me needs to get out, into the street.

As I walk to the train, Jae's face keeps coming back to me. Gray and expressionless. The man in front of me is walking too slowly. I find an opening to pass him and imagine brushing my shoulder against his, just one little touch, one little sign to show him that I'm the one in control.

But I'm not. I have no control over Jae's health or whether he stays or leaves. And as Alice pointed out, I've even given up control over the artwork he's trusted me to deliver. I certainly have no control over the group of strangers Alice is introducing me to tonight or whether they'll like The Project enough to get on board.

Descending into the subway station, I think about what it would really mean to move forward with The Project—to create a vision of a place where hate doesn't win. I wonder what it would feel like to push through all this fear and guilt and allow myself to believe in this one thing. For all of us.

As I swipe my MetroCard, the ground rumbles. I pick up my pace.

‖VOICE

WHEN I GET to the bar where Alice told me to meet her and the artists, we're the first two there. I'd agonized over what to wear because I want to make the right impression—want everyone to understand what this book should be, what I meant when I said *nonnormative bodies*. In the end, however, I chose my form-fitting black vintage dress with the little embroidered flowers. The most feminine version of me Alice has seen since we were sixteen.

"You look nice," she says.

I laugh it off. "Drag suits me, I guess."

She puts two fingers on the front of my shoulder and pushes. "Stop."

Even though this Alice is more reserved than the one who kissed me at the bar, behind her composure I detect a wildness.

She's holding herself back. I like the attention—until it occurs to me that I've dressed this way for her.

I lift my portfolio onto the table. "Be careful," I say as she opens it.

"Duh." She pulls out the drawings and rests them on top. As she thumbs through them, the other artists begin to trickle in.

As soon as I see the first one, a skinny guy in a green knit hat and fatigues, my self-doubt rages. These are all accomplished artists, putting their stamp on the real, living and breathing New York City. And here I am with my little paper facsimile, flimsy and precious, on its way to a gallery to be exhibited and sold to the wealthy. Alice introduces us. His name is Mateo. He watches over Alice's shoulder as she holds up a few pieces of New York. "Wow, this is dope," he says. "Chévere."

Two others arrive, another guy and a woman with a short bright pink Afro and lipstick to match, then a third, by some mercy, neither male nor female. This is Ray. Ray with a shaved head and a tattoo around the neck, like a collar, with serpents and flowers and letters that appear to make a word, which starts on one side and winds its way around the back to the other side, but I can only see the letters on the left and right: *BA* and *CE*. Ray, whose gender I can't decipher and I'm ashamed for trying, is the most beautiful person I've ever seen. In my dress, I feel out of place. And yet full of a longing I can barely contain. A longing to feel as comfortable in my body as Ray seems to in theirs.

But now that everyone is here, it's time to get down to business; I have to try to impress them. So I focus on the pages in front of us, hoping that what's begun to fill them—my face on the Twin Towers, the words from Gertrude's letter that I've scrawled beneath it, *Lately I've dared to hope*, the stencils of the Sapphic Warriors—won't betray my deepest desires. Hoping, beyond all reason, that it will.

I watch these strangers probe their way through my work, handling each piece like they're considering its worth. Until Phoebe, the woman with the pink hair, who crochets cute images with subversive messages onto chain-link fences, finally speaks. "This is mad cool," she says, opening a few pages of the accordion, "but I have to admit I'm not seeing it—your vision. I feel like I need more to go on. You know what I'm saying?"

"I think so," I say, looking at Alice for help. She gestures with her head like *Go on*. "It's just, I was kind of hoping you all would bring your own vision to the theme. Like, to make it feel authentic." I'm squirming.

"So you want to leave it wide open?" she says.

"Well, as long as it fits within the theme."

Phoebe does not look convinced.

Mateo chimes in. "Yeah, as long as you're gonna make a lot of money off us, it's open, right?" He and Phoebe laugh.

I want to die, and I'm sure my face is bright red. I stammer, "No, I mean . . . I—"

"I'm just messing with you," Mateo says, leaning into me in a friendly kind of way. "Alice vouched for you. We know we're getting paid if this thing sells."

Alice shakes her head at Mateo, but she looks amused.

"What?" he says. "We have to look out for what's ours, right?" Then he turns to me.

"Of course," I say. "Absolutely."

He smiles like he's entertained by my naivete. "For real though," he says. "I get that you want us to do our thing like we would on an actual building. But you have to get that no way is it going to look right unless we overlap and shit."

The others nod.

My heart starts to beat again. "Yes, exactly. Actually, that's what I want," I say.

"Then how are you imagining it would work—you know, logistics-wise?"

"The plan is to swap pages at some point so we can work off each other's stuff."

Everyone is quiet.

"But if any of you have a better idea," I say, "I'm definitely open." Already this feels like a disaster.

Ray, who's been silently flipping back and forth between a couple of my pieces, finally speaks up. "I think it's pretty impressive. Especially this army of Sapphic Warriors. Can I ask what the inspiration was?"

Looking at Ray's closely shaved head and perfect erasure of gender, I freeze, afraid anything I say will sound dumb. "A bunch of things, I guess." I pause. "My goal was to make a city that I would want to live in."

"Yeah, I hear that." Ray looks back at the Warriors thoughtfully and then, with a little bow of the head, says, "You can count me in."

I exhale.

"You know, I have been thinking about an idea for a collage," says Mateo. "Right here, at the top of the Chrysler Building. I've always wanted to get up there." He turns to me like he's just thought of something. "But would paste warp the paper though?"

"I could give you some dry adhesive," I say.

"Cool."

"Speaking of logistics," says Phoebe. "Would everything have to be flat on the page? Cause I'd love to crochet something but haven't figured out how to get my needle through an actual building yet."

Everyone laughs. "Depends on what you have in mind. The accordion can accommodate a bit of bulk, but I wouldn't want to get to the point where it doesn't really look like a book anymore when it's closed."

The conversation continues. For a while, they talk animatedly, sharing ideas and shuffling the pages around, and then finally they all agree to sign on. Relief washes over me. Alice and I explain that each of them should take a few spreads and share them with friends, so when all is said and done, we might have ten to twelve artists contributing. In ten days we'll all swap, and in another week or so we'll meet back at the bar with the finished pages. That will give me a little over a week to bind the book and get it to the gallery. It's tight, but doable.

We divide the pages and tape them between layers of cardboard, then hand them out like party favors. Ray takes one from me and says, "Thanks for including me. This is really awesome." Then I watch as Ray disappears through the door with a piece of my imagined city tucked under one arm.

‖ COVER

WHEN I GET home, I find a message on my voice mail from Gertrude. "When are you coming to get these photos? I'm not getting any younger, you know." It's been a little over two weeks since my trip to Long Island to meet her. I hear Alice's voice in my head telling me to call back and honor our history. But isn't that what I'm doing with The Project? If I just focus on finishing that, I can show it to Gertrude, and I imagine it would mean even more to her than some article. But again I hear Mateo and Phoebe's initial coolness toward my whole concept and Jae and Mi Sun wondering when I'll be ready to deliver something that will wow Frank Maresca, and insecurity rushes back in. Is it naive to assume this thing will work out? I might have to write an article after all.

It's too late to return Gertrude's call, so in the morning I muster the nerve. Then when Clare, the hospice nurse, puts her on the phone, she sounds weak, like she's using the last of her energy to get me these photos. It confirms that writing the article is not actually a choice.

"You'll come on Sunday," she says. "Clare says eleven o'clock is a good time, and we mustn't cross her. Does that work for you?"

"Of course," I say.

"Then it's settled."

AND SO A few days later, I'm back at Penn Station, watching timetables flip through a rainbow of colors and rereading the last few texts from Jae. I've been regretting our awkward visit earlier this week, fearing I pushed him too hard. Just when he seemed to be letting me in a little, now he's back to keeping me at arm's length. He still texts me once a day with an update, and I've been hoping that means he's improving enough not to have to go home with his mom. But this morning I asked if I could come by before I go to Long Island, and he said he'd rather rest. I wish I could tell if he's giving up on me or if he's giving up altogether—losing his will to fight the infection. I don't know which I fear more. I should probably be staying in the city for as long as he's sick. But for a few hours Gertrude needs me too.

It's midmorning, just me and the drunks in the station—men sleeping with brown paper bags—and the students who've stayed out all night. Soon I'm on the platform, and the conductor is yelling about time. And then once again I'm on the train, and I'm looking out the window, and a woman runs by. She seems to be running to catch the train, but it isn't leaving for eight minutes. I want to yell out to her, let her know she doesn't have to work so hard.

Then, about two and half hours and many stops later, I'm in Stony Brook, on the platform, looking at the orange cab stand. I take a step forward and the ground goes soft. I'm far from home, from friends. I can't afford to lose my body here. I hold the railing and count my steps—seven—down to the ground. The train pulls away behind me.

The cab spits me out at Gertrude's house. This time I'm alone as I pass the little garden—bursting with color and life. This time it's Clare who lets me in the front door and leads me through the entryway, past the table filled with photographs standing in plastic frames. She's small and full of a calm energy that makes me like her immediately. I follow her to the living room, where Gertrude has been arranged on the couch, sitting with pillows propped under her arms, behind her head, and under her knees, as if she's no longer capable of holding herself in place. This is not exactly the Gertrude I'd met some weeks earlier. It's a slightly thinner, frailer version. She's laboring to breathe, but she has the same intensity in her gaze.

Clare says, "May I offer you some bread and tea?"

I've never seen a dying person before. I don't know what I expected, but I'm tongue-tied. I shake my head, thank her with a few movements of my mouth, which barely make a sound.

"I'll be right in the kitchen if either of you need anything," she says. "She's comfortable for the most part, but she's been going in and out of lucidity. If she gets confused, just remind her of the basics: your name, where she is, what year it is, things like that." Clare seems like she's used to fear. She says, "You'll do fine. Gertrude is thrilled to have a visitor."

I nod. Her confidence puts me at ease. I sit in the chair that's been drawn up next to the couch and look at the painting on the wall, an art deco portrait of a woman, her face mapped into fields of bright color. I say hello to Gertrude.

With friendly eyes, she says my name, but it's more like a confirmation than a greeting, proof she remembers who I am.

"That's right," I say. Like she's a child.

I look at the painting again. Shades of orange, blue, and green. The woman is bald. I look at the books piled on the coffee table. All German titles except for one. *Great Expectations*.

"You're here for the pictures," Gertrude says.

"Yes, to publish with an article about your father."

She closes her eyes. "Yes."

I don't know if she's nodding off to sleep. I try to follow the painter's strokes with my eyes, but they're too smooth.

A moment later Gertrude opens her eyes. "Dawn Levit," she says again. "The bookbinder."

I try to smile.

"The bookbinder with secrets."

I shift in my chair. "I don't know about that."

"Of course you do. Come. Lean a little closer. I won't tell."

I laugh uncertainly. I don't know what she's talking about, even though I've had a strong urge to confess to her. Does she suspect I've been lying? Or does she think she knows something about me? About my gender?

She says, "Remember how I always used to keep your secrets?"

I'm confused. "I'm not sure I do."

"Come on. How I'd sit with you, as close as we could get, thinking no one could hear us? Remember how Papa used to go crazy every time I ran over to your house? 'What is it now?'

he'd say. Remember? 'Did you forget one page of your home-work? Did you spill a drop of ink? What excuse is it now?'" Gertrude laughs. "Goodness, how he'd go on. And now look at you, sitting here, in my living room, in the light of day. We can tell him there was nothing to be scared of. Can't we?"

The chair beneath me is suddenly too small. "Gertrude," I say. I clear my throat. "It's me, Dawn Levit. I'm writing an article about your father—about his bookbinding."

"What? Yes, of course. Dawn. I know that." Gertrude smooths her hair and waves away my reminders. "You're the one that brought that book cover back to me."

My face fills with heat. I feel like the woman in the paint-ing, as if I too am dividing into fields of color. Gertrude looks away. When she looks back at me, her eyes begin to water. "Marta always had secrets too," she says. "I'm so sorry. I wish she could forgive me."

"Forgive you for what? It sounds like you were good friends."

"My friendship was the last thing she needed." Gertrude sits up taller. "She had everything. We both did. Our families were both safe and well in New York, after everything we'd gone through to get there. . . ."

Gertrude trails off. After a moment she sizes me up in that way of hers, no longer looking so fragile but almost as sharp as the day I met her. Except now I try not to shrink away.

She says, "Tell me, Dawn. Do you have a girlfriend?"

The question startles me, and the first thought that comes to mind is I don't want to disappoint her. I don't know how to describe Lukas and me, so I say, "It's complicated."

She laughs. "It always is, my dear."

She seems to be laughing at herself as much as at me. Her

words hang between us like a new understanding. "That's true," I say.

She holds her hand up to signal I should wait as she reaches for her glass of water. After taking a sip, she says, "So don't let it be. Complicated."

Now I'm the one who laughs. "If only it were that easy."

Gertrude shakes her head conspiratorially. The faucet turns on in the kitchen, reminding me we're not alone. She says, "The important thing, my dear Dawn, is not to hide."

I nod.

She says, "Do you understand my meaning?"

I want to tell her I do, or I think I do. That she's saying I should live proudly, in the open, like the people in her stories. But I also want to tell her that whatever strength I've recently discovered feels tenuous at best. That I don't know if I can actually be like her, planting my message around in public, even though I'm finally trying again. Once more, I have a desire to confess—this time about my failure to express myself, especially through art, and about all the hope I've invested in The Project. "I'm trying," I say lamely.

"What's that?" She leans toward me.

I sip from the water glass Clare set beside me. My hands fidget. "I'm an artist," I say, "and I'm trying to express myself that way."

Gertrude waits for me to say more.

"There's this piece I'm working on, for my first time showing in a gallery, but I'm afraid it won't work out, at least not how I'm intending. I can't find a way to convey clearly what I want it to be. And even if I do, I don't know how to trust it will make any difference."

"Nonsense," she says. "Art is a wonderful way to make a statement." She shifts around like she's struggling to get comfortable, and when she settles again, she seems distracted. She says, "I made art once."

"Your Sapphic Warrior books," I say. "I know. I've been thinking about how brave you and your friends were."

"No, no, not me," she says. "I gave up too easily."

"I'm sure that's not true."

"It is." The thought seems to make Gertrude disappear into herself. She takes another sip of water and says, "But how would you know?" Suddenly she seems agitated, and I'm struggling to keep up. I watch her chest rise and fall with her breath, the movement exaggerated. She gathers herself. "Let me tell you a story. About that letter you brought. About Marta."

I lean closer.

"She was too good to say anything to me. It was Papa who did. He tried to do it kindly. He was always protecting me. He said that Marta's mother didn't want me coming around so much. She didn't think it was 'natural' for a girl who looked like me to be sitting so close to her daughter, touching her hand. Papa told me Marta's mother said everything must change, that Marta wouldn't engage me in any conversation more than what was required to be polite. 'Pleases and thank-yous only,' he said. But Marta never turned away from me. She never did. She should have."

I want to wipe Gertrude's tears, but I don't know if it would be okay to touch her.

"I'll never know what she thought," she says, and starts to cry harder.

As I look frantically around the room for tissues, Clare's

voice comes from behind me. "Is everything okay? Ms. Kleber? Gertrude?"

Clare's holding a box of tissues. I give her my seat and she dabs at Gertrude's eyes while I steal glances toward the front door, thinking I should go. "Gertrude, isn't it so nice that Dawn came to visit you?"

Gertrude holds on to Clare's wrist.

"Dawn is here to pick up the photographs of your family, remember?"

I want to disappear.

"What?" Gertrude straightens herself out. "Yes, yes, the photographs. Clare, can you please get the envelope from my desk? There's an envelope for Dawn."

Clare rises. "You try to relax." She turns to me. "I'm sorry. Perhaps it would be best if we cut this short. I haven't seen her get quite this emotional. She might be taking a turn."

Hesitantly, I sit with Gertrude while Clare goes to the study to retrieve the envelope.

Gertrude asks for my hand. "Dawn the bookbinder." She holds my hand with both of hers, a little too tightly. "You'll write a nice article about my father? He was a good man. That's the important thing to get across. He was just bound by the rules of his time, as you can imagine. And it always seemed to cause him grief, the blending in. I always hoped that if he'd lived just a few more years, he would have been able to let down his guard, even just a little. I would have loved to see that."

Clare returns and hands me the envelope.

"Of course," I say to Gertrude. "I'll write the article."

"And you'll keep those photos, because I don't need them where I'm going."

I smile.

"I'm serious," she says. "Use them in that artwork of yours. I'm sure you'll think of something wonderful." She closes her eyes.

"I promise." I look at Clare. She nods. "But I need to get going now. It was nice to see you again. I'm looking forward to finishing up the article." What else can I say? *Feel better? See you soon?*

"Thank you for coming," she says. "You have no idea how much it means to me. And to see you, sitting here in my living room." She starts to cry again. "I'm just so sorry for the harm I've caused you."

"Don't be silly," I say, attempting to soothe her. "You haven't caused me any harm." Then I realize she must think she's talking to Marta again.

As Gertrude cries, Clare sits with her, holding her hand, trying to calm her by going through the basics—what day it is, where they are—as I wait for a chance to say goodbye. The chance doesn't come, so I show myself to the door.

WITHIN MINUTES, I'M in the cab again, headed back to the train station, rattled by Gertrude's tears and apologies. What could possibly have happened between her and Marta to cause her so much guilt? What have I been missing? I vow again to try to track Marta down. But it's too late to reunite her with Gertrude, and maybe that impulse was all wrong to begin with anyway. I have no idea what those two went through.

I'm on the train back to New York when I open the envelope. Inside are a handful of photographs and a smaller envelope. I pull out the photographs and set them on my lap. There are seven, different sizes and shapes. In some, Gertrude's father is working in his bindery, bent over a book, or facing the camera, posing with a book in hand. I turn one over and find a sticky note covering up handwriting in German. *Father at Bremer Presse in Germany.* In others, Gertrude and her family are dressed formally, posed outside their house. A note on the back of one says *Smallest=me.* The smaller child in the photo stands squinting in the sunlight, wearing a bonnet. I wonder where Gertrude's siblings are now.

I study the photographs, Gertrude with her family. Her father, so proud of his work. It all seems so otherworldly, as if it has no connection to the woman I've met. But at the same time, I feel close to all of them.

I pull out the second envelope. Inside is a letter from Gertrude.

May 24, 2003

Dawn,

So, you have the photographs now if you want them for the article. Certainly you'll want one of Father in the bindery and, I think, one of the family.

Also, more importantly, I'm afraid I have a confession that I've waited too long to share—one of a very personal nature. Since you brought me that letter I thought I'd lost a lifetime ago, it seems fitting I should share it with you. Please keep it out of the article, as it is simply a dying woman's wish to get something off her chest.

You know that I was in love with Marta, but she was also my dear friend. For years I spent time with her, sitting close, smelling her hair, coming alive and dying inside at the same time—never telling her about my love or my confusion or my desire to dress in men's clothing. But as my new friends and I gathered courage, I began to feel invincible. I'd been pulping all the covers we'd removed from our precious novels in order to cover our tracks, but the one you found held special meaning for me. So I "pocketed it," as my students used to say, and late that night, when everyone in my house was sleeping, I snuck to the bathroom and wrote that letter to Marta. Then I tucked it into one of my schoolbooks and carried it around for days before I worked up the nerve to deliver it.

When the moment finally came, however, the letter was gone. You can't believe my horror. If a classmate had found it, I could be expelled—or worse, beaten. And the shame that it would have brought on my family, who was trying to keep a low profile after everything they'd been through. I had no wish to put myself or anyone I loved in danger. But eventually, after a few more agonizing days passed and no one confronted me about it, I relaxed, assuming it had been lost somewhere safe, like under the wheel of a bus.

In any case, it seemed like a blessing. I knew I shouldn't really tell her how I felt. But then one bright

Sunday afternoon, when my hair was freshly cut, very short, and I'd already taken to wearing pants everywhere, Marta and I went out for a soda. I don't know if it was simply my imagination, but that day she seemed to sit closer than usual, to put her face near to mine every time one of us spoke. I made a point to talk about how fed up I'd become with boys and even joked that I would take a girl to the upcoming school dance. Marta looked delighted with that idea, so when we were walking out on the street, I stopped at the window of a men's clothing store to point out the outfit I would buy for the occasion. I was keeping the joke going, you see. I even got down on one knee and made a show of asking her to be my date, to which she took my hand and laughed and said of course. Even under the silly circumstances, my blood raced through my veins, and quickly I realized I'd gone too far—that people could see us. I dropped her hand like hot lava.

But I also made an impulsive decision, to follow through on my invitation from the letter I'd lost, to ask her to the bindery to see what I'd been doing with my friends. As we walked, I made sure to keep a few steps between us, even though I was excited to get to our destination so I could let her into my real world.

But tragically I never got to show her. After a few minutes in the bindery, Marta and I heard footsteps in the hallway. My heart sped up, afraid we were about to be caught by one of Father's coworkers. But the reality was much worse. We'd been followed. Three boys—they looked college aged—sauntered into the

room, smiling, though looking anything but friendly. I
froze, paralyzed with fear, when I saw that one of them
was holding a baseball bat. And their breath reeked of
liquor even though it was the middle of the afternoon.
So you could say I knew they were not there to talk
about bookbinding. Instinctively I grabbed Marta and
hid behind one of the workbenches, but they'd already
seen us. They didn't say a word, and in that silence
I thought my heart would come right up my throat.
Marta was staring at me, her eyes wide, terrified. I
stayed in front of her.

The boys yelled for us to come out, and I knew we
were trapped—and in that moment I was gripped by
fear that the whole thing was my fault. That they had
found the letter I'd written to Marta. So now I had to
protect her from my missteps. Shaking like a leaf, I
stood and asked them what they wanted, and they said
I had no business playing a man so that I could hide
such a pretty girl from them. She needed a real man,
said one of them, approaching me with the bat. And
that was when I snapped. I groped around desperately
for a heavy tool and my hands found a cast-iron
weight. But even as I lifted it in their direction, yelling
threats, it wasn't long before they understood it was
useless. I didn't have it in me to strike them.

The boy with the bat cackled and said, "All right,
that's enough. Give us the girl." He bent down to
where Marta sat cowering on the floor and pulled her
face toward his to kiss her on the mouth. Even as she
struggled, I couldn't swing my weapon—I could only

cry out for her. You should have heard his delight
when he realized, or confirmed, what I was, how I felt
about her.

My heart pounds in my ears.

I imagine Gertrude in her kitchen, standing up and walking
to the window, sunlight spilling across her face and chest, her
arms folded across her stomach, holding everything in.

The train goes quiet, the world outside a film on mute. The
only sound my breathing.

She's been living with this for almost fifty years.

One of the worst things I remember was his
absolute glee as he made for me—plucking the weight
from my hand like it was a feather, shoving me to the
ground, and lifting his own weapon. But as he did,
Marta cried out and lunged for it. And then before she
could get a grip, he swung around, landing a blow to
her head.

I screamed with rage as he left Marta's body lying
on the ground like a sack. They must have panicked
and fled, so I ran to the phone and called my father
because I didn't know what else to do. Mercifully, she
was still breathing, so I sat next to her and watched
every rise and fall of her stomach until a few minutes
later when an ambulance arrived and took her away.

And that was the last I saw of her. My parents
told me that her family moved out of state, to a safer
place, and I never heard from her again. I never knew
if it was because she didn't want to talk to me or her

parents wouldn't allow it, or if she even fully recovered from the attack. But I didn't dare try to find her, because I'd done enough harm for one lifetime.

My father never let me speak about that day. What I didn't understand then but know now is that it was at a time when tens of thousands of people had lost government jobs—or had worse done to them—if they were suspected of being a homosexual, or even associating with one. As you can imagine, it ruined thousands of lives, and many people even committed suicide. The bindery where Father worked sometimes contracted with the government, so he would have been vulnerable. And I'm sure he did not escape Nazi Germany to have to worry about such things in the so-called land of the free. Plus he had always been so concerned about protecting me. At the time I thought he was just being strict. But now I like to think that instead of trying to change me, he was simply trying to teach me to change my behavior, to protect myself from such terrible consequences as Marta and I had experienced. Anyway, I believe these are the reasons why he told the police that the incident was an attempted robbery, and that my friend and I had just been in the wrong place at the wrong time. As if poor Marta was simply collateral damage.

So now you know. I tried to be the hero, but instead I was the fool. I shouldn't be burdening you with all of this. Here you probably thought you found a simple love letter. But you see, now I finally know that it wasn't my letter that gave us away. That my father, may his memory be a blessing, must have found it before anyone else did and brought it to work to hide it where it couldn't be discovered. He could have destroyed it or, worse, punished me for it. But knowing he hid it confirms my suspicion that he was keeping my secret. Maybe he even intended for someone to find it many years in the future, when it would no longer hurt Marta or me because we'd be long gone. Or when it might no longer be against the law for a person to love someone of the same gender—or question their own.

I'm sorry I didn't tell you any of this when you showed it to me. I should have been thankful, or at least relieved, to know that it wasn't my letter that had given us away (even if it was my book-bombing or my careless public display of affection or merely how I looked), and to know that my father tried, in his way, to preserve the truth about me, despite the fact that it could have endangered him. But now you understand why such feelings are not without complication, as are so many things in life. Even if it wasn't actually my fault those boys followed us, I still blame myself for that senseless violence against Marta. Papa had tried to warn me to leave her alone. I'd been too bold, too arrogant, to see the danger I courted. And I've spent my life determined not to repeat that mistake. Unfortunately, I've learned too late that this was a terrible mistake in itself. You see, when you spend all your time hiding, you do avoid danger, but you also avoid life. Or at least the things that make it worth living: gathering with friends in the open, walking down the street in clothes that let the world know who you truly are, holding hands with the person you love.

I'm sure you can see why I don't want the book cover, so I hope you'll accept it. I don't care what you do with it. Keep it, give it to your museum, burn it. I suppose it was meant to have a life of its own, like the stories from the Sapphic Warriors.

I believe it's no accident that you found it, as you seem to be looking for something yourself. Maybe it's direction. Or permission or courage. Whatever it is, I wish you all the best luck on your journey. If my story has a lesson in it, perhaps it's this: go forth boldly, my dear.

Gertrude

‖FORCE

IT'S LATE AFTERNOON by the time I get back to Brooklyn, after I've read Gertrude's letter four more times on the train, after I've barely held down the bagel I bought in Penn Station, and after I've decided I have no choice but to write the article about her father—the man who protected her across continents, who kept her secret instead of destroying it.

AT DINNER, I sit across from Lukas at Hunan Delight. The table between us a mile long. I've changed out of the dress I wore to meet Gertrude, and the stiff collar of my button-up is chafing my neck. But I like the discomfort. The feeling of clothing that isn't meant for me somehow making me feel more alive, reminding me of the woman underneath, of the fact that, at least for now, even in George W. Bush's United States, unlike Gertrude in Nazi Germany and in 1950s America, I am still legally allowed to exist. Tonight I want to be everything, to feel everything.

Lukas looks at me, but his eyes see something else. Something I can't read. It's never been this way before, sitting across from each other struggling to make small talk. I've already told him about Gertrude, and as usual, he didn't want to cheapen anything with the "right words." But the more distant he is, the more I want him. I watch him eat his fake chicken, wipe sauce from his chin. I can't wait another minute to get my hands on him.

"Let's go home," I say.

"I'm not done," says Lukas.

"You'll finish later." I stand to pay at the register. Grabbing some take-out boxes, I return to the table and shovel leftovers in.

"Well, what's gotten into you?" says Lukas.

"Nothing," I say. "You."

He stands and follows me outside. I like that I've finally gotten his attention. I'm tired of being quiet. We're only a few blocks from our apartment, but I can't keep my hands off him. He hates touching in public, so he swats me away, but it only feeds my urge to take charge. As soon as we're in the door, I have him up against the wall.

"Take it easy," he says, kissing me, his garlic breath filling my mouth, my nose. It isn't enough. I grab his hips and knock him back against the wall, ignoring the sharp pain that runs through my right side as I do.

He kisses me harder, and I hold his hands over his head. I want to be the man. And the woman. I open the buttons of my shirt and put his hands on my breasts. He moves his hands to my shoulders and runs them down my back. Something inside me shakes loose. Something that's tired of being so repulsive to him. Some wild and unfettered rage at everyone I've ever loved who hasn't been able to love me back. I think about Gertrude and Marta and how much the world doesn't give one single fuck if good people are loved or hated, if we live or die. I grab Lukas's hands and put them back where I want them, then grab him by the hair and pull him closer. "Take me to bed."

Holding my wrist, he leads me to the futon, where I lie back and pull him on top of me. "Now," I say. "I want you right now. Inside me."

But as I move my hands down toward his pants, he rolls us over and, in an instant, all my desire drains away—I can't take this kind of rejection anymore.

"Hold it," I say, pushing against his shoulders to sit up. "Hold on." I resist the urge to close my shirt.

Lukas pulls his hands away. "What's wrong?" he says. "Did I hurt you?" He looks scared.

"No," I say. "I'm okay." But I'm not. And I'm sick from not saying so. If I want anything to change between us, I have to act. Whether I'm ready or not. I catch my breath. "I just need to know," I say without looking at him. "Do you want me like this?"

Lukas sits up. "Like what?"

I push a stray wavy lock out of his eyes and steel myself. "Why do you think it's cute when Jae talks about getting married and having a family?"

"I thought we already settled this stuff about Jae," he says. His voice is gentle, but I sense some impatience at my bringing it up again.

"That's not what I mean." I take his hand and rest it on my thigh, feel the heat of his fingers through my whole body. "Do you think I'd be cute in an apron?"

He takes his hand from my leg, pretending to inspect his nail polish.

"Seriously," I say. "Is it possible for you to imagine some kind of commitment, some kind of family, with me—if we were to do it our own way?"

"You can't do those things your own way. They're institutions, cultural constructions."

"I know that, but we're not exactly a normal couple. What makes you think that would change?"

"The minute you talk about it, it starts to change." He scoots to the edge of the futon to look for his tobacco. Deflated, I button my shirt. "Where is this coming from, anyway?" he says. "What's going on with you? Is it Gertrude and Marta?"

"I don't know. Maybe I'm sick of having to stand for something instead of just loving you."

"What's wrong with standing for something you believe in?"

"Nothing. But maybe sometimes I want to stop questioning everything a woman is supposed to be and just be whatever kind of woman I am. Maybe I want to get married and have kids and do it without having to fit neatly into a box."

"So do that."

"How? You desperately wish I were a guy. Katherine wants me to be a woman who smiles and uses blush. My art school buddies could only see me as a butch lesbian. At this point my parents would probably settle for me just choosing who the fuck I am." I'm losing control, my voice rising. "And I'm so fucking tired of trying to be what everyone else wants. I need to know who I am."

Lukas finishes rolling a cigarette and puts it in his mouth. I want to rip the thing out.

"Why aren't you saying anything?"

He perches on the windowsill, as if he's about to climb out. "What do you want me to say?"

"Anything. Tell me I'm wrong."

His lips shine in the dim light. He looks like a sad movie starlet.

I draw breath. I say, "Do you wish I was a guy?"

"So this *is* about Jae."

"No. Why can't you understand? I'm trying to tell you the world fucking hates people like me—like us. And their hatred just keeps winning, every damn time. So we don't get anything like the American Dream. We get to be punching bags. Or we get fucking killed."

"Dawn, did you really ever think any different?"

"I wanted to. But look at Jae. He could have *died*, Lukas, and he wasn't even doing anything except hanging out with us. For all I know, he still can die. What am I supposed to fucking do with that?"

"I don't know," he says.

A gentle *thunk* from the DVD player, and the little power light goes out.

"Lukas," I say. "Do you love me?"

He looks down. I wait for him to answer, but after an eternity, only a silent tear runs down his cheek.

The blood drains from my head. Holding back tears, I jump

up from the futon, grab my jacket, and head for the door. As it closes behind me, I hear his voice. "Fine, yes," it's saying.

It's too late.

AS I ROUND the corner away from our building, I find a text from Jae. Finally, he wants to know if I can come by soon. It should be a relief, but I'm too numb to feel anything. I pause and catch sight of a man through the window of the laundromat across the street. He's watching one of the machines spin, his hand lying on top of it as if he's performing a healing. I can't think clearly enough to form a response to Jae, so I continue on, but after I've walked a few blocks, I stop again. I have no idea where I'm going; I just know I have to hold it together. My phone says it's well after eight. It's too late to visit Jae in the hospital. I think about texting Alice, but she isn't my friend. And Amina is on a date. Of course, home—to my parents—isn't an option. I lean against a wall and think. I'm not far from the bindery where I'd interned and there's an old vinyl chair I can sleep in if it comes to that, at least for a few hours.

NEXT THING I know I've arrived and am lugging the gate up, stepping into the smell of paper dust and rice paste. I turn on the lights, stand at the empty workbench, and stare at nothing. Even though I'm fighting with Lukas, I'm thinking about Gertrude again, always Gertrude. When faced with her hour of change, regardless of the outcome, she'd chosen to be Abraham, to step forward to protect Marta no matter how high the cost, no matter if Marta even loved her back. What would my life be like if I lost Lukas? Have I already lost him? And am I losing Jae? My sanity?

I'm being too dramatic, I think. It's a mistake to let myself feel sad. If I start crying, I may never stop. But even so I still picture Lukas, the tear running down his cheek. I walk back and forth, trying to pace away the image of him struggling to say three little words. It's my fault for confronting him. I could be home in bed with him if I hadn't pushed him to admit what I've known and feared for too long—he doesn't love me, and he probably never will. My leg muscles begin to burn, my back aches, but every time I sit down, the stillness fills me with a horrible dread and I'm up again. My fingers drumming on my chest. And then my feet are kicking the workbench, over and over, until my toes are throbbing and I finally give in to the chair and curl up into a ball and just sob.

When I calm down and open my eyes, I'm on the cold linoleum floor, looking at a blue streak of paint and the worn-out wheels of a stool. I turn my gaze up to the window, a small rectangle only a few feet from the brick wall of the building next door. I want out of this claustrophobic feeling. And right now there's only one escape: paper.

Fuck it, I think, and push myself to stand. At the workbench I take out a large sheet and my bone folder. My breath calms as I begin to fold it into a signature, the tool molding into the palm of my hand while I reshape the empty expanse into a less intimidating size. When I finish, I run my fingers over the grainy surface, count the leaves, and confirm eight. I pull out a pencil and sketch Gertrude on her porch. Then I stare at it, thinking about what to do next, and I remember the photos of her father and her family in my bag, how she'd asked me to keep them and use them in my art. My pulse quickens as I pull out the big envelope and line up the photos on the bench. Looking at the American Book Bindery in the background of one, I can't imagine it as the horror scene it became. I wonder if this photo was taken before or after Marta was injured. I rearrange the photos, looking for a story in them—an alternate story—but the one I keep seeing is the one in which Gertrude is trying to save the girl she loves, only to have love become the weapon that strikes her. Suddenly, I have an idea.

I make a quick sketch of my army of stenciled Sapphic Warriors, Gertrude standing in front. Then I add another woman slightly off to the side, also rendered in silhouette. I draw many more hearts rising from the heart on Gertrude's chest, all arcing toward the chest of the new woman, who's holding Gertrude's hand, though her body is hanging limp. The point of the last heart, the one that's finally found its target, has pierced the second woman's chest. I study it for a moment. Then, to finish it off, I add a small pool of red blood next to her and a row of flowers growing from it. *My protest against death.*

Once I'm happy with the result, I check my phone. 10:06 p.m. It might as well be midnight.

The chair in the corner looks like something sinister—a vampire bat pretending to sleep. Like once it has me, it will enclose me in its wings, trapping me in my own fear. But I want to be stronger than a chair, so I go to it and close my eyes and tell myself to man up. It hurts my side to sit. My side always hurts more when I'm tired. Starting tomorrow, everything will look better, I tell myself. Things always look better in the light of day.

AT FOUR O'CLOCK in the morning I wake from a dream in which I was holding a book. It was black and yellow and made of rubber, and every time I looked at it, it was bigger than before, until it was so big I couldn't hold it, but it followed me everywhere like a huge, growing wall I could no longer see past.

The studio is pitch-black. My jaw aches, and my cheek is stuck to the vinyl chair. With my head still half in the dream, I think everything that's happened over the last twelve hours has also been a dream, but it doesn't take long for reality to replace relief. Everything hurts. I want to go home. Instead, I close my eyes again, but sleep won't return. Just the giant rubber book, appearing, changing, then disappearing—like an image behind a water glass when you look at it from different angles. Nauseated, I wake again a half hour later. I switch on the lights and test my limbs. I'm thirsty and my throat is raw.

I walk to the workbench, open my book to the new sketch, and decide it's not bad. Then I dig back into the envelope for Gertrude's letter and read it again, but I stop before I get to the part where the boys enter the bindery. I fold up the letter and return it to the dark.

My workday begins in only four hours, so I call a car service, straighten up the workbench, put away the tools, and ease the book into my bag, grateful that at least I still have time to update my work for The Project. Then I wait in the doorway until I see headlights.

‖SPINE

IT'S ALMOST FIVE o'clock in the morning when I get home. Lukas is asleep on the futon, which is still folded up into a couch, and dirty dishes are piled in the sink. He's gotten as far as taking off his shirt but is wearing his pants and shoes. I head for the shower, making the water as hot as I can stand it. When I come out, he's sitting up, his eyes squinty.

"Where were you?" he says.

"Bindery." I grab some clothes from my dresser and bring them back to the bathroom. They're my usual jeans and T-shirt, which I've still been too afraid to wear much since the attack. But I don't care. I want to get dressed and back out of the apartment as fast as possible.

Lukas cracks open the bathroom door but doesn't look inside. "You slept there?"

I pull the door closed. "Yeah."

"You going to talk to me?" he says through it.

"Got nothing to say." As I pull on my jeans, I realize that it isn't just because I'm scared that I've been dressing more feminine. I've been trying to get Lukas to acknowledge that side of me. But this morning it feels good to embrace ambiguity again. For the first time in a while it feels like who I truly am. I step out of the bathroom and take some granola and a bowl from the cabinet.

As I pour soymilk in and start to eat, Lukas sits down at the table. He looks exhausted, like he can barely hold himself upright. I wonder if he tried to wait up for me, if he was scared when I didn't come home.

"Why don't you make some coffee?" I say. "Or go back to bed. You look sick."

He forces a laugh, like he can't handle what's happening, so he'd rather make it a joke. Then he goes back to the futon and lies down.

I want to scream. Instead I follow and sit next to him. If things are ending, I don't want it to happen like this. I try to muster my strength. "Listen," I say. "I'm sorry I can't do this anymore. At least not right now."

He nods. "Is it because of Alice?"

I laugh. I want to cry. "Come on," I say. "You know it isn't."

He sits. "You know, I'm not forcing you to be anyone."

"I know," I say. "But you don't want the same things I do."

"Maybe I can learn."

My eyes fill with tears. "I want to believe you."

Lukas plays with the sheet.

"Maybe we just need a little time apart?" I say. "This apartment is really small for the two of us."

He wraps his arms over his chest. I love him more than I've ever loved anyone. I feel like I'm losing part of myself. But everything also seems clearer than it has in a long time.

Lukas will no longer look at me.

I kiss his cheek. There's nothing more to say.

WHEN I LEAVE for work, the sun has begun to rise, casting a bluish hue over Brooklyn. I can finally feel the hours I've spent curled in that little chair washing away. A new day is beginning.

I ARRIVE AT the Met at seven o'clock and make my way through the quiet galleries to the library. To my disappointment, Katherine is already in the conservation lab, working on her big green box and listening to Joni Mitchell.

Without pausing her work, she says, "What brings you here so early? Excited to work on your book?" She sets down her paste brush and, patting the box firmly with her hand, says, "Stay." Then she laughs. "That's a little bookbinding technique I never taught you. One-word commands. They work every time."

I want to smile, but I must do something else with my face because she says, "It couldn't kill you to laugh a little. That was a joke." Then she starts singing. "They paved Paradise to put up a parking lot . . ."

I walk to my workbench, uncertain what to do. I don't want to take The Project out in front of her. I sit on my stool and pull tools from the drawer. Katherine's back to work, mixing acrylics, trying to match the color of the box.

"What is that?" I say, killing time.

"Oh, it's the wildest thing." Katherine holds a piece of newly painted linen up to the light. "This is a Duchamp, believe it or not. It came to me through a friend who restores sculpture because it's made of binder's board covered in book cloth. He thought I'd know better what to do with it. Quite thrilling, isn't it?"

"A real Duchamp?" I say. "What's inside?"

"Nothing, for the moment, but usually a stack of individual prints, which are actually in almost perfect condition. I'm just repairing the box. The whole thing is a collection of notes on *The Bride Stripped Bare by Her Bachelors, Even*. But the box is considered an artwork in its own right."

"That's really cool."

"Come look," she says, indicating the stack of prints with her elbow. "Just don't touch."

Grateful for the diversion, I walk to her bench.

"If you want to know the truth, it's the first project I've worked on that's actually made me a bit nervous. I mean, what do you do if you ruin a Duchamp?"

"I can't imagine," I say.

She straightens up. "I guess I just can't ruin it, then."

She has a way of saying things that makes them sound final. A done deal, an incontrovertible truth. She's hard to figure out. Throwing herself fully into everything she does and yet never completely satisfied with anything. Always the authority on femininity and yet chose a career over having children. She's made this whole meaningful life for herself and yet still holds on to such traditional ideas about how other people should live theirs. I wonder if she's happy. I wonder what that even means.

When I run out of things to look at, I go back to my bench.

Katherine says, "So, how's Lukas?"

She's just making small talk, but I'm afraid if I answer her, I'll start crying, so I shrug.

She laughs. "Quite the romance, eh?"

"Something like that." I pull a book out of the press and try to start working. But I can't stop thinking about him, picturing him on the couch sleeping while my whole world is crashing around me. I blurt out, "I think we're breaking up."

"Oh," says Katherine. "I'm sorry to hear that."

And then I do start crying and I don't even care anymore. I'm not looking at Katherine, but I hear her paste brush pause, then clunk lightly against the workbench.

"Come over here," she says.

I sweep my bangs out of my eyes and wipe my tears with the backs of my hands. Then I turn and walk to her bench.

"Quit hunching," she says. "And look at me."

I do as she says.

"Good. Now tell me what's the matter."

"I think Lukas and I are breaking up," I say again.

"You already said that. Tell me what's going on."

I tell her that it's complicated but Lukas doesn't seem to love me anymore, and she says there's nothing complicated about that—it happens all the time.

"Is that supposed to make me feel better?" I say.

She laughs. "I suppose not. But I think this is a good thing. Maybe he's the reason you never smile."

I roll my eyes. "I don't need to smile. There are plenty of

people who walk around smiling who aren't happy, so it's not doing them any good."

"Touché. But you don't seem happy either. And all I'm saying is, maybe if Lukas doesn't love you, you're better off without him."

I start to cry again. "I'm sure that's easy to say when you're the kind of person who can always find someone else."

Katherine sits back on her stool. "Dawn, you're a pretty girl. If you took better care of yourself—"

"No, see, that's exactly what I mean. I *do* take care of myself. Just because I'm not the kind of person who smiles and wears high heels—"

"You didn't let me finish."

I cover my face with my hands. *I'm not a girl*, I want to say.

Katherine says, "What I'm trying to say is I can see you're confused, or whatever you want to call it—I don't care. But you shouldn't let that stop you from caring about your appearance. Because, like it or not, that says something about you."

"I can't just pretend to be some girly girl."

"That's not the point. It doesn't make one bit of difference if you wear high heels or combat boots. Whatever you choose, I just want to see you wear it proudly. For god's sake, if you want to put on a suit and tie, put on an Armani suit. And if you want to wear a dress, then wear a McQueen. Or do something in between, but commit to it. You owe that to yourself. Do you understand what I'm saying?"

"I think so." Even though I don't necessarily agree with her emphasis on fashion, I'm more than a little moved to learn that she understands me more than I'd thought. She's trying in her way to tell me the same thing Gertrude had. I look down at my

T-shirt and jeans. "I'm wearing the heck out of this T-shirt," I say.

She shakes her head. "You're certainly one of a kind. I'll give you that."

As soon as I sit back down to work, my phone buzzes. Lukas wants to know if I'm okay.

Then Amina comes in, carrying a big bag. She's always in by 7:45 a.m. "What are you doing here?" she says.

Katherine doesn't miss a beat. "She and Lukas are breaking up."

"What?" Amina comes straight over.

"Thanks," I say to Katherine. "Anyway, we might be breaking up. Might."

"They're breaking up," she says.

"Is it because of the things you were telling me?" Amina says.

"Basically, yeah."

"Can I give you a hug?" She drops her bag and opens her arms.

I say, "I don't want to cry on you."

Amina feigns a stoic expression. "Of course, best not to."

I hug her quickly.

"Seriously though," she says. "If you need a place to stay for a bit, you can crash with me."

"Thanks," I say. "I'll figure it out."

"Don't be proud," says Katherine. "You need your friends during a breakup."

"We may not be breaking up," I say again, but no one is listening, and by that point I'm not even sure I'm listening to myself.

Amina takes her bag to her workbench and starts to unpack.

I cook paste and tear strips of Japanese tissue. My project today is a book of George Grosz's drawings, which I open to a page with a large tear along the right side. It's running through a line drawing—*The Saleroom*. A woman stands with her side and most of her back to the viewer, arms above her head, hands gripping a bar, her profile half covered by her right arm. She's naked, and the tear in the paper has missed her breast by half an inch. I sprinkle eraser crumbs over the paper and rub them lightly with a piece of cotton, then brush them away with my horsehair brush. Dabbing my thinnest watercolor brush into the paste, I carefully follow the edges of the tear, then rejoin the paper and coax the fibers back together with a dry brush. I paste a strip of Japanese tissue over the tear to reinforce my repair, brushing the edges into the original paper until they disappear and turn the tear into nothing more than a faint damp line. The woman whole once more. I think of Marta.

I'd requested to work on this book as soon as it came into the lab. I thought it would be interesting to spend time with Grosz, an artist who openly objected to the Nazis and was forced into exile, but who nevertheless believed nothing he did made a difference and sunk into depression and alcoholism. I get the sense from his work—the intensity of the violence and sexuality, the ugly distortion of bodies and faces—that he saw past the surface, and he knew that behind it lay something even more sinister than what he could capture with his brush. I wonder if he would have known the full extent of what was happening to homosexuals and trans people in America. Or if anyone knew how far the Lavender Scare was going. How was it possible that we'd just fought and won against the Nazis and only a few years later we were using their surveillance tactics?

At least now I can play a role in preserving Grosz's work. While I'm still figuring out my own. For the rest of the morning, I try to let go of thinking about the Lavender Scare and about Lukas. I do my best to let myself get lost in the books, in putting them back together, in the joy of having hands that can fix things, and in the comfort of being surrounded by friends.

BEFORE I LEAVE for lunch, I change the blotters surrounding my paper repair. With the tissue almost dry, the water line has disappeared; the woman's wound is healed. I feel a renewed sense of hope about finding Marta—or at least learning where she is now and maybe something about her life, so that I can put Gertrude's mind at ease before she passes away. So on my way out for food, I stop once again at the reference desk to ask for advice. After Vika lists a few things I've already tried, she says, "What about obituaries? I know it's a little morbid, but if she's deceased, and especially if she died in New York, you're likely to find an obituary at the public library."

I don't hesitate. Returning to the branch where I'd found information on the Lavender Scare, I explain what I'm looking for. The librarian helps me do some digging and eventually sets me up at a microfilm reader with a copy of the *New York Times* from 1983. My breath picks up as I scan its pages and find an obituary for one Marta Kohn (née Brahm), originally from Munich, whose family escaped the Holocaust and settled in New York, then moved to the Chicago area when she was sixteen years old.

My emotions are all over the place. Excited I've finally found Marta, disappointed to learn she's deceased. Sad I'll never get to meet her or put her in touch with Gertrude so that at the very least they could finally say a proper goodbye. Nevertheless, I continue to read. In Chicago, Marta met her future husband, David Kohn, and he died tragically in a car crash only a few years later. After that, Marta resettled in New York with their young daughter. The article goes on to list her various jobs and passion for community service, but it doesn't mention if she ever remarried. At the end, however, after it explains that she died of complications due to cancer, it says: "In addition to her daughter Barbara, Marta is survived by her longtime close friend Sylvia, with whom she lived for the last seven years of her life."

I sit back and my eyes well up with tears. Then I read it again to make sure I've understood correctly. That Gertrude was right about Marta after all. Right to look for a code in her smile. Right to think she would have gone to the dance as her date. I can't wait to tell her—especially that Marta didn't let what happened that day at the bindery stop her from eventually sharing her life with a woman. As I collect my things, my arms gather speed. And practically running to the door, all I can think about is what it could mean to Gertrude to know that in a way, Marta had gotten the happy ending that she and the Sapphic Warriors had been so determined to write.

Outside, I stop on the sidewalk, flip my phone open, and dial, watching people and cars pass by as the phone vibrates in my ear. But with every ring that goes unanswered, my excitement dims. Finally Gertrude's machine picks up, and I say, "Hi, it's Dawn. I just got some good news and wanted to share. Give me a call as soon as you can." I want to say more, but not on her machine, so a bit grudgingly, I hang up, hoping she'll call back today.

As I walk to the subway, my mind begins to wander. I remind myself that Jae is finally ready for a visit, so I text him back, feeling more hopeful about him than I have in a while too.

‖STRIDE

THE NEXT DAY I have lunch with Amina and, looking down at a stain on my shirt, tell her I need time away from Lukas and I'd like to take her up on her offer of crashing for a little while. She hugs me and says Blossom will be so excited for the company and do I mind sleeping next to a cat? I say of course not—it'll be good to have someone tiny and warm by my side.

It's a Tuesday, but she invites me to start moving my things over as soon as I want. Then it occurs to me that I've never really "come out" to Amina about my gender. Not in so many words, anyway. As she talks about another failed date she's been on, I sift through all the ways I can explain—or hide—myself while I'm staying at her place. I wonder if I should tell her about the anglerfish.

"Have you ever experienced that?" she says. "You're on a

date and some random thing happens in front of you and it ends up affecting the mood of the date?"

"You mean like witnessing a car accident?" I say.

"Yeah, like that, only it was a little dog taking a dump right next to our table and then stepping in it. The way things were going, it felt like a clear signal."

I giggle. "I'm sorry to hear it. In his profile he seemed so . . . decent."

"He was. It was weird. Like, everything should have been right, but we were talking just over each other's heads or something."

"Was he at least as handsome as his picture?"

"Yeah." Amina sips her iced tea. "But only in his looks."

I admire her clarity about things. I go to put my hand on her shoulder, but by the time it gets there I'm afraid she'll think it's weird, so I end up just kind of patting her awkwardly. I say, "Listen, thanks again for letting me crash. I don't know how I'm going to make this up to you, but I will."

"Nonsense," she says. And she gets up to throw her waste in the garbage.

THAT NIGHT ON my way home, I reread the response that finally arrived from Jae late in the afternoon. He changed his mind about the visit. *Too much stimulation today.* But I'm too overwhelmed to try to interpret what he means.

Back at the apartment with Lukas, I have to shore up my resolve not to say forget everything. In order to do that, I start packing, but that makes it worse because so much of our stuff has gotten mixed up together. Every stack of CDs I go through becomes an exercise in whether or not I have the strength to leave more pieces of him behind. Even our clothes have gotten confused and put away in the wrong dressers. As I fish through a drawer full of T-shirts, I separate one deflated, lifeless shirt from another, and the ones that have to stay slump back into the darkness. What makes it all even worse is that Lukas is acting like nothing has changed. He's dancing to Wu-Tang Clan over a pot of lentil soup, making us dinner, ignoring the suitcase and the boxes and garbage bags, ignoring the sounds of drawers opening and closing. He's doing the thing he always does, refusing to have the feelings that any normal person would be expected to have, and I don't know what would make me feel worse: if he doesn't care I'm leaving, or if he feels like he needs to pretend it doesn't matter.

It's when I get into bed for the night that he finally seems to acknowledge what's happening. With his clothes still on, he lies next to me and stares up at the ceiling. I turn toward him and he kisses me, gently at first, his lips barely grazing mine, and then deeper and more intensely until I lose myself and can't stop. We make out for almost an hour, but our movements are more tentative, already becoming those of strangers. When it's over, I'm even sadder because it doesn't change anything inside me.

The next thing I know, I'm waking from a dreamless night with his feet next to my face. He must have gone to sleep with his head on the opposite end of the bed, like I used to do with my friends as a kid when we needed to sleep in a single bed together but didn't want to get too close.

‖BOND

OVER THE NEXT few days I bounce around, from work to my apartment to Amina's place to drop stuff off. I move the bulk of my things into a small storage unit in Brooklyn and scour classified ads for apartments or rooms for rent. Whenever I'm at the apartment with Lukas, we can't help making out, even though our bodies barely recognize each other.

ONE NIGHT, WHEN Amina is out and I have the apartment to myself, I get a call from Clare. She tells me Gertrude passed away peacefully at home two days ago, surrounded by friends. I thank her for the news, and for a few moments after we hang up, I stare out the window at the blank sky, worrying that I have no right to be sad. After all, I'd barely known her. Yet in the short time since I've sought her out, I've grown to like her, and also to feel some responsibility for her, for helping her find a little bit of peace at the end of her life. I've been thinking about her more than usual, painfully aware of how lame it is that I never responded to her letter about Marta and what happened that day in the bindery. That I never tried again to tell her what I'd learned from Marta's obituary. I wonder if she even got my message.

I scan Amina's apartment and all that surrounds me is loss. But when my gaze lands on my portfolio standing against the arm of the couch, my mind begins to run through everything Gertrude had been telling me. That she wanted me to learn from her own years of giving in to fear and shame. She wanted me to be true to myself, whatever the perceived cost. And even though I miss Lukas, I have to hope that letting him go, at least for now, is a first step. It's a leap of faith, to trust myself like that.

Perhaps it's time to trust Gertrude too. I look back at my portfolio. Maybe I need to believe that she really wanted me to include her photos in my art. It's possible she hoped that if I shared some of what she tried to communicate to me, it would help her assuage her guilt. Or shame. And if I can lift some of that burden for her, even after she's gone, then I'd like to do it. Musing over Alice's pop art concept, over the eye project, and over Gertrude's penetrating gaze in that photo of her I'd found, I start to see a new image form.

I go to Amina's computer, search the Internet for a picture of Warhol's *Marilyn Monroe*, and print it. It's black and white, but it'll work for now. I take out my photocopy from the library and cut both Marilyn's and Gertrude's faces into strips, fitting them back together into one picture—a strip of Marilyn's forehead, a strip of Gertrude's eyes, a strip of

Marilyn's nose, then Gertrude's mouth and Marilyn's chin. I imagine what it will look like in color, Marilyn's vibrant hues against Gertrude's black and white, Marilyn's perfect femininity against Gertrude's rejection of it. I love the effect. It's still Gertrude, but not in a way anyone would recognize. And it makes the kind of bold statement she's been trying to encourage me to make.

I search for more iconic portraits of feminine women, then masculine men, so I can contrast Gertrude's ambiguous gender with them too. Then I plan out how I'm going to print them all in The Project.

‖REBELLION

IN THE MORNING, I call Jae. I haven't had a text from him since yesterday morning. But his mother answers and says he can't come to the phone. I ask if he's okay and tell her I just want to say a quick hello, but she insists he's resting. At lunchtime, I try again and get the same answer.

"Can you tell me when would be a good time to come by?" I say.

"I'm sorry," she says. "We're leaving tomorrow. There won't be time."

"What? Tomorrow?" Why wouldn't Jae have told me that? In the background I hear his voice. "Mutti, who is it?"

"I'm sorry," she repeats. "I have to go. Jae needs his lunch." She hangs up.

I call the hospital and ask to speak to a nurse. She says that if Jae doesn't want to come to the phone, there's nothing they can do. I explain that it's his mother who won't let me speak to him, but she says they can't get involved in that either and suggests I send a card. "Why would I do that," I ask, "when he's being released tomorrow?" She tells me to calm down and I realize I've begun yelling, so I apologize and tell her I don't know what to do, and she says a few deep breaths might be a good start.

I start to text Jae *What the fuck?* then delete it and write, *Everything okay? Been trying to call.* After an hour goes by and I don't hear from him, I decide screw it, I'll go to visiting hours anyway. Once I'm there, his mother won't be able to turn me away.

I look back at my phone and find no reply from Jae, so I type, *See you soon.*

WHEN I GET off work, I walk to a little café, where I pick up two shiny chocolate chip cookies. Then I hail a cab to the hospital, telling myself that I can stand my ground against Jae's mother. But the cab smells of cigarettes, which makes me worry that if she thinks I've been smoking on the way over, that will somehow sully my claim on his friendship. When the cab pulls up to the hospital, I discover that in my nervousness I've eaten my whole cookie and almost half of Jae's, grabbing chunks from the bag without looking.

Gripping the bag, I take the elevator to the third floor, but rather than going straight to Jae's room, I stop at the nurses' station. "Is Jae Kwon still here?" I ask.

"Yes," a familiar-looking nurse says.

"Is his mother with him?"

"I don't know."

"Okay, can somebody check?"

"I'm sorry, we have other patients to look after."

I'm about to argue, but the nurse excuses herself, saving me from that humiliation.

I walk down the hall and turn right and there's Jae's mother, standing outside his door, talking with a doctor. When she sees me, she raises an eyebrow, so I wave and duck into the room, where Jae is sitting on a bed next to a pile of folded clothes. He looks at me with blank eyes.

I hold out the crumpled brown bag. "I got you a cookie. Well, actually half a cookie. It was all they had."

"Thanks," Jae says, forcing a smile, but he doesn't take it.

"Chocolate chip," I say.

Still nothing.

I point to the pile of clothes. "What's this? Packing?"

"I guess so."

"Want help?"

He shrugs, so I put down the cookie and move his clothes into the suitcase on the other bed.

Then his mother comes in. "What are you doing?" she says. "Jae is supposed to be putting those on."

"I'm sorry—I was trying to help."

"You can see he's not dressed, can't you?"

Jae is still in his hospital gown.

"I'm sorry," I repeat.

His mother sighs. "I told you we wouldn't have time for visitors today."

"Mutti," says Jae. "Enough."

She fixes him with an exasperated expression and drops the clothes back on the bed next to him.

She walks out of the room, and I turn to Jae. "What's going on?" I say. "Why doesn't she want you talking to me?"

"Once again, my friend, not everything is about you. It's just Mutti being Mutti."

"And that's okay with you?"

"It is what it is."

His mother returns and looks at me with spent eyes. "Can I talk to you in the hallway?" She turns back to Jae. "Get dressed. I'll be back to check soon."

I follow her into the hallway.

"What do you want?" she says.

The directness of the question catches me off guard. I want so many things, it's overwhelming. I want her compassion. I want someone to understand what I've been going through. I want to give up like Jae's doing, but also to shake him back to reality. I want to scream and cry and not be afraid everyone would think I'm crazy. His mother is looking at me. The way she holds her sweater closed, she might be holding herself together. I say, "I want my friend."

She shakes her head. "Does that look like your friend?" She gestures into the room. "Does it look like my son?"

I look at the floor.

"I understand this is hard for you. But I'm trying my best to get Jae out of here because this place is doing no good for his psyche." Her eyes are wet. "He needs to get home. And I need to limit distractions so he'll stop fighting me."

"What if he needs to get back to his life here?" I say.

At that, her tears flow freely. She stands in front of me trembling, her hands twisting a tissue. I reach out and touch her shoulder and she comes closer, so I put my arms around her and she leans against me and cries. Before I can think what else to do, she breaks away and composes herself. "I'm sorry," she says. "I just don't know what to do. He's been here for too long, and no matter what they do to help him, something else goes wrong, and we've all been so scared, but I need to keep things positive. For him. To give him the confidence he needs." She brings the tissue to her face and closes a few buttons of her cardigan. She touches my hand. "Excuse me," she says, and walks back into Jae's room. I want to grab her and tell her I'm the one who's sorry—for being selfish—but that I still think she's going about this all wrong. For Jae to get better, he needs his own space, his friends, his plants and his garden.

Then again, what if she's right? Who am I to say? And what have I been able to do for him?

As I look in the room after her, however, I see him still sitting on the bed, the clothes still next to him in a pile, and I can't help but smile. A tiny rebellion, but it's the first sign of the old Jae I've seen in a long time. And he has the paper bag in his lap. He's eating the cookie.

‖HOME

DAYS FEEL LIKE years as I draft Gertrude's article, work on my art for The Project, and wait to get the pages back from Alice and the artists. I hate how easily I'm getting used to life without Lukas. We still talk every day, but I have so much to take care of that it's getting hard to keep up. I found an apartment in the East Village through someone at work who has a friend who was looking for a roommate. His name is Rashid, and she described him as quiet and gay, which both sounded perfect. Even better, he'll be away for six months.

It's now a matter of days before I'll be moving in with Rashid, or at least into his empty place. I've been staying late at work to use the computer so I can gather my notes for Gertrude's article into an outline. I'm no writer, so I've also broken down and asked Katherine to help me, and she's thrilled to have a project. Every day she reports to me with some new bit of information she's unearthed or advice about organizing the content. One morning, when I arrive at work, she's at her desk waiting for me with her final edit. I've finally worked up to wearing a men's shirt and tie to the lab, so I approach a bit hesitantly. But she gives me an encouraging smile—subtle enough that I'm the only one who notices—and it fills me with gratitude.

I love what she's done with the article. Somehow she's helped me capture the story I wanted to tell—one of craftsmanship and community that draws a direct line between the artistic impulse and the pursuit of social justice. It explains how a fellow craftsman helped Hermann Kleber and his family out of Nazi Germany and how Kleber was able to go on to create a safe, comfortable life for them in the States, among bookbinders. Of course Katherine doesn't know the story about Marta, but I like the article better this way. It's what Gertrude would have wanted. I tell Katherine it's perfect, and she sends it off to the *Grolier Club Gazette* and a handful of other journals.

IN THE EVENING Amina helps me carry the last of my things over to my new place. Some people have gathered on the steps of the apartment building next door and are listening to reggae. When they see us approach, they wave for us to join them, and Amina tells them we'll be right back.

But I'm still wearing the men's shirt and tie, and I didn't anticipate meeting anyone. "Yeah, *you'll* be right back," I say, and Amina pretends to hit me with her box. My phone buzzes. When we get up to the apartment, I drop my stuff and check it. It's Alice. Finally, my pages are ready. *Meet tomorrow, same place, same time?* I should be excited, but now that it's really done, there's something scary about it, facing my own artwork without knowing what I'll find. I write, *Yeah. Thanks!* and walk into my new bedroom to throw my phone somewhere far away.

"What's up?" says Amina. "Something happening with Jae?"

"No, just some news from a friend." I look out the window. "It's all good." Someone's arrived next door with a guitar. He's settling in and talking over the music. It occurs to me that with Rashid away for so long, no one in the world even knows where I am except Amina, Lukas, and Jae. The fact that some things are coming together while others are falling apart has been playing games with my head. It will only be a matter of days now before I learn if Gertrude's article will find a home. And Alice has come through for The Project, and before I know it, I'll have my first gallery show in Manhattan. But who will care?

The sound of guitar music rises from the street, and Amina says she refuses to stay put. Despite my protests and complaints that I need to change my clothes, she drags me out the door and downstairs. "You need to stop brooding," she says. "Get to know your new neighbors."

Outside, we see the reggae is no longer coming from the radio. Two of the guys are now playing live—the one with the guitar and another on drum—and people are stopping to watch or dance on the sidewalk. Amina makes herself comfortable among the small group gathering on the stoop and waves me over, and even though I'm vehemently shaking my head, someone else pulls me into the small sea of bodies that's

308 II JENNIFER SAVRAN KELLY

now swaying on the sidewalk. I take a step backward, but the man who pulled me in still has my hand, and he moves my arm along to the music. Amina is dancing too, on the stoop, and she yells, "Woo!" And then seeing her having so much fun, I let myself get swept up in the rhythm and the singer's soulful voice, and then a beer is in my hand, and I'm dancing—first with a man, then a woman, and another. Thanks to the music and the drink, I forget what I'm wearing or I don't care. Perhaps Jae was right. I need to stop thinking everyone is out to get me. I wave to Amina, who's laughing along with some stranger, and for at least this evening, for as long as these men are playing their music and everyone is dancing and a new life may be possible, it feels good to forget myself.

LATER THAT NIGHT, Jae texts me. Three words. *Home with Mutti.*

I hug the phone to my chest. *Glad to hear it*, I write. Though I don't like the idea of Jae's home being so far from the city. *When can I visit you out there?*

Soon.

‖EVERY/BODY

THE NEXT EVENING after work I take the 2 train downtown to meet Alice and the artists, intentionally arriving a bit late so I don't have time to be anxious.

The only empty seat is next to Ray, so I slip into it. I notice Ray's outfit, a simple short black dress over baggy jeans and combat boots. Breath that smells nutty and sweet.

"I want to thank you all for doing this," I say. "Please drink up. It's on me."

Ray raises a glass. This time I'm close enough to read the tattoo. *BALANCE*.

"Shall we?" says Alice, lifting one of the portfolios from the ground. Mateo stands and clears a spot on the table. I get up to help, and minutes later I'm pulling out the pages, laying them in front of me. My heart sinks. A woman with wings spread wide, her face tattooed. A giant nude, fractured in the cubist style. A woman with green skin and horns, peeking over a fence. Why had I been so cagey about what I wanted? Why hadn't I just said what I meant by *nonnormative bodies*? They've all seemed to miss the point. But as my eyes explore, I begin to notice things. The cubist nude has no discernible gender and towers proudly over tiny people that have been painted on the sidewalk. The green woman's face is a mask, and her hand, which is about to peel it away, or perhaps finish putting it on, is a man's hand. I uncover more pages and see strangely rendered cartoon faces with polka dots and stripes, word bubbles hovering next to them, saying things like *This is a cover* and *Please see me*. Two Black men are kissing, silhouettes of flowers blooming in the background, in an homage to my mural depicting Gertrude and Marta in front of the Sapphic Warriors. *LⱯVE IS LⱯUDER*. A pink-and-blue eye surrounded by flower petals, crocheted on the side of a bus. A strange collaged sci-fi creature whose body parts are labeled *Marginal Privilege, Amassed Oddity, More Dangerous Than You Think*. Four genderless bodies in a kaleidoscopic formation. *OUR BODIES OUR LIVES. RƎVOⱢUTION*. A giant black-and-white close-up of a man's bearded face from the nose down, a ring through his septum and hoops in his ears, red lipstick being applied to his full lips. *COURAGE HAS NO GENDER. LOVE PEOPLE. WAKE UP, DREAM BIG. WHAT DOES IT MEAN TO BE FREE? WHAT DOES IT MEAN TO BE LOVED? WHAT DOES IT MEAN TO HAVE PRIVILEGE?*

I'm trying not to cry, but I have to lean back so I don't get any tears on the work. Everyone's been bent over, looking at the pages, but now they're looking at me. I want to cover myself. I want to sob with relief.

WHEN I GET home, I lay the portfolio on my desk, wishing I had someone to show it to. I know I'm asking to be disappointed, but I can't help it—I call Lukas.

His voice mail answers. "I don't know why I'm calling," I tell it. "I got the pages from Alice and her friends and they're kind of awesome, and I think I finally have a title. Anyway, call me back if you want."

Then I text Jae. I type, *I'm thinking of naming The Project "Every/Body,"* and then delete it. It's not time to be talking about myself. *Hey, just wanted to say I'm happy to give you whatever space you need, but I also want you to know I'm here when you're ready.* I close my phone and set it down, hoping his mother was right and he's healing up at home. I guess no matter what I think of her tactics, she really is doing what she believes is best for him. That's probably the important thing—for him to be with the people who love him most, even if they drive him crazy. And even if I hate it.

The whole thing's been making me think about my own parents. The last time I saw them, it was a couple of years ago, not long after the art show they walked out on. They asked to come to Brooklyn to meet Lukas and take us out to dinner. In the restaurant, Dad rested his hand on Mom's. They sat close together and laughed at each other's jokes. Basically, they seemed happy together, and I couldn't help but think that it was because I was gone. It was the only thing that had changed. They had their easy life back, and were just making sure I was doing okay so they could check off that box. When they offered me money outside their car, it only confirmed my suspicion.

"You came here to check on me, so consider me checked on," I said, handing back the money. "I guess you still don't like what you see. So you've done your duty and you're free to go."

"That's not fair," said Dad. He put his arm around Mom, as if she was the one who needed comforting. "You need to give us a chance one of these days, and when you're ready to do that, you know where to find us."

He opened the car door and ushered her in. My stomach turned. My dad has always had this way of making me feel like shit and then manipulating me into thinking I'm the one who caused it. But I didn't want to leave things like that. I wanted to tell them to come back, that if they were serious, then we should talk about it, but in that moment, I was too upset to bring myself to go after them. Since then, it's been necessary phone calls only. But that's another weird thing about memory. That night I was sure they'd come to write me off, but as time has gone by, I've feared that I misunderstood and they were really trying to start making amends for all the hurt that led up to that moment. Maybe they'd been extending an olive branch.

My phone buzzes with a response from Jae. *Thanks. Come whenever.* He can't know how much I want to—it's all I want. But now that I have the pages for The Project back, I can't, not just yet. I write, *Only 11 days to bind book for show. Right after?* I don't hear from him right away, so I'm afraid I've shut him down again. I walk into the kitchen, where the dishes are piled high and Rashid has left instructions for how to capture a rat if one should show itself while he's away. He's drawn a little diagram showing a stick figure with devil horns, a *V* for eyebrows, and a broom, and a rat more than half the size of the stick figure.

My phone buzzes again. *Of course. Good luck. Or whatever you say for a bougie art opening.*

Fuck you :), I write, and pace the kitchen, imagining myself fending off an army of giant rats while I wait for his reply. Which doesn't come. I wash the dishes and pour myself a beer, flip through the pages of my book again, slowly, taking everything in—the enormous green woman/man, the tiny people on the sidewalk, the secret details in the background, like cracks drawn through things that at first appear perfect, and hands reaching up from nowhere to block bullets. Then exhaustion lassos me into bed. I look at my phone again and find Jae's reply: *m*/. Before I turn out the light, I type one more message. *I love you, bro.*

IN THE MORNING, I get ready for work as usual, but the huge portfolio complicates my routine. I need the equipment at the museum to bind the book, but that means braving Katherine and the others' reactions to my first work of art in years. I can't work at the bindery in Brooklyn because my old boss let me know it won't be available for a while. She's working on a massive project and her studio is full. I'll have to face peoples' reactions soon enough, I think. Soon the book will be out in public for anyone to see. I pick up the portfolio and carry it to the door, then stop. I turn around, bring it back to my room, and leave it on my bed. Not quite yet.

WHEN I GET to the lab, Katherine looks up at me from her workbench with a grin that's almost too big for her face.

"There's an envelope for you on your workbench," she says.

I look at her. Then at Stacey and Amina, who are both waiting for me to go get it. I walk to the desk and pick it up. The return address is from the Grolier Club. For a moment, I forget about The Project. I catch my breath.

"That was fast," I say. "Should I open it?"

"Quit stalling," says Katherine.

Amina and Stacey come over too, and the three of them make a little semicircle around me as I open the envelope. Like a fort. And I realize they've always been a kind of fort, I just haven't ever noticed.

The letter is short and to the point. The editors are very pleased to notify me that they've accepted my article "Handwork and Social Justice in Nazi Germany and 1950s America" for publication in their summer issue. I imagine Gertrude sitting at her table. Who would she have told when it published? And would she have liked it? Either way, I'm so happy to be fulfilling this promise.

Katherine is beaming. She says she knew I could do it, and Amina squeezes my arm.

"How does it feel to be famous?" she says.

"Will you keep your job, or do you plan to travel the world now?" says Stacey.

Katherine claps her hands twice. "All right, get to work."

FOR THE REST of the day, I enjoy my job more than I have in a long time, now that I'm no longer just a fixer of other people's art, but someone who's making my own work again—and even contributing to the field with my article. Also, I have to admit that I might not have been able to do either without Katherine's help.

In the evening, as I leave the library, I make a split-second decision to go look for her. I find her in the office upstairs chatting with one of the catalogers, so I wave, and she motions for me to wait.

When she comes out to meet me, I say, "I just wanted to thank you again."

"I know," she says. She hugs me—a quick, awkward embrace—and her cheeks are flushed as she pulls away.

AT HOME, I pull out my sketchbook. Then my phone rings and Lukas's name appears. I pick it up and stare at it until the third ring.

"Hi," I say.

"Hi."

"How's it going?"

"I got your message yesterday about the book," he says. "That's awesome."

"Yeah, pretty crazy it's coming together." Our voices sound formal. A business transaction.

Lukas says, "I miss you."

I swallow hard. He's never said that. I tell myself he's panicking. Soon enough he'll meet someone he can actually love and will barely remember why he wasted so much time on me. "Me too," I say.

I picture him sitting on the futon with his head in his hands, the way he always looked when we were arguing.

"Listen," I say. "I don't know if I would have even trusted

316 II JENNIFER SAVRAN KELLY

my idea if you hadn't believed I was onto something. So, thank you. It's meant a lot to me."

"I'm glad," he says. "But I should go. I just wanted to make sure you're doing good. And, you know, that's really awesome about the book."

"Thanks. Really."

"Okay, well, bye."

"Bye," I say, and keep the phone to my ear until the line goes dead.

WHEN I WAKE in the morning, I discover another message on my voice mail. "Yeah, hi, it's Ray. I was just wondering if you wanted to get a drink sometime. Anyway, now you have my number, so . . . call me back?" My heart goes a mile a minute. I'd been so intrigued by Ray's beauty and confidence that I never imagined Ray could see much of interest in me. When it sets in, I'm more excited than I've been in a long time. I play the message again and then put my phone on the bed, stealing glances at it as I get ready for work, too nervous to go near it until I'm ready to call Ray back.

When it's time to head out the door, I have to reckon with the portfolio again, which is where I'd left it the previous morning, leaning against the wall like a lover daring me to stay or go—last chance. I have nine days to finish the book. But this morning, something has shifted. If one thing is becoming clear, it's that I no longer have anything to fear from Katherine or anyone at work. I grab the handle and make for the door.

‖ENDPAPERS

WHEN THE WEEKEND comes, for the last time I step off a train on Long Island to visit Gertrude, but not as far east. Only in Elmont, at Beth David Cemetery, where she's been buried next to her parents. At the cab stand I pause, a sense of finality setting in, the full realization that it's not Gertrude I'll see but her tiny plot of land. Not even a garden.

THE CAB TAKES me through the iron gate at the blocky stone entrance, down a narrow street, to the blocky office, where I ask an elderly man how to find Gertrude's grave. He looks it up on his computer and gives me a map, recites some directions, and walks me to the door. His hand is on my back as he sees me off.

Soon I'm walking among graves, the sun shining strong in my eyes, the air tasting of earth and stone. With Gertrude gone, I've found myself thinking again about religion. About whether I should make another visit to Temple Israel or at least reach out to the rabbi. But I've realized that what I'm craving is not God or even spirituality, but ritual—the way Judaism used to always help me mark time and keep my world organized, give a certain order to the chaos. In the fall, eating apples and honey. In the winter, lighting eight candles. In the spring, squeezing every last family member around one table to read from the Haggadah. It's always rituals that confirm for me that something important has really occurred.

In other words, I've been looking for a way to say goodbye.

After a few minutes I'm in front of Hermann and Helga Kleber. They're buried side by side with one joint headstone, their last name engraved across the top, beneath a star of David. Helga on the left, *Beloved wife, devoted mother, beloved sister and grandmother*; Hermann on the right, *Beloved husband, devoted father, beloved brother, uncle, and grandfather*.

And next to them is Gertrude. Her grave still fresh. I wonder what her headstone will say.

I couldn't remember where people get the small stones they leave on Jewish graves, so I brought my own, and they're tugging gently down on my pockets. I pull them out. Three. First I place two by Hermann and Helga, and then I take a moment. The cemetery is quiet. Only a few other people arriving, and one or two cars parked along the edge of this small road. Looking at the ground, which is squishy under my feet, I can't believe Gertrude is beneath it, when only weeks ago I was sitting next to her, listening to her give me advice. I bend down to get closer, to see if I can feel any of her energy. A warm breeze rushes past. I set the last small stone near the head of her grave and return to standing, my desire for closure not quite satisfied, but with nothing left to do unless I want to say a few words.

I step back and examine all three graves, still and lifeless, even as my memories of Gertrude remain very much alive. And as her story, and her photographs and likeness, remain alive in my work, the work that may not have come to exist without her, the artwork whose life is only just beginning. This is when it hits me, when I understand the rabbi's sermon about Abraham and Lot, and my eyes fill with tears. At last I know who I've been and who I need to become.

Bending down one last time to touch the ground, I say thank you to Gertrude. "Thank you for being my visitor, for taking me by the hand and showing me it's time to act."

ONLY ONE DAY before the deadline, I'm standing at my workbench finally about to finish *Every/Body*. I've been working in the conservation lab every night for a week, measuring and remeasuring boards and paper, painting cloth, throwing it away, painting more until, at last, I've come up with something that doesn't thoroughly disappoint me.

From the outside, it doesn't look like much. Solid brick red, like a wall, with *Every/Body* spray-painted in bubble letters, one of Alice's eyes inset in the o. But waiting between the covers is a living, breathing city with its own story to tell. It gives me the same feeling that lured me in when I went digging under the endpaper for Gertrude's letter: that the book is keeping some secret but inviting the reader inside to discover it.

As I prepare to complete the last step, covering the bare insides of the covers with endpapers, I set the pages in front of me and flip past the title page to a blank leaf where Ray has painted what looks like a large tear in the bottom-right corner of the paper. It's filled in with an image of a person painting words on a brick wall. *They said there was no place for us,* and at the end of the book it continues, *but they were wrong.*

A few days ago I'd mustered the courage to call Ray back, and next week we're going to meet for drinks. Tonight, however, I have other important plans. Jae is feeling well enough to come into the city to meet for dinner. He wants to come to the gallery opening, but he's still not sure he's ready to make small talk with a crowd of strangers, so I should consider this a test run. When I finish with *Every/Body*, I'm going to head to the sushi place.

I'm excited to see him, but I've given myself an extra hour before dinner, which I told myself was to make sure I'd have enough time to finish the book, but really I want time with it before I have to let it go. So gently, I turn each page, holding pieces of the city in my hands, painted with beautiful bodies— bodies usually relegated to the shadows—watching their faces appear and disappear as each page comes to rest on the one before. When I get to the end, I stand the book up and stretch it out like an accordion, so that it opens up to one continuous image, one skyline, one city, one little world I wish I could live in. And for the moment, I can.

Then I lay the book back down and open the back cover. The last thing left to do is paste down the second endpaper. Protecting the book block with a sheet of newsprint, I place the paper against the board to make sure I've cut the paper to the right size. Then I pause and look at my bag resting at the foot of my stool. I've been carrying the book cover from Gertrude around for weeks, deciding whether I want to give it back to the museum. But in the past few days, the answer has become obvious. Carefully, I pull it out. I place it on the back side of the endpaper and trace it lightly with a pencil. Then I brush paste onto the paper, avoiding the rectangle I've drawn so that it will remain dry. Setting the cover of *Turn Her About* on top of the bare binder's board, carefully I cover it with the endpaper, which I smooth down with my bone folder. Now Gertrude's story will remain her own, private but no longer completely secret. A protest against loneliness.

The Project is finished.

Running my hands over the back cover, I wonder if it had been coincidence or fate that led me to Gertrude and then decide it doesn't matter. More likely, for every shitty thing that happens, an equally good thing is just waiting somewhere to balance it out. Or what we call coincidence is just life tumbling over itself, sifting some shit we didn't even know we needed out of the mess. Because both the things we need and the things that will hurt us are everywhere. As Lukas said, to recognize one from the other requires only that we pay attention. And I hope that I was able to help Gertrude too, at least to show her what forgiveness can look like, even if I never had a chance to say the words. I hope that maybe I was a visitor for her too.

I check the time on my phone. Only a half hour until I'm supposed to meet Jae. Placing *Every/Body* on my workbench, I set it up carefully to dry. Then I leave the museum. I walk down the street in my engineer boots and red dress. For the first time in as long as I can remember, I haven't planned who to be. I just got dressed in the first thing I liked. Maybe it's progress. Or maybe I'm too tired to care. But I want to believe progress, and I figure that means something.

Stopped at a traffic light, I puzzle over the remnants of some graffiti, only a few words still legible:

> end of   *the climbing*
>   *And oh my god, it seemed*   *the top*
>   *strength*
>   *when how brutal*
>   *really worth it.*

WHEN I FIND Jae at the sushi bar, the first thing I notice is he's wearing an eye patch.

"Fuck. Still?" I say as I wrap him in a bear hug.

He shrugs as we pull apart. "How else am I supposed to keep getting sympathy from you?"

"What?"

He looks like he's trying to stifle a smirk.

"Are you messing with me?" While I examine his face for a clue, I see sitting on his shoulder one of those little fuzz balls with sticky feet and googly eyes. It has a little makeshift beak. "What the hell is that?" I laugh. "Is it supposed to be a parrot?"

"Argh, matey."

"Oh my god," I say, punching his arm. "You fucking scared me for a minute."

"Come on," he says. "You have to admit it's a good look for me."

"You're a lunatic."

He puts his arm around me and we head to the back of the restaurant and claim a small table. In the dim light we need to look hard to see each other. He takes off the eye patch and picks up a menu, and as he reads it, he bends it back and forth. Every time his shoulder moves, the parrot bobs up and down.

"I've missed you like crazy," I say.

"Ditto. Thanks for being so patient with me."

"Actually, I think the score is even on that."

Jae sets the menu down. "So, I missed my interview with the CPA."

I laugh and rest my hand on his. "You'll be back on your bullshit soon enough."

We go through the motions, ordering food and beers, and a strong sense of calm settles over me. It's the same calm I felt with him at the top of the Empire State Building—but not because we're somewhere beyond the bustle of the city. Because we're part of it. And now I get what he meant when he said it's good to be reminded of how small we are. There's something beautiful about putting yourself out there when you don't know who's going to listen or care, because one day someone will think it matters. And that will be more powerful than anything.

Jae asks if I want another beer, and I say yes and he waves to get the server's attention. Then he leans forward and says, "So, is it finished?"

For a moment my heart speeds up because I think he means Lukas and me—is it finished between us? But then I realize he's talking about *Every/Body*, so I relax and say, "I think so."

And he smiles, and the smile reminds me of when we first met and he said he got the feeling we'd make good friends.

"I didn't think it could turn out so well," I say, and I've never been so grateful to be wrong.

ACKNOWLEDGMENTS

I'M SO GRATEFUL for my agent, Beth Marshea, for her tireless support and guidance, and for my first agent, Trevor Ketner, who believed in this novel and helped me shape it into something that could find a perfect home at the most unlikely time—in the middle of 2020. There are not enough words to thank my editors. Abby Muller's insightful guidance and perseverance led me to reimagine this book in ways I never anticipated and made the editorial process feel like a true partnership. Betsy Gleick and Mae Zhang McCauley steered the book (and me) expertly and thoughtfully to the finish line. Thanks as well to Brunson Hoole, Christopher Moisan, Travis Smith, Steve Godwin, and the whole Algonquin team. Thank you to Delia Davis for copyediting and to Jaya Miceli for designing the arresting cover of this book.

I made what I consider to be my first formal attempt at

writing narrative fiction in my late thirties, several years after my son was born. At a time in my life when I believed I'd started too late, two authors read my early work and encouraged me anyway. I can never express the depth of my gratitude for my mentors J. Robert Lennon and Amy Wallen. Thank you for believing in me. Thank you also to Diane Zinna and AWP's Writer-to-Writer Mentorship Program for the opportunity to work with Amy. This program has meant so much to writers with nontraditional paths who crave formal education and community.

Special thanks go to two of my undergraduate professors who, years ago, first dared me to dream: Diane Fortuna, whose passion for great writing could bring her to tears while reading from *The Norton Anthology of English Literature* to a lecture hall filled with hundreds of students, and Ira Livingston, my teacher and good friend, who rightly encouraged me to pursue a creative path.

As I drafted and revised this novel, I was honored to receive support from the Barbara Deming Memorial Fund/Money for Women, the Community Arts Partnership of Tompkins County (CAP), and the Constance Saltonstall Foundation for the Arts. Special thanks to Robin Schwartz at CAP for your years of support for our local artistic community and to Lesley Williamson at Saltonstall for making such a comfortable, welcoming space for artists (complete with laundry-basket standing desks!).

Every writer knows that no book would get written without the help and support of dear friends and other writers. A hundred million thanks to my talented and wise novel-writing group, Melanie Conroy-Goldman and Bob Proehl, who helped steer me through multiple drafts of this story. Special heartfelt thanks to my short-form writing group, Kathryn Henion, Sarah Jefferis, Brenna Fitzgerald, Kate Blackwood, and Darlene Gold, who read early drafts of the opening chapters and spent countless hours listening to me talk about my publishing dreams. Amy Reading has turned feedback and encouragement into art forms of their own, and Melanie Greaver Cordova's insights always lead to something better. Brian Hall, Nora Fussner, Scott Ondercin, Martha Rand, and Fred Schneider read an early draft at the Colgate Writers Conference and set me on the right path. Susan Specter spent hours proofreading—catching typos and mistakes while making me laugh all the way through. JT Tompkins invited me to read from an early draft at one of Ithaca's local treasures, the Grayhaven Motel.

I'm grateful for the support and inspiration of many other dear friends and writers. Big love to Amy Whitney, Gary Hodges, Pamela Tan, Chris Holmes, Elvira Katić, Adam Berenstain, Chris Bainbridge, Scott Hitz, Michelle Hitz, Emily Hopkins, Kenneth McLaurin, Elbonee La'Trece Stevenson, Jackie Swift, Everett Fox, Gina Nutt, Ange Romeo-Hall, Eleanor Henderson, Michael McGandy, Christopher Gonzales, Leslie Daniels, Paul Cody, and Elizabeth Holmes.

Thank you to Rabbi Daniel Kirzane for granting me permission to include ideas from his sermon about Abraham and Lot; to Jeremy Wilcox for his engaging walking tour of the street art of the Lower East Side of Manhattan; to Rhian Ellis for answering my frantic questions about meningitis; to Mijin Cha for educating me about Korean names; to Eric Rosario for saving me from my inadequate Spanish; and to Mona

Eikel-Pohen and Angelika St. Laurent for helping me with the German language.

Thank you to Ithaca Coffee Company for allowing me to occupy your space for so many hours while my son was in Hebrew school and I scribbled away. And a huge virtual donut for Ralph Walker and the #5amwritersclub on Twitter. Thanks for keeping me company during so many early mornings while I drafted, revised, and revised some more. Nothing beats the power of community to get you out of bed before dawn to write in the wee, quiet hours.

Unending gratitude and love to my family: Mom, Ken, Stacy—my sister in life and letters—Eric, Rachel, Maia, Marie, Rob, Kathy, Matt, Josie, Tabitha, all the Breiters and Kellys and Benedettis, and my kitties Daffy and Moishe (RIP, sweet Phil).

And especially, always, to Chris and Elijah.

‖ENDPAPERS‖

Questions for Discussion

QUESTIONS FOR DISCUSSION

1. Dawn narrates *Endpapers* in the present tense. Why do you think the author made this choice? Consider where Dawn is at the beginning of the story and where she is at the end.

2. In 2003 in the United States, there were no pronouns in mainstream use for gender-nonconforming people, nor were words such as "nonbinary" or "genderfluid" in mainstream use. Therefore, Dawn does not consciously choose a pronoun for herself, and other characters in the book use she/her for Dawn. How do you think this affects Dawn's feelings and experiences? Do you think she might have experienced life differently if her story was set in the 2020s, when people are beginning to use and accept they/them pronouns and describe themselves in terms such as nonbinary or genderfluid? If so,

how does language contribute to one's experience and understanding of oneself and others?

3. Lukas argues that the consideration of legalizing gay marriage means "gay people might now be allowed to live, as long as they do it like straight people." What do you think of his position? Are there inherent differences between the way LGBTQIA+ and straight people live? Should there be? Do you think current marriage laws do or somehow should reflect that position?

4. What, if anything, did you know about queer history in the United States or the Lavender Scare before you read this book? Is there anything this story makes you want to know more about? What are some events, bills, or laws that affect or specifically target LGBTQIA+ people right now?

5. Dawn and Lukas's shared queerness both enriches their relationship and challenges it. From your point of view, how much of their challenges arises out of their sexual orientation and gender identities, and how much does miscommunication or failure to communicate play a role?

6. Dawn spends a lot of time looking at street art because it's both inspiring for her own work and comforting in the aftermath of 9/11. She says, "The only thing that felt straightforward was the street art—whatever feelings it inspired, at least the messages were clear. Like those of the original graffiti artists—the Black and Latino kids who wanted to create a nonviolent way to connect and make their voices heard." Do

you notice street art where you live? If so, how does it affect you?

7. Gertrude confesses to Dawn that, as a teenager, she snuck her friends into her father's bindery so they could replace the covers of their lesbian pulp novels with rejected covers from more culturally acceptable books. She also tells Dawn that "since those pulp novels painted such a dire picture of our futures," she and her friends took a step farther by writing their own lesbian love stories with happier endings and leaving them on store shelves for customers to discover. Why do you think the queer pulp novels of the 1950s were so popular, even though they painted such a dire picture of queer life?

8. After getting attacked outside Mars Bar, Dawn visits a temple and is drawn to a Shabbat meditation that reflects on how to approach an "hour of change." Throughout the second half of the book, Dawn repeats to herself the following question from that meditation: "Shall we draw back . . . or cross over?" What do you think it means to Dawn to draw back? To cross over? Do you think she does one or the other by the end of the book? Both?

9. Alice questions Dawn's desire to collaborate with multiple artists on her project for her first gallery show, saying she prefers to have more control over her work. Dawn responds, "It seems like a better idea to have multiple styles, like real graffiti in a real city." What did you think of Dawn's choice to collaborate, and how did you feel about the outcome?

10. Katherine tends to be blunt and judgmental, which leads Dawn to hide her true self from her. Then she surprises Dawn by saying, "If you want to put on a suit and tie, put on an Armani suit. And if you want to wear a dress, then wear a McQueen. Or do something in between, but commit to it. You owe that to yourself." What do you think Katherine is trying to tell Dawn? Is she simply making a statement on fashion or speaking to something bigger?

11. Jae is a grounding force for Dawn until they get attacked at a bar and Jae's head injury leads to serious complications that affect him physically and mentally. Then Dawn needs to learn how to be a grounding force for him. How successful do you think she is, regardless of how Jae reacts to her from moment to moment?

12. Dawn is bothered by how casually Dr. Mink seems to accept that Jae's been attacked for coming across as gay, and Jae is bothered by Dawn's arguing with Dr. Mink about it. He tells her, "You have to stop assuming everyone's a piece of shit." Do you think this assessment of Dawn and her behavior is accurate or fair? Why or why not?

13. The book takes place roughly two years after 9/11, and one of the men who attack Dawn, Jae, and Lukas at Mars Bar is wearing an American flag shirt. In the hospital, Jae picks up on Dawn's feelings of guilt over the attack, and Dawn tells him they need to be more careful. He responds with, "Our country has declared war on evil, right? . . . So everyone wants a target, and when you have yellow or brown skin, you get to be the

target." Why do you think the author set the book in this time period? How might Dawn's and Jae's experiences be the same or different today?

14. In Gertrude's letter to Dawn, she says she still blames herself for the attack on Marta in her father's bindery, because she was too bold to notice the danger her appearance and actions could lead to: "I've spent my life determined not to repeat that mistake. Unfortunately, I've learned too late that this was a terrible mistake in itself . . . When you spend all your time hiding, you do avoid danger, but you also avoid life." How do you feel about this statement? Have you ever taken a risk in order to be true to yourself? If not, have you ever wished you had?

15. Both Dawn and Gertrude blame themselves for the attacks that cause their friends serious injury. Do you think either of them was to blame? Why or why not?

16. Dawn spends a good deal of time wondering if it was coincidence or fate that led her to Gertrude. At the end, she decides it doesn't matter: "Both the things we need and the things that will hurt us are everywhere . . . To recognize one from the other requires only that we pay attention." How do you feel about this perspective? Have you ever experienced a coincidence that changed your life in some way?

© DARCY ROSE

Jennifer Savran Kelly (she/they) lives in Ithaca, New York, where she writes, binds books, and works as a production editor at Cornell University Press. *Endpapers* is her debut novel, and their short fiction has appeared in *Potomac Review*, *Black Warrior Review*, *Green Mountains Review*, *Iron Horse Literary Review*, *Grist: A Journal of the Literary Arts*, and other publications.